Marguerite Kaye w...
her home in cold and usually ...
Regency Rakes, Highlanders and Sheikhs. ...
published over fifty books and novellas. When sh...
not ...ing she enjoys walking, cycling—but only on
...vel—gardening—but only what she can eat—and
cooking. She also likes to knit and occasionally drink
...rtin s, though not at the same time. Find out more on
...r website: margueritekaye.com.

THE EARL WHO
SEES HER BEAUTY

Marguerite Kaye

MILLS & BOON

First Published in Great Britain 2021
by Mills & Boon, an imprint of HarperCollins*Publishers* Ltd,
1 London Bridge Street, London, SE1 9GF

www.harpercollins.co.uk

HarperCollins*Publishers*
1st Floor, Watermarque Building,
Ringsend Road, Dublin 4, Ireland

The Earl Who Sees Her Beauty © 2021 Marguerite Kaye

ISBN: 978-0-263-28425-6

09/21

MIX
Paper from
responsible sources
FSC® C007454

Printed and bound in Spain
by CPI, Barcelona

This book is dedicated to my dear friend and fellow writer Sarah, Duchess of York, who generously allowed me to create one of my characters in her name.

I hope I've done her justice, and I have not forgotten my promise to give her the happy-ever-after you imagined for her in the second book in this duet.

Prologue

~~~❦~~~

Lavrio, Attica, Greece, March 1862

Dominic took his usual outside terrace seat at the little café on the harbour, nodding a polite good morning to the man sitting at the neighbouring table. Dull February had finally given way to spring, with the cloudless azure sky segueing to turquoise as it bled into the Aegean Sea in the bay. He had arrived in the early morning for the livestock market. The fishing boats had already left harbour. He could see them now, strung out like an armada in the lee of the island of Makronisos. Closing his eyes, he lifted his face to the sun. The air was heavy with salt but still fresh, his favourite time of year before the blistering dry heat of June, and the damp, draining swelter of August to come.

'*Kaliméra*, Kýrios Caldwell,' Andreas said, setting down a small cup of pungent Greek coffee. 'To what do we owe the pleasure? The market, I suppose?'

Dominic nodded. '*Kaliméra*, Andreas. I bought a fine goat.'

The café owner rolled his eyes theatrically. 'Goats are stubborn creatures. Nearly as stubborn as wives.'

Dominic laughed. 'Luckily, I wouldn't know about that. Anyway, I like that about them. Goats I mean, not wives. I'm stubborn too.'

'I kept this for you. An Englishman from Athens left it here yesterday. A tourist. I think this newspaper is almost as ancient as the ruins he came to see,' Andreas said, setting it down on the table.

'Three months old, not quite three thousand years,' Dominic said, looking at the publication date. '*Efcharistó.* I'll have a flick through it, though I confess to having no interest in events taking place in the land of my birth.'

'You are more Greek now than English, I think,' Andreas said. 'Good choice, in my humble opinion!'

'I tend to agree.' Dominic sipped his coffee, grimacing. Though he'd been coming to this café on market day for almost five years now, Andreas still automatically made it with sugar as the locals preferred. It was a compliment of sorts, he knew, even though it wasn't to his taste.

Idly opening the newspaper, which was *The Times* dated the twenty-ninth of January this year, he recognised none of the names in the births and deaths column on the front page. A cursory glance at the Announcements which took up the next two pages opened a window onto a completely alien world. Footmen, grocer's assistants and mathematical tutors seemed to be required in vast quantities. A gentleman requiring singing lessons after ten in the evening made him raise his eyebrows. There were tickets for sale on steamers heading to every corner of the globe, and numerous shops, houses and businesses were advertised for sale. Benevolent funds appealed for money to support orphans and consumptives. The announcement of a charity ball in aid of the veterans of the Crimean War made his lip curl. The men who had been maimed fighting for their country should not need to rely on charity.

He turned the page over in disgust. Court reports. A colliery accident. His eyes skimmed absently onward, half of his mind already compiling a list of provisions he required before collecting the goat and returning to his small-holding, a short distance along the coast. He turned another page, and his attention was caught immediately by a headline.

Was the Sixth Earl of Bannatyne the Last of the Line?

The print was perfectly clear, but the words swam in front of his eyes. Dominic stared down at the page. Resisting the impulse to crumple the newspaper and hurl it into the bay, he forced himself to read on.

It has been revealed that one of the most illustrious victims of the tragic and fatal train collision on the London and South Western Railway line ten days ago was the Sixth Earl of Bannatyne. Jeremy Thorburn inherited the title from his father Wilfred, the Fifth Earl, only four years previously.

His Lordship, who was in his thirty-eighth year, was a keen amateur botanist who collected many rare samples for the gardens at Kew while on his travels in the tropics, and lately established his own

*fernery in the grounds of the family seat
in Hampshire.*

*The Sixth Earl died unmarried and was,
like his father, an only child. In the absence
of a legitimate claim being substantiated
the title will lapse and the estates will fall
to the Crown. Anyone with relevant information which might assist the executor's
enquiries is requested to contact...*

After he had finished reading, Dominic sat
staring sightlessly out at the familiar and beautiful view for some time. Then he read the piece
again.

'Anything of interest?' Andreas paused at his
table, a stack of empty crockery carefully bal-
anced in one hand.

Blinking, Dominic shook his head. He
drained his cup of cold coffee, put a few coins
on the saucer, folded the newspaper up and put it
in his pocket. 'As you said, it's ancient history.'

Chapter One

❧❧❧❧❧

Hampshire, June 1862

It was a beautiful fresh summer's morning, the sun beaming down from a cloudless sky as Prudence Carstairs set out on the well-trodden path towards her destination. Though she wore her ubiquitous wide-brimmed bonnet, the risk of meeting anyone on this short walk was minimal enough to allow her to leave off the detachable veil and enjoy the fresh, unfiltered air. Her gown of peacock-blue Indian cotton printed with delicate floral sprays and twisted woody stems matched the bright promise of the day. The fabric was a gift from her sister Mercy, but the design was all her own, the neckline high, the gown free from fashionable ruffles, sashes and swags. Such furbelows offended Prudence's preference for clean lines. Her undergarments were her one indulgence. Though she wore only one petticoat, it was striped silk with a deep scalloped hem. Her steel-hooped crinoline had lately arrived from London and was the very latest flat-fronted model. Thanks to her own minor modifications, it swayed easily as she trod lightly along, humming quietly to herself.

The gates to Hawthorn Manor sat permanently open, one of them lying at a drunken angle against the gatepost where the hinge had given way. The scrolled wrought iron was rusted through in places, the family crest almost indecipherable. Refurbishing them was one of the many tasks on the long list of renovations and improvements for the gardens which remained undone.

The sweep of the driveway brought the house into view, and Prudence took her wide-brimmed bonnet off with relief, a ritual she had instigated when the house had been closed up, and which never failed to lighten her mood. Hawthorn Manor was built in the classic English style, parts of it dating back almost three hundred years. Four years ago, it had been in a dreadful state. Now, after an enormous amount of hard work, it had not only been restored but completely modernised too. She had been looking forward to seeing the gardens similarly transformed, but the ambitious plans to restore and replant, to redesign and to renovate were all now in limbo.

Rather like herself. She turned the heavy key in the lock of the front door and entered the cool stone-flagged hall. Setting her basket down, she was in the process of hanging up her bonnet when she noticed a coat occupying her usual peg on the rack. Her hat fell unnoticed to the ground as she gazed in astonishment at the trespassing garment, an overcoat made of dark blue wool. Tentatively, she touched it as if it might be a figment of her imagination, but it was real enough, much worn, the lining torn, but of good quality, for the tarnished buttons were almost certainly silver.

Her heart began to race. The door had been locked, but it was well-known locally that the Manor was unoccupied. Would a housebreaker brazenly hang up his coat while he searched for loot? A crash, followed by the muffled sound of a man swearing made her jump in fear, stifling a scream. She was already in panicked retreat, halfway back towards the front door before she managed to stop herself. Hawthorn Manor was in her care, albeit an unofficial curatorship.

Forcing herself into action, blanking her mind to the potential dangers, Prudence began to creep up the stairs, step by tentative step. The noise seemed to be coming from the bathroom, an opulent room which she had designed, and which had been created in one of the smaller bedrooms which lay across the hall from the master suite. Listening intently, she could hear the distinctive spatter of the shower which was positioned over the bath.

'What on earth?' Prudence muttered under her breath as she heard the protesting squeal of the taps. Whatever the intruder was doing, he would have his back to her, giving her a very small advantage. Garnering her courage, she rushed towards the bathroom and flung open the door.

The man whirled around, and Prudence shrieked. He was tall, extremely forbidding and wholly naked. His hair was long, reaching down to his shoulders, and raven black. A thick beard of the same colour covered most of his face, and a smattering of hair was sprinkled over his very broad and muscled chest, which was tanned walnut-brown. The tan stopped in a line just below his narrow waist. Her eyes travelled lower in shocked fascination until she got a glimpse of—a hastily grabbed towel.

'What the *hell* do you think you're doing barging in on me like this? Can't you see I'm trying to take a bath?'

Jerking her head up, her cheeks blazing, Prudence encountered a gaze that was both furious and incredulous. The eyes, beneath brows drawn together into a heavy frown, were the deep blue of a summer sky. 'This is private property,' she said, striving to inject some authority into her trembling voice. 'I have no idea how you managed to get in, but...'

'Through the front door.' Cursing viciously under his breath, he tied the towel more securely around his waist. 'What I want to know is how *you* got in?'

'*I* have a key,' Prudence retorted, astounded by his effrontery.

The pipes clanged again, and a fresh deluge of water sprayed from the shower. 'Damn this infernal contraption.'

'It is not an infernal contraption; it is a very expensive shower bath of the latest design. For goodness' sake, get out of the way.' It was the work of a moment to make the plumbing safe, but sufficient to thoroughly soak her hair. 'There, it's not difficult if you know what you are doing,' Prudence said, retreating to the door once more.

'Are you the housekeeper? I was informed that the place was empty.'

'Which explains your brazen behaviour.'

His response, to her astonishment, was a rumble of laughter. 'I certainly wouldn't have attempted to take a bath if I'd known you were going to burst in on me. Are you going to try to arrest me? I assure you, it would be a big mistake.'

His manner unsettled her. This man, a complete stranger with unkempt hair and a ragged beard, was acting as if she were the intruder, and not he. His tan was not the type to have been acquired under the English sun, yet his accent was indisputably English, and educated.

'What do you mean, a mistake? This is private property. You have no right...'

'I have every right. I also have a set of keys.'

'Where did you get them?' she asked, highly suspicious.

'From Mr Lionel Doncaster, of Doncaster and Sons.'

'From Jeremy's lawyer?'

'*My* lawyer, for the time being, at least. One of many things I appear to have inherited.'

Inherited! Prudence stared dumbfounded at the stranger. 'Who *are* you?'

'I am Jeremy's brother, if by Jeremy you mean the Sixth Earl.'

'Don't be ridiculous, Jeremy didn't have a brother.'

'I assure you he did. The lawyer was as surprised as you, but he was forced to change his tune when he saw my papers.'

'But that's not possible.' Prudence continued to stare, too astounded to care about the fact he was wearing nothing but a towel. 'You don't look anything like Jeremy.'

'Since I have no recollection of ever seeing him, either fully clothed or naked, you have the advantage of me.'

'I have *never* seen Jeremy naked! I have no idea what you are implying...'

'I'm not implying anything,' the man snapped. 'I am simply trying to establish who you are and what you're doing here.'

'My name is Prudence Carstairs, and what I'm doing is looking after this property.'

'Prudence...' He gave a crack of laughter. 'You were very badly named, for you are neither prudish, since you're having a conversation with a half-naked man, nor indeed prudent, if you really do believe me to be a housebreaker.'

'What else was I to think when I saw your coat on the rack?'

'You thought a housebreaker would hang up his coat and then take a leisurely bath before plundering the contents of the house?'

'It is common knowledge that the Manor is unoccupied,' Prudence said defensively, for that was precisely what she had thought. 'For all I know, you might have been planning on spending the night here.'

'Then perhaps it would be *prudent* for you to seek assistance in ejecting me, Mrs Carstairs, for that is exactly what I plan to do, since the house belongs to me.'

'It is Miss Carstairs, and how do I know you are who you claim to be?'

He indicated the towel wrapped around his waist. 'I really don't want to have a debate about the laws of inheritance while I'm...'

He broke off suddenly and, too late, she realised that her face was completely exposed. Worse, she was positioned in the full glare of the sunshine. Her hand flew to her cheek, confirming that her carefully arranged hair had been displaced when she was shutting off the shower, exposing her scar to the unforgiving light, making her feel as naked as he. She never exposed her face like this to anyone, save her closest family. Frantically, she tried to pat her damp hair back into position.

'I'm sorry,' he said. 'I didn't mean to stare.' Contrary to her expectations, however, the man looked neither horrified nor embarrassed. Nor did he avert his eyes. 'A very old injury, by the looks of it,' he added.

She wished she had kept her bonnet on. She ought not to have let her guard down and got into the habit of assuming she was safe here from unwelcome attention. Prudence turned her face to the side, still frantically trying to rearrange her hair over her face. 'A childhood accident.'

'You needn't be embarrassed, Miss Carstairs, I've seen a great deal worse.'

He spoke gently enough, but her hackles rose. 'In a freak show at a fair, do you mean?' To her horror, she found herself on the verge of tears. It had been so long since anyone had seen her laid bare, and it was her own careless fault. 'Is that supposed to make me feel better?'

His expression darkened. 'I meant on a battlefield.'

'Oh.' Momentarily distracted from her mortification, she wondered if this accounted for his unkempt appearance. 'Have you just returned from a campaign?'

'Not unless you count the battle I have been fighting with the lawyer over the last few months to establish my claim.'

'I'm not surprised he was sceptical. We have always thought—I mean everyone thought, including Jeremy—that he was an only child.'

'Yet here I am, in the flesh.' The man whose name she didn't yet know looked down at this point, grimacing. 'Rather too much flesh. Fascinating as this discussion may be, I am at a decided disadvantage. If you will excuse me, I will put some clothes on before we continue.'

Prudence was about to gratefully seize the opportunity to remedy her own feeling of nakedness when it occurred to her that he might simply be intending to escape.

'I have no intention of absconding,' he said, seeing her hesitate. 'All I crave is a bath and a bed, and since I assume you are not going to allow me either of those until you have assured yourself I won't make off with the family silver...'

'It's safely ensconced in a bank vault in London,' she said, deciding that whether he made off or not, she had to retrieve her bonnet. 'I will wait for you in the parlour. That is downstairs, the first door...'

'I will find it.'

Prudence backed out, managing to whisk her skirts out of the way just in time as the door slammed shut. Shaking, she stood for a moment, trying to collect her wits, to no avail. It was not yet noon, but the occasion, she decided, called for a stiff drink.

Chapter Two

Dominic sat on the edge of the bath, waiting until he heard Miss Prudence Carstairs head downstairs before he went in search of the clothes he'd discarded in a neighbouring bed-chamber. The rough wool trousers and jacket he had travelled in were very much the worse for wear. The suit had been acquired in a hurry from Lavrio's only tailor, and was intended to be worn as Sunday best, or for *mezé* on a Saturday night at the local taverna. Departing from Athens on the first leg of his voyage, Dominic had not looked radically out of place, but as each stage brought him closer to his native shores he had become more and more conscious of his odd appearance. Pulling a Holland cover from the dressing table mirror, he grimaced at his reflection. The suit strained at the shoulders and was only just long enough in the leg and, combined with his unkempt hair and beard, he was forced to admit that he looked every bit the opportunist vagrant Miss Prudence Carstairs had assumed him to be.

Who the hell was she, this self-appointed caretaker who was intimate enough with the deceased Earl to call him by his given name? 'The last straw, that's who,' Dominic growled, turning away from the mirror.

He wished he'd never read that damned newspaper report. He had tried to put it from his mind, but his immediate, visceral reaction had been naggingly persistent. It was impossible to ignore the cruel irony. The fates had conspired to render him part of the elite echelons of a society which it had cost him dearly to renounce. He couldn't live with that long term. So he'd settled on delivering a pre-emptive strike, coming here to claim the privilege he abhorred in order to reject it once and for all.

Though he hadn't expected the process to be so tediously exhausting. The days since he'd arrived in London merged one into the other, an endless round of meetings with legal types who all looked the same to him. Despite the reams of correspondence which had preceded his arrival, he had been greeted with scepticism and endless questions. By the time the lawyers' mood had turned from suspicion to acceptance and then to warm congratulation, Dominic was almost beyond caring. The list of properties and sureties and investments associated with his inheritance seemed endless, and the associated paperwork requiring his immediate attention had brought him yesterday to the end of his tether. A house which had been shuttered and abandoned for six months had seemed the perfect bolthole. The moment the keys were in his hands this morning, he had headed for the train station at Waterloo.

Save that the house had not been altogether abandoned, and his solitude had been very rudely interrupted. Under any other circumstances, he would have found the whole episode amusing, and Miss Prudence Carstairs intriguing. Right now, exhausted and reeling, he simply wanted her gone.

After opening the door first on a dust-sheeted dining room and then on a cupboard stacked with artwork and tapestries, he located the parlour, where the shutters had been thrown open to let in the morning light. The walls were panelled with oak, but the cream damask of the curtains and the white painted ceiling made the room seem much brighter. A chaise-longue sat in the window embrasure and two wingback chairs faced each other companionably at the empty hearth, all of them still draped in Holland covers.

His uninvited guest was seated at a three-legged table in the middle of the room, but she jumped to her feet as he entered. 'I have taken the liberty of procuring a flask of brandy from what Jeremy called his medicine cabinet. Would you like some? I know it's early, but I thought, in the circumstances...'

'An excellent idea. The sun must be over the yardarm somewhere.' Dominic took a seat opposite her. The flask was set out with two crystal goblets, one of which had already been put to use, a fact which he found oddly reassuring. He poured himself a large measure and topped up the other glass without asking. The brandy was mellow and old, very unlike the familiar harsh burn of the local Greek ouzo he occasionally indulged in. The cognac warmed him and steadied his erratic pulse.

Opposite him, Miss Carstairs took a small sip before pushing her glass to the side. She was sitting with her back to the light and had put on a wide-brimmed bonnet which shielded most of her face. Beneath it, he could see that her hair had been carefully arranged over her right cheek. The long thin scar which ran in a diagonal from her hairline across her forehead, slicing down through her right eyebrow along her cheek, was completely concealed, save for the jagged end at her top lip. The wound he had seen vividly in the bright glare of the bathroom was actually very pale pink, fading in the fleshier part of her cheek to white, but the stitch marks were clearly visible, puckering the skin, the product of the most rudimentary surgery—and God knew he ought to know, having witnessed far too many incidences. She had beautiful skin, the kind of complexion that would have been called peaches and cream, were it flawless. Her hair was dark blonde with golden highlights. What age was she? Anywhere between thirty and thirty-five, he reckoned. Gently born and single by her own admission, what the devil was she doing here?

Her eyes were an arresting grey-green, deep-set, heavy-lidded and thickly lashed. The contrast between the two sides of her face had been painful to look at, but more painful still had been the expectation that he would look away in disgust.

'I'm afraid I cannot offer you tea,' she said.

'I prefer coffee, if it comes to that,' Dominic said.

'I doubt there is any coffee in the pantry. In fact, there is not much of anything.'

'I have made arrangements for provisions to be delivered from London later today, since Doncaster warned me that the house had been lying empty.'

'That horrible man! When he came to take away Jeremy's valuables and all his papers, he dismissed the entire household and closed the house up without making any provision for essential maintenance. I told him that if the fernery was not properly regulated the plants would die, and as for the new plumbing— But he paid no heed to me.'

'Miss Carstairs, I am still not clear what, exactly, your status may be. How do you come to have a set of keys that the lawyer knows nothing about?'

'Jeremy gave them to me and, since the lawyer didn't specifically ask me to return them, I kept them.'

'Do you live here?'

'No, of course not! I live with my brother, at the Old Rectory. If you are implying that my relationship with Jeremy was in any way improper, you couldn't be further from the mark.'

Dominic took another long swallow of brandy, closing his eyes as it burned a fiery path towards his very empty stomach. 'Look, I'm sorry. I've had a trying few days following an extremely tedious and testing few months. I can appreciate that my turning up here unannounced has come as something of a surprise.'

'That is something of an understatement! If I had known you would be here…' She broke off, dipping her head, her hand smoothing the hair which covered her cheek in a gesture that was obviously ingrained.

'I made the decision on a whim,' Dominic said, touched. 'If I had known, I would have given you some notice of my arrival.'

'If I had known, I would not have walked in on you like that,' she snapped, glowering. 'I am sorry that my appearance upset you.'

'Miss Carstairs, I was stark naked and attempting to take a long overdue bath. You certainly startled me, but your *appearance*,' he said, deliberately trying to catch her eye, 'did not upset me.'

Her shrug told him she didn't believe him, and he couldn't blame her. Her 'freak show' remark spoke eloquently of a lifetime's painful experience. 'If you really are Jeremy's brother,' she said, her gaze lowered, firmly fixed on her empty glass, 'your arrival will cause an absolute sensation in the village.'

'No!' Dominic cursed violently, making her jump. 'Under no circumstances—I do not wish my presence here to be known.'

'Why on earth not?'

Ironically, he now had her full attention, and wished he had not. 'I came here for peace and quiet.'

'But if you really are Jeremy's brother, then you are the new Earl. Everyone will wish to make you welcome.'

'I will not be assuming the title. I have absolutely no interest whatsoever in joining the ranks of privileged, useless...' He paused to draw breath. 'I have no interest in being fêted. I would be much obliged if you would refrain from telling anyone that I am here.'

Her expression hardened. 'In that case I need to see cast iron proof of your identity. It is an established fact that Jeremy was an only child. He had no other close relatives. That is why proceedings are underway to have the estate handed over to the Crown.'

'Proceedings which have now been halted.' Resigned, Dominic got to his feet. 'Wait a moment.'

As soon as the door closed behind him, Prudence dropped her head into her hands. *Oh, God, oh, God, oh, God.* This whole situation was embarrassing beyond belief. If only she'd remembered to put her bonnet back on as soon as she had spotted his coat on the rack, that would have been one less humiliation. The fact that the man, who might or might not be who he claimed to be, had been considerate enough to make light of her disfigurement only made it worse! She knew from bitter experience just how unsightly other people found her. Every inch of her face had been exposed to him in the unforgiving light upstairs. Every time he looked at her, she knew he must be seeing her scar, no matter how well hidden it was now. It was no consolation at all that she had seen him similarly exposed, for he had absolutely nothing to be ashamed of!

She lifted her head, listening intently. She thought she could hear his footsteps on the stairs but she couldn't be sure, so she made for the window to keep a watch on the driveway, just in case he made a break for it, though what she intended to do if he did, she had no idea. Could he really be Jeremy's brother? If so, why had his existence been obliterated from history? And why, if he was the new Earl, was he so determined to keep his presence here a secret? And if it came to that, why was he set on rejecting the title he was claiming he'd inherited? None of it made any sense.

'Were you worried I was about to abscond?'

Prudence whirled around, blushing. 'I was opening the window,' she said, turning back to lift the latch and make good on her lie. 'It's stuffy in here.'

He sat back down at the table and began to rifle through a thick folder of papers. 'The deeds to this house.' He pushed the papers over to her. 'Happy now?'

Prudence took her chair and picked them up. 'Mr Doncaster would not have given you these unless he was certain, but…'

'And here is a copy of the parish register, noting my birth.'

'"Dominic Matthew Thorburn",' she read. '"Father the Fifth Earl. Mother the Countess. Born in this parish June 1827".' She checked the date then looked up, dazed, to find his eyes intent on her. 'Jeremy would have been two years old in 1827. His mother died in childbirth when he was an infant.'

'Contrary to what everyone believed, however, the child did not perish with her.'

The implication was clear enough, but so outrageous that Prudence was stunned into momentary silence. 'That was you?' she finally managed. And when he nodded, 'What happened to you?'

'I was given away, to a childless couple who were grateful enough to swear to keep my true origins a secret.'

'Why?' Prudence asked, astounded. 'Why would a man who has just lost his wife give away his son? Wouldn't you think that the child she had left behind would be even more precious?'

'Not if it was a cuckoo in the nest, which seems to me the most likely explanation.'

'But you are registered as the Earl's son, here in the parish register.'

He shrugged. 'Legally, since I was born in wedlock to his wife, I was his property. Since she conveniently died and spared him the scandal of declaring her an adulteress, then all he had to do was rid himself of the evidence of her crime.'

His tone was indifferent, but she couldn't believe he could be. 'So he had you adopted,' Prudence said softly.

Another shrug. 'After a fashion, though the transaction was both unofficial and covert.'

'I can't believe it. No,' Prudence added hastily, 'don't take umbrage. I don't mean that I don't believe you, I mean I can't believe it happened.'

'You can have no idea how much I wish it had not.' He held out his hand for the documents, sliding them back into the folder. 'It is ancient history, there is absolutely no need for you to get upset on my behalf. I am not.'

His expression was so stern, it was clear the very last thing he wanted was sympathy, never mind empathy. 'Have you always known the truth about yourself?'

'I had no idea until my father died—that is, the man I believed was my father.' The new Earl—for it was undoubtedly he—took another sip of brandy, his fingers curled tightly around the short stem of the glass, for the first time betraying emotion. 'I found the copy of the parish register in his papers, along with a letter from the Fifth Earl.'

'Oh, my goodness, that must have been a terrible shock.'

'My mother—I mean his wife—died when

I was fourteen. We'd never been a particularly close family, not surprisingly since I wasn't actually theirs, and my father was more than happy to pack me off into the army.'

'At fourteen! Isn't that very young?'

He shook his head, his eyes lighting up. 'I loved it. I felt at home, right from the beginning.'

'Are you on leave now?'

His smile immediately faded. 'I left five years ago.'

'I see.'

'I very much doubt it.'

She flinched at his tone, at a loss as to what she had said to upset him. 'So when you discovered that you were not—I'm sorry, I don't think you mentioned your name—the name you grew up with?'

'Caldwell. Dominic Caldwell. As far as I am concerned, that is still my name.'

'So your adoptive parents kept your first name, at least. May I ask, when did your father die?'

'Back in fifty-three.'

'But the old Earl was still alive then!' Prudence exclaimed. 'You could have sought him out, written to him at least. You must have been curious.'

'Are you imagining a happy reunion? He gave me away, Miss Carstairs. He already had an heir of marriageable age, he didn't need a spare, and certainly not one who had been born on the wrong side of the blanket.'

'You were intrigued enough to establish that much.'

'It wasn't difficult, and I was never interested in discovering more. The army was my family. I'd just been promoted, we were about to go to war, I had other far more important things on my mind. As far as I was concerned, the matter was closed.'

But Prudence couldn't agree. 'You had a brother only two years older than yourself. I'm sorry, I know it's none of my business, but...'

'It is absolutely none of your business. I wasn't interested nine years ago when I learnt of his existence and I am even less interested now that he's dead.'

Shaken, for she could not imagine herself being so callous in a similar position, she took a large gulp of her brandy. 'So why are you here?'

'To draw a line under the Bannatyne dynasty and sever my connection with it, which means disposing of what there is by way of property and sureties and shares and whatever else is listed here,' he said, indicating the folder. 'I don't want any of it.'

'You're going to sell up and give it all away? But Hawthorn Manor has been the ancestral home of the Earls of Bannatyne for... I don't know, two hundred years.' And her own *raison d'être* for the last four, Prudence thought, dismayed.

'As far as I'm concerned, the Sixth Earl was the last in the line. I have no use for the title, and I have no need for the money.'

'But...'

'I have more than explained myself, Miss Carstairs. I am still in the dark, however, as to the purpose of your presence here.'

One look at his expression made it clear that he wasn't going to answer any more questions, and indeed why should he? No matter how proprietorial she felt about Hawthorn Manor, she was now the interloper. The realisation was disheartening in the extreme. 'I have been keeping the fernery going,' Prudence said. 'And the house, to an extent, running the water, lighting the range every now and then, trying to prevent all the excellent work undertaken to restore and modernise it being undone. I was closely involved in the renovations, you see. When Jeremy inherited four years ago, this place was very run-down, the gardens quite neglected.'

'So you're an architect?'

'Nothing so grand. I have an interest in de-sign and since Jeremy was more interested in the fernery, he was happy to delegate overseeing the work on the house to me.'

'I'm afraid if you're imagining that I will con-tinue to employ you, you'll be disappointed.'

'I wasn't employed, as such.'

His brows shot up. 'Then I'm not surprised he was happy to delegate to you.'

'The situation,' Prudence said awkwardly, 'was mutually beneficial.'

'If you say so. In my experience, the aristoc-racy are notorious skinflints. Though they're more than happy to spend a fortune to bribe their way up the ranks of the military and will mort-gage themselves to the hilt to honour a gam-bling debt, paying a tradesman for his services is anathema to them. Or a tradeswoman, in your case. I'm afraid I won't be needing your services, either as a designer or a caretaker.'

'I am not actually offering you my services,' Prudence retorted. 'The house is finished, it's only the gardens that require work now, and they were never my forte. What's more, I have no ambition to make a career out of being a caretaker.'

'I didn't mean to offend you, Miss Carstairs.'

'I'm not offended.' Simply heartsick, knowing she had lost her haven. Clement, infuriatingly, had been right to warn her that the current situation would come to an end sooner rather than later. 'I am sorry to have doubted you.'

The Earl surprised her with a crack of laughter. 'You ought to have seen Doncaster's face when I walked into his office. Though in his case I was fully dressed, he was every bit as taken aback by my appearance as you were.'

Recklessly, Prudence swallowed the last of her brandy in one gulp. 'I am not surprised, if you were wearing that suit.'

'It's the best that Lavrio's lone tailor could provide.'

'Lavrio! On the Attic peninsula?'

'You can't possibly know it?'

'I know *of* it. It was known as Laurium, and famous for its silver mines in ancient times. My brother,' Prudence explained, cutting herself short, 'is a scholar of ancient civilisations. Do you have an interest in archaeology?'

'I live on a smallholding with a few goats and

chickens. I have absolutely no interest in digging up the past.'

'But isn't that what you are doing? Coming back here, establishing your identity…'

'Establishing my claim,' he interrupted her. 'I know who I am, and it has nothing to do with all this.'

'Establishing your claim then,' Prudence said, exasperated by his pedantry. 'In order to sell up.'

'In order to sell out.'

'Sell up, sell out—surely it is the same thing.'

'Not to me.'

'Well, it seems to me that it amounts to a form of madness,' Prudence said.

'Doncaster agrees with you. Personally, I don't give a damn what he or anyone thinks.' The Earl got to his feet. 'Since I have now convinced you of my right to be here, I'd appreciate it if you left me to the solitude I sought.'

Prudence pushed back her chair, feeling quite sick. This could very well be her last visit to Hawthorn Manor. She had always known the day would come, but for it to happen so suddenly, without a chance to prepare herself was awful. 'What about the fernery?' she asked. 'The temperature needs to be regulated. Then there is the water supply. And the range. There is a knack to lighting it…'

'I'm sure I will manage.'

'Will you? If you've been living in the wilds of Greece, I can't believe you have any understanding of modern plumbing. Or heating. Or even cooking.'

'I can light a fire.'

'There's a great deal more to modern kitchens than…' Prudence bit her tongue. Hawthorn Manor was not hers. If he wanted to wreck the plumbing, he had every right to do so. 'We don't have a gasworks in the vicinity, so the lighting is a combination of oil lamps and candles. If you decide you do require any help, then you can find me at the Old Rectory.' She waited but there was no response, so she dropped a curtsey. 'Good day.'

Once outside, she shuddered. Well, that had been a horrendous experience. It would be a long time before she let herself be seen uncovered again.

Chapter Three

Dominic woke with a start. Confused and disorientated, it took him a moment to remember where he was. After he had locked the door following the departure of the inappropriately named Miss Prudence Carstairs, he had fallen into the first bed he had found, sinking into a small mountain of mattresses, pulling the Holland dust sheets over himself and dropping into a deep and dreamless sleep.

The bedframe creaked now as he sat up, only to come face to face with a large ginger cat with a ringed tail staring unblinkingly at him. 'How long have you been there?'

The animal took this for an invitation and jumped onto his lap, purring loudly. 'No point in buttering me up,' Dominic said, scratching the cat's forehead. 'I've nothing for you, though by the looks of you, you're used to catching your own dinner.'

On cue, his own stomach rumbled, reminding him that he had not eaten since he'd left London yesterday morning. What he really wanted more than anything was a cup of coffee. It was to be hoped that the provisions he'd ordered had arrived, for the alternative was a foraging trip to the village he'd passed when walking from the train station yesterday morning and he was not in the mood to face the polite enquiries of complete strangers.

'But there's nothing for it but to do just that if there's no coffee,' he muttered, dislodging the cat and pushing back his makeshift sheet.

His watch, which he'd placed under the pillow out of habit, told him it was still very early. The day loomed long, laden with tasks he didn't want to do and decisions he didn't want to make. The vain hope that he'd be able to complete this business in a few weeks had already been extinguished by that damned lawyer, who had made him feel like an ignorant fool. Not that the man would have guessed. Not that that made Dominic feel any better. One thing was certain, the next time he was forced to consult him, he was going to be better dressed and better informed.

He flicked the cover of his watch closed, enclosing the familiar shape of it in his hand. His thumb traced the engraving on the back.

Presented to Captain Caldwell on the occasion of his promotion
A mark of respect from the Men of his Regiment of Foot, February 1853

He had carried it every day, on campaign and into battle. The gold casing was scratched and dented, but the mechanism never let him down, nor did his men. If only the same could be said for the officer class he had served under. His fist tightened. The memory of his shameful departure still tormented him. His anger—at his treatment, at his own stubborn refusal to back down—could still overwhelm him. Until that incident, he'd had an unblemished record. A lifetime of loyal service, of exceptional achievement, and all of it in tatters.

Dominic cursed. He had been true to himself, and that was what mattered. He set the watch back down on the bedside table. That life was over. The task now was to rid himself of this life he had inherited and get back to the simple one he'd made for himself. A bath, if he could persuade that new-fangled contraption to deliver up water, some clean clothes and coffee, in that order. Then he'd be ready to face the task he'd come here to complete, of investing the wealth of the man who had rejected him in some more worthy cause. Although what that should be, he hadn't the foggiest notion.

The taps in the bathroom refused to cooperate, forcing Dominic to stand under the shower rather than take a bath. It was a surprisingly pleasant sensation to have the tepid water rain down on him, but it ran out after a few minutes and, downstairs in the kitchen, the tap was also dry. The substantial piece of cast iron set into the fireplace was, he presumed, the range, but how to light it was another puzzle. Since he didn't have any water to fill the kettle, however, it was hardly a priority.

Dominic cursed the previous Earl for his renovations, and he cursed Miss Prudence Carstairs, with her enthusiasm for modern plumbing. What was wrong with a village well and an open fire, dammit? The ginger cat mewed plaintively at the kitchen door and, though the animal must have other means of getting in and out of the Manor, Dominic opened it for him, watching as he padded off, tail held high. He was going to have to go round to the Old Rectory, wherever that was, and beg Miss Carstairs to initiate him into the mysterious workings of his temporary abode. In actual fact, he was glad of the excuse to see her again, though he'd much prefer to do so with a cup of coffee inside him. There must be another source of water somewhere.

The fernery! There must be a water supply there. Dominic picked up the kettle and stepped out of the back door. It was a lovely morning, the sun shining down, the sky pale blue and almost cloudless, but he shivered in his shirtsleeves. It felt like a typical winter in the Attic peninsula. Acquiring some warmer clothes was going to be a priority. Which way was the fernery? He could see nothing beyond a high, wildly over-grown hedge. What should have been a lawn at the front of the house, he now recalled, was more like a hayfield. Doncaster had been very deter-mined not to spend money when he'd closed the house up, though that hedge looked like it had been untended for a lot longer than six months.

There was a path leading round the side of the house to the front, where he would, he hoped, be able to get a clearer view of the gardens. Still grasping his kettle, Dominic was about to fol-low it when the cat came bounding out from a gap in the tall hedging, followed by, of all people, Miss Carstairs. She didn't see him at first, her wide-brimmed bonnet having been supplemented by a veil, excluding him from her view, and her face from his sight. Her gown was grey-blue, made high to the neck, with long sleeves, of some filmy material that fluttered in the breeze, giving him a glimpse of a petticoat beneath. This was a lacy garment, deeply ruched and festooned with ribbons, in stark contrast to the simplicity of her gown. A woman of hidden layers, he thought fancifully.

'Miss Carstairs.'

She jumped theatrically, clutching her hands to her breast. 'You startled me.'

'I beg your pardon.'

'I came to check the fernery.' She kept her head down, but her tone was defensive. 'I didn't get a chance yesterday.'

'My fault.'

'The water supply…'

'Seems to have run dry,' Dominic said, holding up the kettle.

'The cistern in the house is most likely empty.' She eyed him accusingly. 'Did you run a bath?'

'A shower. A very brief one.'

'The water supplier only turns on the taps

every other day. It is running today, but in order to fill the cistern you need to turn on the tap in the scullery.'

'Miss Carstairs, is it too much to ask that you show me?'

'I would happily have done so yesterday.'

'If I had not sent you off with a flea in your ear, you mean,' Dominic said. 'I owe you an apology. We got off on the wrong foot, and it was entirely my fault.'

'To be fair,' she said, 'I did catch you somewhat off-guard.'

'Somewhat! Do you think we could start afresh? If you can show me how to fill the kettle and light the range, I will be forever in your debt. I am in dire need of a cup of coffee. Luckily, my grocery order has arrived.'

He stood back to allow her to precede him through the back door and, after a moment's hesitation, to his relief, she nodded. 'Very well, since it is a matter of life and death.'

'Thank you.' The Earl placed the full kettle on the lit range. In the bright morning sunlight streaming through the kitchen window, with his unkempt hair glinting blue-black, his eyes seemed more extraordinarily blue, his skin more deeply tanned. There were crow's feet at the corners of his eyes, frown lines etched between his brows which made him look older than the thirty-five years Prudence knew him to be, but beneath the ragged beard and unconventional attire there lurked a very attractive man. Who was smiling tentatively at her.

'You made it look so easy.'

'It is easy, if you know what you're doing,' Prudence said, choosing a seat at the table with her back to the window. 'I have a mechanical mind. I like to understand how things work. There is a system to heat some of the rooms in the winter using steam, similar to the one operating in the fernery.'

'I'm cold enough to need it now.'

'It's the height of summer!'

'I was thinking only a few moments ago that I'm going to have to acquire some warmer clothes.'

'I can give you the name of my brother's tailor in London if you like,' Prudence said.

'Thank you, I may take you up on that. I normally dress to suit myself.'

'So you don't have a wife and children waiting for you back in Greece?'

'I choose to live alone.'

Which, Prudence thought, was an odd way to put it, but just then the kettle came to the boil and the Earl gave a sigh of relief, giving his entire attention to quickly and efficiently making a large pot of coffee.

'There's no milk, I'm afraid,' he said, setting it down on the table, along with cups and saucers and sitting himself opposite her. 'It would require a trip into the village, and I'd obviously rather avoid that.'

'Frank will be disappointed,' Prudence said, bending down to scratch the cat's forehead. 'He's very fond of a saucer of cream.'

'Is that his name? He woke me up this morning.'

'He's a champion mouser and keeps the Manor and the fernery free of vermin.'

'Then that's one less thing for me to worry about, I suppose.' The Earl poured two cups of very dark, evil-looking liquid, pushing one towards her and immediately took a sip of his own. 'That's better.'

Prudence was torn. She could try to drink the coffee with her veil in place, but it would be tricky, or she could push it back. She knew that her bonnet and her hair would cover most of her face and, besides, he had already seen the whole thing, but still she hesitated.

'Is it too strong?' the Earl asked, getting to his feet. 'Let me look and see if I can find some sugar.'

He turned his back on her, making a show of opening and closing doors and drawers that she knew could not possibly contain sugar, unless he had put it there himself. Prudence took advantage of the deliberately created opportunity to quickly push back her veil. The Earl slammed another cupboard door shut. 'I'm sorry,' he said, still with his back to her. 'I'm afraid I can't find any. I must have forgotten to order it.'

He must have known from the outset that there was none. 'It's fine,' Prudence said, touched, 'I don't have a sweet tooth.' She took a sip of the coffee as he sat back down opposite her and tried to suppress a shudder.

Unsuccessfully, for the Earl laughed. 'It is an acquired taste. Andreas, who owns the harbourside café in Lavrio, insists on serving me *metrios*, which is coffee with sugar in it, though he's known me for five years and I have lost count of the number of times I've told him I prefer *sketos*, which is without sugar.'

'Do you speak fluent Greek?'

'*I* think so, but my neighbours would probably beg to differ. The trick is to talk as if the words are caught in the back of your throat.'

As he finished his coffee and poured himself another cup, Prudence debated with herself. Once she had recovered from the shock yesterday, she had spent the rest of the day wondering about the huge gaps in his story, and the inconsistencies in his behaviour. Strictly speaking, none of it was her business, but she was intrigued enough to overcome her customary reticence and, if she was honest, still nursed a residual hope that the Manor was not completely lost to her just yet.

'I have been wondering if I misunderstood you,' she ventured. 'Are you really planning on giving up your inheritance? Because most men would consider themselves incredibly fortunate to inherit an earldom and all that comes with it, and you—forgive me, but it sounds as if you have been living a very simple life. Are you truly going to give away a king's ransom?'

'Yes.'

'How?'

'I have no idea yet. I am still trying to understand the extent of it.'

'Yes, but…' Prudence pushed her almost untouched coffee to one side. 'You must see that to choose what I assume is relative poverty, to eschew the influence the title would give you and all the comfort—it makes no sense.'

'It does to me.'

His tone warned her that she had already gone too far, but she ignored it. If she must give up her refuge, she wanted to understand why, and this might be her only opportunity. 'You are clearly an educated man, and no fool, whatever Mr Doncaster thinks. If you are afraid that you will not be accepted...'

'If you're thinking me intimidated by rank and privilege, you're well off the mark, Miss Carstairs. I was a captain in Her Majesty's army and surrounded by those who claim to be from the first families in the land.'

'As Earl of Bannatyne, you would be one of them.'

'Precisely,' he said. 'The very last thing I wish to be.'

Prudence frowned down at the viscous coffee in her cup. 'So you choose not to be titled, but why choose also to be poor?'

'The money isn't mine.'

'It is, according to the law. You've established that yourself. It seems to me that you've gone to a great deal of trouble to acquire something you don't want.'

'The satisfaction is in being able to dispose of it. Then there can be no question of any of it belonging to me, the title or the trappings.'

'I'm sorry, I simply don't understand.'

He sighed, drumming his fingers on the table. 'They gave me away.'

'To a family who took care of you,' Prudence interjected hotly. 'They clothed you and fed you and kept you safe. Instead of bemoaning your fate, you should be grateful.' As she was. Thinking of how very lucky she had been made tears spring to her eyes. She blinked rapidly, aware of his gaze on her and determined not to betray herself any further.

'You seem to have strong views on the subject,' he said.

'Anyone would, who reads the press. London is full of homeless children that nobody wants. You are lucky to have been given a decent home.'

'I'm not disputing that.'

'And fortunate to have discovered, in the army, a place where you truly belonged,' Prudence persisted.

'Not any more.'

'Well, no, for you have retired, but…'

'I did not say I had retired. I left.'

Pedantry again, Prudence thought, refraining from rolling her eyes. 'You left and have been living alone in Greece without any family. And now you are here, back where you started, so to speak...'

'And I'm going to make sure that is where any hold it has over me comes to an end,' the Earl said, enunciating his words carefully. 'It could not be further from what I want, from who I am.' His fingers were curled tightly around his empty cup. 'Why, after all I have been through, would I allow a man who had rejected me at birth to dictate to me from beyond the grave? I won't have it.' The handle of his cup snapped. He stared at it blankly, then set it down carefully in the saucer. 'I simply won't have it,' he repeated, more mildly. 'Do you see now?'

What on earth could she say to that? She had been mistaken to draw any parallels with her own situation, and she was quite intimidated by his chilling tone, and so she nodded.

Fortunately, it was all he seemed to expect. 'Good,' he said.

'If you are going to remain here though,' Prudence said, 'while you...while you dispose of your inheritance, it will take some time, won't it? How will you explain your presence?'

'I don't know. I'll say I'm one of Doncaster's minions, here to make an inventory, since no one is likely to guess the truth.'

'No, that is for sure. I suppose it may work, for you bear no resemblance to either Jeremy or the previous Earl, who were both very fair in colouring.'

'Confirmation, as if it matters, of my lack of connection.'

'To the Earl perhaps, but Jeremy would have been your half-brother. Why are you so determined to disown him?'

'He's dead. I'm not disowning him, though I'm beginning to wonder if there was more to your relationship with him than you would have me believe. You rarely miss an opportunity to mention him.'

'That is not true! You just don't like to hear his name. I told you that there was nothing in the least improper...'

'Perhaps his intentions were most proper?'

'What?' Her anger was turning to astonishment. 'You cannot possibly be imagining that Jeremy and I were betrothed?'

'Why not? From what you've said he gave you

a free hand in rebuilding this place to your own design. He was what—thirty-seven? I can understand him wanting to put his house in order first, but he must have known that it was long past time to be thinking about his successor.'

'Thus sparing you the burden of inheriting,' Prudence threw at him.

'I don't know why you are getting so angry; it is an obvious conclusion to draw, especially since you assumed responsibility for looking after the place.'

'You could not be more wrong.' She pushed her cup away so violently that coffee splashed all over the saucer and the table. 'The notion that Jeremy and I...that he would even consider...it's utterly ridiculous.'

'Because of your disfigurement?'

She was so unused to anyone directly mentioning her scars, Prudence was quite dumbstruck.

'Shouldn't I have mentioned it?' he asked. 'Isn't it better to acknowledge such things than to pretend they don't exist? That is my experience, at any rate.'

'Your experience, my lord, is with battle scars.' She pulled her veil back down over her face, infuriated by the gentleness of his tone, for it could imply nothing other than pity, even though she agreed with the sentiments. 'A battle scar is a badge of honour, a scarred woman is an object of ridicule, but it was not my disfigurement which prevented Jeremy from asking me to marry him. My sister Mercy is one of the most beautiful women in England, and Jeremy wouldn't have considered asking her either. I know you think it very selfish of him, but he was no more interested in marrying than you. In fact, the more I think about it, the more I think you were brothers, for he too hid himself away from the world, albeit in a rather grander environment.'

She fully intended to rile him, and she succeeded. 'You know nothing of my circumstances,' he said testily.

'And you know nothing of mine, but that doesn't stop you from assuming that you do. I have spent the last four years working here, transforming what was almost a ruin into this beautiful, modern... And...and...and you come along, bemoaning the fate which handed it to you, determined to rid yourself of it as if it was a plague house. Do you have any notion of how fortunate you are?'

'Luckily I have you to point it out to me,' he

said, through gritted teeth. 'I would have much preferred to continue to live the life I chose for myself, undisturbed. Do you think it was pleasant, having to prove to that damned lawyer who I am? Do you think I enjoyed the way he looked down his nose at me, interrogated me as if I was a criminal? And I'd have been spared it all if your blasted Jeremy had simply done what every other man does and settled down with a wife and got himself an heir.'

'*You* have not done so, and Jeremy never would have,' Prudence declared, pushing her chair back. She never lost her temper, she rarely let herself express any extreme emotions, but she was too angry now to care about the consequences. 'Jeremy was what is euphemistically known as a confirmed bachelor. The Ancient Greeks understood such leanings but, in the eyes of the world we live in, he was an aberration, a crime against nature, just as I am. That's what we had in common, my lord—I beg your pardon, my temporary lord—and that's why we would never have made a match of it. We were both misfits, but Hawthorn Manor brought us together. Jeremy had his precious fernery, and he gave me the task of restoring the house. A woman so ineligible that no one would imagine him moved by anything other than pity. The arrangement suited us both very well, but his untimely death put an end to that.'

Across the table, the Earl was looking utterly dumbfounded. As he should! 'You are not the only son that the old Earl rejected,' Prudence said, making for the door. 'You have that in common with Jeremy too.'

The kitchen door was slammed shut. Dominic continued to sit at the table in stunned silence as Miss Carstairs stormed back to the Old Rectory in high dudgeon. The conversation had gone horribly wrong, but he couldn't understand how. What had happened to the fresh start they had agreed to make? He had gone to a great deal of trouble to explain himself when he didn't need to, and he thought she'd understood. But no, back she came with her accusations of his ingratitude. She hadn't understood at all. He had been patronising after that, though he hadn't meant to be, and she had taken complete umbrage at the mention of her scar. He had gone to such trouble to try to put her at her ease regarding it, and had succeeded too, for she had put up the veil from her face and had seemed to have forgotten its existence until he'd reminded her. Ought he to go after her and apologise, or explain? But to what purpose? How dare she tell him how fortunate he was? She knew nothing about his life, nothing at all.

All the same, he wished he'd handled it better. Dominic cursed viciously under his breath, picking up the coffee pot and checking that there was still enough hot water in the kettle. He wasn't used to company, that was the problem. He certainly wasn't used to being called to account. In fact, the last time that had happened...

With a yelp, he pulled his hand away from the burning heat of the kettle's handle. Do. Not. Think. About. That. He spooned fresh coffee from the grinder into the pot and took it back to the table. He'd made a complete arse of this morning. Though he now knew how to light the range and turn on the water. He rolled his eyes, signally failing to be lifted by this silver lining.

He'd upset her. She was clearly not the type to lose her temper, she'd lashed out in defence, and that was his fault. Dominic poured himself a coffee and took a large gulp. When had he last eaten? He wasn't hungry. His head ached. He was cold. And very, very weary. It wasn't yet noon, but he was in no mood to open the folder of paperwork, and he had no other call on his time.

His mood plummeted. What the hell was he doing here? A tourist had left an out-of-date newspaper in a café in Lavrio and Andreas had kept it for him, rather than wrap the potato peelings in it. What were the chances?

'A thousand to one,' Dominic said, staggering to his feet and heading for his bedroom.

'A hundred thousand to one,' he said, kicking off his boots and toppling onto the bed, pulling the dust sheet over him.

'A million to one,' Dominic muttered. 'Sorry again, Miss Prudence Carstairs. Very, very sorry,' he mumbled, and then sleep claimed him.

Chapter Four

Prudence stepped out of the bathtub and wrapped a towel around herself. The bathroom in the Old Rectory was small, built into what had been the dressing room of the main bedchamber once occupied by her parents, and now by Clement. The tub was simple, panelled with mahogany, with none of the luxuries of a shower attachment and a very erratic water supply which often failed to provide more than a few inches of hot water. This morning she had been fortunate and had relished the opportunity to linger in the tub.

Opening the stained-glass window to clear the steam, she crossed the hallway to her own bedchamber. She usually avoided the full-length mirror until she was fully dressed, but today she forced herself to stand in front of it. The curtains were still drawn, but the morning sun filtered through a gap, generating a hazy light. Her hair was piled high on top of her head, leaving her face exposed. She traced the scar from where it began on her scalp, across her forehead, the slice of skin that divided her right eyebrow, along the deeper indent of her cheek, where she had to press hard on the skin to feel anything. The compulsive habit of touching her tongue to the deep gouge at the top of her lip had been broken a long time ago, but she did it now, deliberately. Her lips were soft on either side, but the groove, with its stitch mark, was ungiving. When she was a child, her parents had planted their kisses on the undamaged left side of her mouth. Mercy and Clement always kissed her left cheek. No one else ever touched her. Jeremy, despite his familiarity with her disfigurement, could never even bring himself to look straight at her. She hadn't worn a veil when she was working at Hawthorn Manor, but she had always taken care to cover what she could of her scar with her hair and her bonnet. Only since he died had she become considerably bolder. And now her brief period of freedom was over.

Despite what she'd said yesterday, the new Lord Bannatyne had almost nothing in common with his brother. From the moment she'd seen him, stark naked and furious, she'd been aware of him in a way that she'd never been aware of any man. That was what had fuelled her ire yesterday. That was what made his pity so much harder to take.

Was it pity though? One of the things she hated more than anything was the way some people pretended her disfigurement didn't exist. Growing up, her parents, with Clement and Mercy following their lead, had been stoically silent upon the subject. She had, until that dreadful incident at Mercy's eighteenth birthday party, all but allowed them to persuade her that her appearance was nothing out of the ordinary. Her illusions had been shattered that catastrophic day on more than one account, and every other subsequent experience of exposing herself to public scrutiny had been torturous. Her brother and sister, as a result, were extremely protective, and Prudence felt horribly guilty for resenting this. They loved her but they were misguided, and she had no idea how to change that.

Dominic Caldwell was different. He had looked at her and he had not looked away in horror, but neither had he pretended that what he saw was flawless. No one had ever been so matter-of-fact. He hadn't been disgusted by her.

Before they'd both lost their tempers yesterday, she could almost have convinced herself that he was interested in her—and not only because she was the means to his precious morning coffee. The change in mood had been her fault, she could see that clearly now. She resented his careless disregard for the place she had come to treasure as her refuge from the world. She was irked with herself because, against her better judgement, she'd been intrigued by him and, yes, attracted to him.

She did not for a moment imagine it was mutual, but the fact of her attraction embarrassed her. She was thirty-two years old and she'd never been kissed. Thirty-two, ineligible in every way and, in the eyes of the world, an old maid. She had accepted that her age and her face made the longings of her youthful self, to love and be loved, an impossible dream. She had no such ambitions now, yet her body refused to accept the pointlessness of longing. Beauty made a woman desirable, but the lack of it didn't remove her desire.

Prudence closed her eyes, letting her lips rest on the back of her hand. How would Dominic Caldwell's kiss feel, the graze of his beard on her skin, the touch of his tongue on her lip? And his hands, sliding around her waist, pulling her tight against him, or feathering up her arm? Her fingers reached her shoulder, and the tip of her other scar, and her eyes flew open.

'Look,' she instructed her reflection, which showed her chest and throat flushed. 'Turn around, and look.' The mark on her back ran from her shoulder in a diagonal, the skin thick where the stitches showed, so much more crude than those on her face. The wound must have been deep. Not a knife, but something heavy and jagged. She shuddered, turning away from the mirror, dropping the towel and grabbing her fresh chemise, which she had laid out ready on the bed. Not until she had donned the full armour of her undergarments, crinoline, skirt and blouse fastened high to the neck, did she turn to the mirror again, to arrange her hair. And that she could do without looking.

Dearest Mercy,

I am very, very sorry to hear that you are once again unable to visit us this summer. Forgive me if I say that I think His Lordship is being selfish in keeping you from us though doubtless your husband would say that we are being selfish in wish-

~~ing you to abandon him for a mere few weeks~~.

I understand how ~~desperate~~ eager you are for a child, but you have now spent the last five summers at the spa in Baden-Baden to no avail. Is it possible that the issue is not with you, but with...

Prudence crumpled up the draft letter and threw it into the wastebasket. It was wrong of her to crush Mercy's hopes, even if she did think them futile. What Mercy herself thought, she had no idea for she would never write about such an intimate subject and they had not seen each other for more than a year, an issue which she would happily lay entirely at Mercy's husband's door, if only it were true.

The doorbell clanged. Remembering that it was Lizzie's day off, Prudence got reluctantly to her feet. Even if Clement heard the bell, it wouldn't occur to him to answer it, even though the chances were it would be a courier with a rare book or an obscure academic paper for him. Morning callers were a rarity, actively discouraged by Clement, who didn't like to be disturbed when he was working, and by Prudence, who wished to protect her privacy within the confines of her home. She checked her hair before she opened the door, careful to show only the left side of her face.

'Miss Carstairs,' Lord Bannatyne said, sketching a bow. 'I beg you will spare me a few moments of your time.'

Her initial instinct was to close the door on him, for he had caught her completely unawares for the second time in two days. Realising that she would appear ridiculous, never mind rude, and remembering that she had in fact been wishing to apologise, she remained where she was. The day was balmy, a perfect English summer morning, but her visitor was wearing the heavy woollen overcoat she'd seen hanging in the hallway at Hawthorn Manor. He had not shaved, his hair looked as if it had not been introduced to a comb in at least a week, but the lines of exhaustion had gone from his eyes and he was smiling tentatively, and he really did have a very, very attractive smile.

'Have I come at an inconvenient time?'

She had not invited him in. He did not want to discuss whatever was on his mind on the doorstep. And she did not particularly wish Clement to wander out of his study and find her loitering with a stranger. Prudence opened the door, stepping back into the shade of the hallway. 'Would you like to come in?'

'If you are sure I'm not disturbing you?'

She shook her head. 'Only from writing to my sister and, to be honest, I was happy to abandon that task. Go straight on, the parlour is the first door on the right. Would you like some tea—or coffee?'

'No, thank you. I've already had a surfeit.'

Which gave her no opportunity to rush upstairs and throw on a veil or a bonnet, and would, she concluded, simply draw attention to her horror of being seen. On the other hand, he had already seen her face and not been horrified and… and anyway this was her home. She took her usual seat with her back to the window by the empty grate, where the flowers she had picked that morning were already beginning to wilt. 'Please,' she said, 'make yourself comfortable.'

He took the chair opposite her, looking extremely uncomfortable. 'Miss Carstairs, I owe you an apology. Yesterday, when I questioned your relationship with the Sixth Earl, you quite rightly took umbrage. I compounded my rudeness by mentioning your appearance. That was presumptuous of me.'

His straightforwardness took her breath away.

She caught herself as her hand strayed to her cheek. This time, she would match his honesty with her own. 'No, you were right,' she said, and immediately felt it to be more than true, and a huge relief to admit it. 'There's no point in pretending—not once you know it exists, I mean.' Heat prickled at her throat, but she forced herself to continue in the hope that he might actually understand. 'It's not as if I can ever forget it's there or fool myself into thinking that it doesn't matter. But no one ever mentions it, you see, so yesterday, when you did, I was taken aback. No, that is to put it much too mildly. I was flabbergasted, frankly. But there's no need to apologise for it.'

He was silent for a moment, staring at the flower arrangement in the grate. 'When a soldier is wounded, whether he is scarred for life, or loses a limb or even two, his first concern is not for himself, once he knows he's going to live, it's for his family's reaction. I've seen many examples of a conspiracy to pretend that he's perfectly normal, when he's had half his face blown off, or both his legs.'

'Are you telling me that I ought to be grateful for having got off lightly?'

'No, not at all. I meant it only… I was going to say that I understand, but you'll think I'm patronising you again, and I came here to make my peace with you. I'm not used to explaining myself. I don't want to get off on the wrong foot again.'

She was touched, not only by his obvious sincerity but by his having made the effort when he had no need to explain or account for himself. 'I don't want to either,' Prudence said. 'I am glad you called, for I want to apologise too. It's not your fault that you have inherited Hawthorn Manor and all that goes with it.'

'But what I've inherited is the place you've come to think of as your own,' he said wryly.

'I'll need to come to terms with that. I've just realised I don't even know how you came to hear of Jeremy's death.'

'By complete chance. I read about the train crash in a three-month-old copy of *The Times* left in a café by a tourist. I didn't even know the Fifth Earl had died, and so learnt about both at the same time.'

She stared at him, aghast. 'I cannot imagine how you must have felt.'

'I wished I hadn't read the blasted paper,' the Earl replied. 'I went home and tried to put it from my mind, but I couldn't.'

'You mean it, don't you, when you say that

you don't want it. What will you do with the money?'

'I can't even begin to comprehend how much is involved,' he said, grimacing. 'Nor did I appreciate, until that last session with Doncaster a few days ago, how complicated it would be to sell up. As well as Hawthorn Manor and a stack of London properties, there are shares in railways, in a pickle factory, in a shipyard, and Lord knows what else. According to Doncaster they all follow a different selling process, depending on the way the particular company is governed—at least that's what I think was the gist of what he said.'

The lawyer, Prudence thought, had clearly tried hard to befuddle his client. 'I believe that lawyers make the simplest of matters sound ridiculously complicated. All that legal jargon, the clauses and sub-clauses, the "heretofore" and the "pertaining to" and the "notwithstanding"—I'm not sure if it is to show off or pull the wool.'

She was rewarded with a faint smile. 'Are you an amateur lawyer as well as a house renovator?'

'Ha! I don't know when you were last in England...'

'About nine years ago.'

'Goodness! Well, things have not changed

very much with regards to the roles of mere fe-
males, despite the fact that there has been enormous progress elsewhere.'

'Shower baths and steam heating and so on,
you mean?'

'I know it's odd of me to be interested in such
things, but I always have been. Do you know, according to *The Builder* magazine, every house in
the city is now being built with a scullery and a
water closet? Of course, one is not supposed to
mention such things...'

'Why not?'

'It is not polite to mention functions of the
body, of course. A lady would no more admit to
a need to use a lavatory than she would confess
to being with child.'

'Now that puts me in a quandary, for you are
undoubtedly a lady, yet you seem to be—how
shall I put it—rather fascinated by plumbing. A
woman who reads the—what did you call it?—
The Builder magazine to boot?'

'Contrary to popular belief, women do have
brains, and some of us even apply them, when
we are given the opportunity.'

His smile faded. 'I regret that I am depriving
you of the opportunity, but...'

'That's not what I meant.' Though it was, in

part, she acknowledged to herself. It was wrong of her, but she still nourished some residual resentment. She angled herself in her chair again, turning her face away. 'I am fortunate in having been able to take the opportunity that Jeremy offered. As a middle-aged spinster wholly dependent upon my brother to put a roof over my head, Clement would have been well within his rights to demand that I devote my time to providing his domestic comforts. Luckily for me, it would not occur to Clement to demand such a sacrifice. He would, frankly, be appalled if I whiled away the hours painting fire screens or embroidering slippers or fashioning peggywork rugs for him.'

'I commend him, though I have no idea what a peggywork rug is.'

'An abomination,' Prudence said with grim humour, turning back to face him. 'It is wool knitted into strips on a frame, and the strips are then sewn into rugs. A tedious business and the result not worth the effort. One of those pastimes invented by men to keep women uselessly occupied, in my opinion.'

The Earl laughed. 'Are you a radical, Miss Carstairs?'

'Not at all. I am fortunate, that's all, to be

spared the need to have a husband to formulate my opinions.'

'And to have a brother who encourages you to formulate your own, I gather?'

'Yes,' she agreed, wondering what Clement would make of their visitor, before realising that her vehemence had caused her to once again let down her guard and forgot to shield her face from Dominic. What was it about him that made her more lax than normal? Perhaps, she thought wryly, it was because they had both seen each other naked, in different senses of the word, during their first encounter, and had nothing to hide from each other.

'What have I said to make you smile?'

'Nothing.' The situation was far from amusing, for goodness' sake.

'Miss Carstairs,' he said, 'it's what passes for a lovely day. I don't suppose you are free to take a stroll round the gardens of the Manor with me? Though, from the little I've seen, they look more like a wilderness.'

'Prue, did that package arrive from—? Oh! I do beg your pardon; I didn't know we had a visitor.'

'This is my brother,' Prudence said, getting

to her feet, extremely flustered. 'Clement, this is—this is…'

'Caldwell,' the Earl said, standing up and offering his hand. 'Dominic Caldwell. I'm here to tie up the Earl of Bannatyne's estate.'

Clement was dressed in his usual working attire of trousers and a waistcoat with a pristine white shirt. Her brother was absurdly good-looking, with straw-gold hair, cornflower-blue eyes, a near-perfect profile and a clean-shaven square jaw. This combination, topping the wholly unearned body of an athlete had, over the years, caused many a young lady and several of more mature years to sigh wistfully—in vain. The Earl, Prudence observed, was struggling to come to terms with his preconceived stooped and dusty scholar metamorphosed in front of him into an Adonis.

Her brother looked equally dumbfounded. 'Clement Carstairs,' he said. 'How do you do? Are you here at the lawyer's request—what is his name?'

'Doncaster. And yes, you could say that,' the Earl replied.

Clement, eyeing the other man's odd suit and ragged appearance, looked utterly unconvinced, and moved closer to Prudence. 'What business have you with my sister?'

'I understand that hers was the inspiration behind much of the restorative work done at Hawthorn Manor,' the Earl replied. 'I was hoping her expertise might be of benefit in carrying out my evaluation.'

'I would have thought Doncaster would have sent a man who already had the necessary expertise,' Clement said. 'How do you know about my sister's involvement, in any case? She had no official role. It seems very odd to me, come to think of it,' he added, turning to Prudence, 'that a complete stranger came calling and you admitted him without summoning me. You're not exactly known for encouraging casual acquaintance.'

'Mr Caldwell and I bumped into each other at Hawthorn Manor the other day, when I was checking the fernery,' Prudence said, wishing fervently that for once Clement had kept his nose in his books, for his presence was threatening to destroy this chance to return to Hawthorn Manor. 'Once I had assured myself that he was who he claimed, I offered my assistance.'

'You will forgive my scepticism, Mr Caldwell,' Clement said, turning back to the

Earl, 'but your appearance is rather unconventional, and my sister does not venture out in the world much.'

'Clement! I may not venture out much, but I am not naïve. I have seen proof of Mr Caldwell's credentials. He's not imposing on me, if that's what you're worried about. I'm happy to help.'

'You certainly know more about the Manor than anyone, even poor Jeremy.'

'Your sister will be perfectly safe with me, Mr Carstairs. You have my assurance.'

'If I thought for a second she might not be,' Clement responded mildly, 'I would not have been so readily persuaded. Notwithstanding your unorthodox appearance, it's clear you are a gentleman. Be aware, however, that if my sister informs me otherwise…'

'For heaven's sake, Clement,' Prudence exclaimed, exasperated. 'You are treating me like a child.'

'Sorry, Prue,' her brother said ruefully. 'It's only—no, sorry. You will excuse an older brother from interfering, Mr Caldwell, my intentions—but Prue is right, she is perfectly capable—though I will say this, if you are one of Doncaster's underlings, I'll eat my hat.'

'Is your brother always so protective of you,

or was it me?' the Earl asked as the door closed on Clement.

'I rarely give him the opportunity,' Prudence said, torn between exasperation and embarrassment. 'Unlike some people, he doesn't think my mind is as damaged as my body, but I wish he would remember I'm a grown woman who can make her own decisions. I'm sorry, you are more than likely regretting calling on me now.'

'Only if your brother's dire warnings have made you wary of my company.'

'I'm still not at all sure why you wish to have my company, Mr Caldwell—I presume that's how I am to address you?'

'Perhaps you could use my given name, since it is the one thing that has been mine from my birth?'

'But I barely know you.'

He smiled. 'I think we've already progressed beyond formal introductions, don't you?'

The image of him naked popped into her head and she quickly banished it, though not in time to prevent herself blushing. 'Dominic.' She forced herself to look up and smile. 'Then you must call me Prudence.'

'Prudence, would you care to take a walk around the gardens of Hawthorn Manor with me?'

Panic seized her. Poor Prudence Carstairs would never, ever consent to such a thing. But hadn't she been silently railing at being labelled Poor Prudence in the eyes of the world—and, yes, in her brother's eyes too—for years now? For whatever reason, this man saw a different Prudence. Not to mention the fact that he was offering exactly what she longed for, more time at her haven.

She smiled, this time daring to meet his eyes for a few seconds. 'Dominic, if you will grant me five minutes to collect my bonnet and gloves, I would be delighted to do so.'

Chapter Five

It was almost noon as they entered the gates of Hawthorn Manor, the sun high in the sky and even Dominic had to admit that there was some warmth in it. The prospect of the house was very English, a sweeping driveway still distinguishable from the lawn despite being suffocated with weeds. The lawn itself was unmown, filled with wildflowers and grasses. The cow parsley was dying back, but he could see daisies and creeping buttercup, groundsel and nettles. Hosts of butterflies and dragonflies fluttered and hovered, bees droned, and the air smelled lush and verdant, of earth and fecundity. It was nothing like the dry, salty air, the dusty, harsh tang of a Greek summer. His goats would make short work of this grass. Their milk would be sweeter for it, the cheese creamier. He'd keep a very small herd if this was his land, just enough to provide him with milk and feta, and keep the grass down a bit.

His daydream was interrupted by Prudence. 'I think it's rather lovely, like a wild meadow,' she said, 'but I expect you'll want to get it scythed.'

'No, I prefer it as it is,' Dominic said, turning his eyes towards the house. It was, he supposed, handsome, in a very traditional sort of way, the stone mellow with age, in contrast to the slates of the obviously new steeply pitched roof. Tall chimneys and a row of dormer windows broke up the roofline, mirrored by the row of windows peering out from the basement. A huge conifer was growing at the eastern corner of the house, which was blocking the light from the lower windows, one of the many rooms he hadn't even investigated yet. He would have the tree cut down and plant…

Enough! He gave himself a shake. 'Which way shall we go?'

'If we follow the drive, we can go through the old rose garden,' Prudence said. 'You were miles away. Are you missing home?'

'I'm missing the weather,' Dominic replied with a theatrical shudder, but the truth was he'd barely thought of his smallholding. 'Though I won't be too sorry to miss July or August, if I have to. The heat becomes oppressive, and it gets horribly humid. It's impossible to do anything in the afternoons except sleep or—even in August there's usually a breeze on the beach.'

'I've never been to the seaside. Do you swim every day?'

'Almost. Even in the winter, the Aegean is warmer than the waters on the coast here.'

'So that's why you are so tanned.'

Prudence spoke almost as if to herself. Dominic's memory of their first encounter was primarily of his own shock and embarrassment, and then of Prudence's mortification at his having seen her scar. Though she was wearing her wide-brimmed bonnet, she had not pulled the veil down, and while her hair was still carefully arranged over her cheek, and she had taken care to have her left side closest to him, she seemed to relax more with every step she took further into the Manor gardens. She was wearing a pale blue skirt today, and a high-necked cream blouse embroidered with little blue flowers that might have been forget-me-nots. There was a natural elegance about her, a grace in the way she walked, and in the long, narrow line of her spine, in the enticing curve towards her waist, the span of it made tiny in comparison to her skirt. A row of buttons marched down the front of her blouse, over the swell of her breasts, tempting him to wonder what she wore underneath. How many layers would there be to unwrap before…?

'We go through here,' Prudence said, once again startling him. 'Have I an insect on my blouse, or a smut?'

'I was wondering how you manage that contraption under your skirts?' Dominic asked, which was at least approximating the truth.

'My crinoline,' she answered primly, 'if that's what you're referring to, is a Thomson's Crown model. It has narrow bands of steel, with a watch-spring mechanism which makes it, so the manufacturer claims, the most flexible on the market. It is also a great deal less cumbersome and much lighter than the layers of petticoats it was designed to replace.'

'Practical Prudence,' he teased. 'Was it indelicate of me to ask?'

'Extremely. Don't they have crinolines in Greece?'

'I haven't come across any, though that isn't saying much. I don't quite lead the life of a hermit, but there has been no woman in my life for some years now.' He stopped walking, surprised by his own confession. The garden they were in was a large square, completely enclosed by the tall hedging. Paving had been completed around the perimeter, but the markings for the meandering pathways which had not yet been laid were largely obscured by weeds. The roses had been throttled by briars, though a bright tangle of buds and blowsy blooms could still be seen and the air was heady with their perfume.

'Did you say this was a rose garden?' he asked. 'The hedges would need to be cut right back,' he went on, wandering over to the ancient moss-covered sundial which stood at the centre of the space. 'The sun is high in the sky now, but by September the garden will be in shadow for most of the day.'

'Jeremy was not particularly fond of roses. He intended this to be an outdoor extension to the fernery.'

'I like roses, but they're a spring flower in Greece. The summer sun scorches them. Shall we take a seat over there, in the shade?' Dominic said, spotting a stone bench.

'Never say you are too hot?'

'I was thinking of you.'

Frank bounded up to them as they sat down, brushing himself against Prudence's skirts, and she stooped to scratch his head. The cat twined himself around Dominic's legs a couple of times before settling down under the bench and falling immediately asleep.

'I'm sorry,' Prudence said, 'that I blurted out what I said about Jeremy yesterday.'

'I don't share his tastes, but I'm neither shocked nor disgusted, if that's what you're worried about. I am curious though, how you knew that he was a confirmed bachelor, to use your own phrase. Did he tell you himself?'

'Goodness, no! *That* was not a conversation he would have dreamed of having with a woman, no matter what her age or experience. He would have considered it both vulgar and shocking.'

'Then how?'

She had removed her gloves at some point while they were walking, and now frowned down at her hands. 'I don't know, exactly. I wouldn't say we were friends, we did not confide in each other, but he listened to me, showed an interest in my opinions. You've no idea how unusual that is. To most people, the ones who know me, I mean, I'm the invisible woman, a damaged spinster with no expectations. I'm very easy to ignore.'

She spoke lightly, without a trace of self-pity. It made him furious on her behalf, imagining what she must suffer, though he knew she would think him presumptuous. Though she had several times forgotten to shield her face in the course of their conversations, had even met his gaze on occasion, her expression animated, time and again she'd remembered and turned away, or tugged at her hat brim or her hair. Such ingrained caution spoke of a lifetime of degradation. Even her brother, who clearly cared deeply for her, thought her too fragile to fend for herself. He wondered if that too was a result of bitter experience, and his antipathy towards the man faded. Yet he was misguided, as Prudence herself had said. She was vulnerable, but very far from pathetic. She had a mind of her own, an acute and unusual one too, though the only person who had shown any interest in it, save for her brother, had ironically been a reclusive aristocrat! She was extraordinary and yet she had no idea she was.

'Speaking for myself,' Dominic said awkwardly, for he had no idea how to explain any of these musings, nor how to deal with what he was feeling, 'I have found you impossible to ignore.'

'That's because you've twice caught me trespassing.'

'I sought you out today of my own accord.' She looked up at him then, holding his gaze for a few heart-stopping seconds, and Dominic wondered if she was feeling as confused as he. 'I find you fascinating,' he said, meaning it sincerely, though keeping his tone flippant for fear he might alarm her.

'By your own admission, you've been living like a hermit,' Prudence said, resuming her sidelong gaze, 'so you were bound to find almost anyone interesting. It just so happens that I'm the first person you met.'

'Then it's as well we've not taken each other in dislike. I am very grateful to the shower bath, for bringing us together.'

He was rewarded with her laughter and her direct gaze. 'It is more usual for introductions to be made by a mutual friend.'

'I don't think you could be fonder of anyone than that shower bath.'

'Alas, I fear you may be right. Though if ever I was fortunate enough to be introduced to one of the new sewage pumping stations which are being constructed in London, I fear it may just steal my heart.'

Her eyes were alight with amusement. She looked so lovely to him, but to tell her would be a catastrophic mistake. 'However we were introduced, I consider it a stroke of luck on my part,' Dominic said. 'Though I'm not sure your brother would share that view. He accused me of being an imposter. He has a point,' he added, his mood darkening.

'He meant that you were clearly not a lawyer's clerk.' Prudence, to his surprise, reached for his hand, touching it reassuringly. 'And the law of the land has confirmed you are no imposter but a bona fide earl. Though I know you don't wish to acknowledge that fact,' she added, and would have withdrawn her hand had he not caught it.

'It's not fair of me to expect you to lie to your brother though. If you wish to tell him the truth in confidence…'

'I don't. I know he loves me, and I know it's ungrateful of me, but I am tired of his wanting to keep me wrapped in cotton wool. He is forever anticipating my being hurt, you see, and there are times when his attempts at protecting me are more painful than whatever he's trying to protect me from.' She grimaced. 'When he introduces me to any of his friends, it's always clear that he's warned them—oh, never mind. What I'm saying is that I see no need to tell him the truth, especially since you are so eager to remain incognito. Besides, you've already introduced yourself as Mr Caldwell. It shall be our secret.'

He was still holding her hand. Now he lifted it to his lips, kissing her fingertips. The gesture took them both aback. When he released her, she remained quite still for a moment before getting to her feet, obviously at a loss. And Dominic followed her, equally discomfited.

Dappled sunlight fell on the huge oval of the sunken fernery, which had first been excavated like a small lake, then lined with rock to create the cavern-like interior, with only the glazed roof on view from the outside, screened by the stand of tall spruce which surrounded it. The door opened inwards onto a gravel path. Inside, the air was hot and humid, the smell earthy and sweet from the moss which grew on the rocks and the distinctive scent from the many ferns which grew in lush abundance. Water dripped from channels cut into the rock into little pools set at intervals along the edge of the path which ran around the perimeter of the fernery. Prudence had preceded Dominic, excited and suddenly nervous about his reaction. It shouldn't matter whether he liked her work or not, but it did.

The small pond containing her first water feature stood at the entrance, a large cast iron bowl with water spouting from a fish. She watched Dominic's face closely as he examined it, delighted to see his expression change from mild interest to intrigue as the spout grew higher and the fish tail began to swish, and then give a shout of laughter as the fish appeared to plunge towards the water, then swivelled upright on its support before repeating the whole process.

'How does it do that?' he asked.

'It's surprisingly simple,' Prudence said, going on to explain the mechanism. 'Jeremy wanted marble dolphins or a statue of David, but I persuaded him that this would be much more fun, and Frank is fascinated by it.'

'You persuaded—good grief, did you design this?'

'And the larger one too. Do you want to see it?' Delighted by his reaction, she took his arm, urging him along the narrow path to the central pool, where her masterpiece stood at the far end. 'There, what do you think?'

Dominic said nothing, but his transfixed gaze told her everything. A huge water wheel turned inside a bronze case, powering the large clock which perched on top of it, the mechanism exposed, the slow tick-tock echoing under the glass roof of the fernery. Myriad cogs and gears linked by chains and pipes were mounted on the wheel casing, all turning in counter-intuitive directions. 'They are quite superfluous,' Prudence explained, 'they don't contribute to the clock mechanism at all.'

'It doesn't matter.' Dominic leant over the railing to take a closer look at the lower section. 'You think that they do, and that's the point, isn't it, to make you think, to try to understand what connects to what, like a giant puzzle.'

'That's exactly the point! Exactly! No one else has ever understood that—not that many people have actually seen it. Even the man who constructed it found it odd. He kept asking me— why have these fripperies when they're not required?'

'But you do need every single bit of it. Are those hawthorn berries, embossed on the casing?'

'Yes! I call it the Hawthorn Wheel.'

'It's quite miraculous. I could stand here looking at it all day. Prudence Carstairs, you are nothing short of a genius.'

'No, I'm not. I only designed it. I don't have the skills to build it. And honestly, in essence it's only a water clock, and even the Ancient Egyptians knew how to construct those.'

'Not like this though. What an incredible imagination you must have.'

'I have a number of other designs, intended for the gardens, but obviously they never came to fruition. To be honest, I think Jeremy only had this constructed to indulge me, I doubt he'd have agreed to any of the others.'

'I would love to see them.'

'They are stored in the turret room. It's not really a turret, it's the room at the top of the stairs above the long gallery.'

'I haven't looked around the house properly yet.'

'But you've been here three days!'

'I'm not actually constructing an inventory, Prudence. That's an artifice, remember?'

'I know, but…'

'What did you mean when you said that hardly anyone has seen this wonderful creation of yours?'

Evasive tactics again, Prudence thought, irked, but if she persisted he would either stubbornly refuse to answer or turn the tables on her, and she had no desire to spoil the mood. 'Jeremy was not quite so much of a recluse as his father, but he did not go out much in society and rarely entertained.'

'Your brother must have seen it though?'

'Yes, though it is far too modern for his taste. My sister Mercy was enchanted by it, and would have commissioned…but her husband has more conventional tastes and, besides, he would not permit…'

Dominic raised his eyebrows quizzically, but Prudence had no desire to discuss Mercy's objectionable husband and took a leaf from Dominic's book of evasive tactics. 'There used to be fish in this pool, but unfortunately Frank discovered them.'

'That cat left me a present this morning, just outside my bedroom door. Half-eaten, so I suppose I should be flattered that he deigned to share his breakfast.'

'You should be extremely honoured. Have you seen enough? Shall we move on?'

'Truly, I don't think I could ever tire of looking at this. What an extraordinary woman you are.'

'I'll start to believe you if you continue to tell me so.'

'It's true,' Dominic said. 'I would imagine that

there are some who would pay a pretty penny for such unusual designs.'

'Do you think so? Oh, but no—I couldn't,' Prudence said, her spark of excitement immediately fading.

'Why not? Surely your brother is not the type of snob to object to a woman making an honest living, especially when you are so talented.'

'It's not that. I mean it's true, Clement would not wish me to…but not because he…and he would be right. I have to wear a bonnet and veil whenever I go out.'

'You're not wearing your veil now. And there's no need for you to wear your bonnet here. You didn't before.'

'I was alone then.'

'Why don't you take it off? There's no one here but us.'

'I can't,' she demurred, though at the same time she was asking herself, why not? There was no one to scream or point or stare or faint.

'Why not? I know what you look like under that brim. You don't need to hide your face from me.'

'I don't. Haven't. Not so much,' she said, aware of how defensive she sounded, remembering the conversation in the rose garden, where she had several times met his gaze and not wanted to look away. 'I don't feel comfortable, I feel naked without a hat, if that doesn't sound too fanciful,' she protested, but she was wondering now if she could.

'Then I won't try to persuade you.'

He looked disappointed. She was disappointed in herself. Prudence tried to untie the ribbon. Her fingers were shaking, and it knotted even tighter. 'Now I truly can't,' she said, trying to make light of it.

'Do you want me to help?'

She nodded. Dominic waited a moment but when she made no sign of changing her mind he carefully untied the knot. She was holding her breath as she took off her hat. She had the distinct impression that he was too, until she set it down on the rocks by the fountain. 'Be careful what you wish for,' she quipped, close to tears.

He said nothing. Instead, he touched her. His finger traced the shape of her scar, from her forehead, down her brow, her cheek, to the indent on her top lip. His touch was gentle, his gaze intent. 'There is so much more to you than this, Prudence.'

No one had ever touched her in this way, yet it wasn't outrage that was keeping her silent. There was no pity in his gaze, but a gentleness that brought tears to her eyes and, to her horror, one of them escaped. 'But this is all anyone sees.'

'Not me.'

'No. I know.'

His fingers twined with hers, and she allowed him to draw her closer. His kiss was the merest flutter, the graze of his beard, the soft warmth of his lips, before he lifted his head, studying her carefully. She made no effort to break his gaze, her heart thumping, wondering if he was disappointed. Was that it?

He said her name as a question, and she finally understood that he was as confused as she was. He had kissed her. Some response was required. She leant towards him, terrified that her inexperience would show, but more afraid that he would think she was rejecting him. Heart thumping, she put one arm around his neck, and he inhaled sharply at her touch.

'Prudence,' he said again, this time not a question but a cross between a moan and a groan, his arm sliding around her waist. 'Prudence,' he said, and she lifted her face to his.

Their lips met again. He kissed her gently, carefully, his fingers on her back stroking, and his mouth gently urging hers open. A soft, lingering kiss that became deeper, the pressure of his lips on hers making her dimly aware that she had had no idea what constituted a real kiss, but it seemed the most natural thing in the world to follow his lead. Her eyes closed and she surrendered to the sensations he was arousing in her. His tongue touched hers and they both shuddered. His hands stroked her back, curled into her hair, feathered the hot skin at the nape of her neck, and all the time their mouths clung together. And then it ended, and Prudence slowly opened her eyes before disentangling herself.

'I'm not quite sure how that happened,' Dominic said.

He looked quite dazed, and his hair was wildly rumpled. Had she done that? She couldn't recall. Her mouth was tingling. She felt tightly wound and euphoric at the same time. Nothing she'd imagined had prepared her for that. 'Do you regret it?' she asked, not because she thought he did but because she thought she should say something.

Dominic laughed gruffly. 'No, though I should. Your brother would probably call me out, if he knew.'

'He is not such a fool. You are bound to be a

crack shot, and I doubt he even knows how to load a gun. Besides, duelling is against the law.'

'Practical Prudence,' he said with a faint smile, taking her hands, studying her intently. 'I didn't mean to—I should have shown some restraint.'

'Are you worried that I might misunderstand your intentions?'

'I didn't have any intentions, save to kiss you. That's what bothers me. I've been perfectly content with my own company for five years, but since coming here, meeting you... I don't know, all this,' he said, making a sweeping gesture. 'It doesn't feel real. But you do. I know I'm not making sense.'

'Perhaps there's no sense to be made of it. You are not the only one who is behaving out of character,' Prudence said, very belatedly realising how boldly she had behaved. 'I all but threw myself into your arms. I've never done that in my life before. I've never been kissed by a man.'

She was blushing furiously. Dominic's hands tightened around hers. 'I suspected as much, and that's what makes it... I've been on my own for a long time, Prudence, but I'm not without experience. Some would say I was taking advantage of an innocent.'

'But you're not, and I know you never would,' she said, disturbed by his sudden frown.

'I swear I would never—you have to believe me.'

'Of course I do. What is it?'

He opened his mouth to speak, then closed it again. 'Thank you,' he said, pressing a kiss to her hand before letting her go. 'The heat in here is overpowering, even for me. Shall we go?'

Chapter Six

'Thank you, dear.' Mrs Botheroyd, the vicar's wife, was five years younger than Prudence but her status as a married woman with a nursery full to bursting meant she felt perfectly entitled to condescend to her. 'I will say this for you, you write a very fair hand and the little changes you suggested are… Yes, I will admit it, Miss Carstairs, you have actually *improved* my own draft. Well done.'

'It is merely an invitation to a summer fête,' Prudence said, suppressing the urge to scream.

'Well, you have depicted it beautifully. Now, if you can copy another—shall we say fifty?— yes, I think fifty. You won't mind, will you? It would be a great help, for I have a list of things I must do and not a moment's free time, and these invitations must go out this week.'

'It's not a problem. I am fortunate to have neither a husband nor children nor a parish to make demands on me,' Prudence said, gritting her teeth. 'My time is all my own.'

Mrs Botheroyd was a kind woman at heart but, like many people, she was uncomfortable talking to a woman whose face was obscured by a veil and was always eager to ensure their conversations were as brief as possible. Today, however, she loitered. 'Well, as to that, Miss Carstairs, I had heard that you were helping to collate an inventory at Hawthorn Manor. Such a very important task. I must say I was most surprised—though I believe that there is a qualified clerk who is actually—but it does seem strange.'

'I know the Manor better than anyone now that the Earl is no longer with us.'

'Lord Bannatyne will be happy with the Lord and the angels,' Mrs Botheroyd said blithely. 'Miss Carstairs,' she continued, lowering her voice and drawing up a chair, 'I cannot believe that it is proper for you to be consorting in this way with a complete stranger.'

In truth, she had been expecting the warning, but it did not make her any more receptive. 'My brother has no issue with my *consorting*, as you put it,' Prudence said, though if Clement had an inkling of what had happened yesterday—goodness, it was almost amusing, trying to imagine what he would make of it. Almost.

'Oh, a brother—even such a dutiful brother as Mr Carstairs,' Mrs Botheroyd said with a small sigh, 'is hardly the best placed to counsel you. As a woman of the world, my dear, I feel it my duty to warn you that working in close proximity to a man, quite unchaperoned, as I understand you are, can expose you to the most unwelcome advances. And, I regret to say, your particular disadvantages make you even more vulnerable, for he is likely to assume you rather desperate.'

The words were kindly meant, Prudence told herself. Mrs Botheroyd was only articulating what was most likely a common viewpoint, and it would be easier simply to say nothing and get on with writing the invitations. But she was tired of hiding herself, her face behind a veil and her feelings behind a mask of bland acceptance. Why should she keep her opinions to herself? They were as valid as any other—more so, according to Dominic, who thought her extraordinary! And she really was sick and tired of being pitied and patronised.

'What do you mean by my particular disadvantages?'

Mrs Botheroyd looked considerably taken aback and immediately got to her feet. 'Come now, my dear. I would have thought it was rather obvious,' she said, vaguely indicating Prudence's bonnet and veil. 'I don't think there is any need to embarrass you...'

'I wear this veil because you are embarrassed by my looks, not me.'

'You are mistaken, Miss Carstairs. I pity you your misfortune, but we are as God made us, after all,' the woman said, her cheeks red, making for the door. 'My intention was to protect you from being preyed upon, but I will say no more. I did not mean to offend.'

But she had offended and though her instinctive response was to deny it, Prudence refrained. 'I am sure your intentions were well-meaning,' she said, 'but your concerns are quite unfounded. Mr Caldwell is a perfect gentleman, and I am confident he would never make any unwelcome overtures.'

'I am delighted to hear it,' Mrs Botheroyd said, already halfway through the door. 'Now, I must go as I am expecting guests for luncheon. You need have no fear that they will disturb you. I will have them shown directly to the dining room, so you may be at ease while you work. Did we say fifty invitations? I think perhaps sixty, to be on the safe side. What a pity that your sister is unable to find the time to open our little fête. Such a very beautiful woman, quite a queen of high society I believe, she would lend such a cachet—but perhaps next year? Oh, that is the doorbell. Excuse me, Miss Carstairs. If you will ring the bell when you are finished, the maid will make sure that you can leave without…that you need have no fears of…oh, what am I saying, you must be familiar with the routine by now.'

The door closed behind her, and Prudence counted to ten before pushing back her veil. She wanted to leave right now, without writing a single card. What was wrong with her? She didn't usually let Mrs Botheroyd get under her skin— at least not to this degree. It had been a relief to speak her mind though, just for once. But that was scant satisfaction since she would now be labelled as bitter and twisted, railing at her fate, on top of everything else.

Sighing, Prudence got to her feet and pushed the layers of lace curtain back to look out at the vicarage's back garden, where several of the little Botheroyd children were playing a game of catch, their very young nanny seated in the shade with her book. She let the curtain fall back into place, worried that one of them might see her. Was it her scar, or her lack of a husband and children that made her an object of pity? If she were unblemished, or if she was married, would she be a different person? Stupid question, for the answer was obviously yes. But she was going to have to live with her scars and her spinsterhood for the rest of her life. Did that mean she must content herself with this unsatisfactory existence, spending her days at other people's beck and call, making herself useful in the most tedious of ways, tolerated but never included? She had no friends, no one to confide in, for Mercy had too many troubles of her own. Was that why she had been so frank with Dominic? If anyone else had taken the time to listen to her, to treat her as if there might actually be a thinking, feeling person behind that blasted veil she had to wear, would she have been more wary of Dominic?

But they had not, and it was he who had looked beyond her veil and her bonnet and her scar. Seeing her creations through Dominic's eyes had reignited the ambitions she'd been forced to suppress since her one and only patron had died. She longed to see them brought to life, to have the audience they deserved. Was it really an impossible dream?

Dominic had stirred more than her creative ambitions, Prudence recalled, sitting back down at the table. She touched the tender skin where his beard had rubbed when they kissed. She had relived those kisses so many times, at times her toes curling with embarrassment at how forward she had been, how shockingly she had behaved, at others, closing her eyes, her body thrumming, reliving the sheer bliss of them. She was convinced that Dominic had felt as she did. Despite her complete lack of experience, she knew he had been as carried away by their kisses as she was. He desired her. Not for a moment had she thought he might be kissing her out of compassion or to try to prove a point, or for any other reason than that he wanted to. Dominic was attracted to her. When he looked at her, he didn't see a pitiful spinster or a scarred misfit. He saw a sensual woman with an extraordinary mind.

Prudence smiled wryly to herself. She really was starting to believe him. Dominic, who had not wanted a woman for many years, remarkably, astonishingly, wanted her. Though whether he would allow himself to do anything about it, she wasn't at all certain. Nor what her response would be if he did. Her smile faded. Why on earth had he been so vehement when he'd sworn he wouldn't take advantage of her? And that thank you of his when she'd assured him that she trusted him, it had been so fervent. It was strange that such an attractive man had lived for so long without female company—had actually avoided it? He was not, like her, lacking experience. Had another woman rebuffed him, or even broken his heart?

Resolutely putting those interesting questions to one side, she sighed, picked up her pen, dipped it in the ink and began to write.

Dominic pulled another paper from the stack in front of him, but the words swam meaninglessly in front of his eyes. He had spent the entire morning wading his way through documents detailing shares and equities and rents and mortgages. Neither of the previous earls seemed to have shown much interest in checking the accounts and, from what he could see, the lawyer had been making a very handsome living from the estate for years. It was no wonder that the man was so resistant to Dominic selling up, for he'd be losing a large portion of his income. The sums of money were immense to Dominic's eyes, and intimidating, for he had no idea what he'd do with them.

And, right now, not much interest either. He pushed the sheaf of papers to one side of the large kitchen table. Outside, the sun was shining for the fourth day in a row. If it stayed fine until the end of the week, he thought dourly, they'd probably consider it a spectacular summer. Perhaps if he went for a walk it would clear his head. He wasn't used to being indoors so much and he was badly missing his daily swim. There must be a kitchen garden somewhere. It was late in the growing season to be planting anything, and he'd probably not be here to harvest it, but he might as well take a look.

Frank appeared, his ringed tail pointed straight up to the sky, as soon as Dominic stepped out of the kitchen door. He had never had a cat, but he rather enjoyed having Frank around. He was useful, he didn't make too many demands and he didn't answer back. In Greece, the farm cats were feral, but perhaps if he could acquire one as a kitten…

Was that what he'd come to? He was thirty-five years old, not a hundred. Dominic pushed open the door and entered the walled kitchen garden. It was divided into four beds, but each was horribly overgrown, a tangle of weeds and grass, the brick pathways almost obscured. The fruit trees which had once been espaliered on the south-facing wall had not been pruned in a long time, and the glasshouse at the far end had hardly any intact panes. The last Earl might have been a botanist, but he'd not been a gardener.

There was a stone bench on the wall beside the glasshouse. Dominic sat down, kicking at the long grass at his feet. He hadn't been aware of being lonely in his cottage in Lavrio, but the idea of going back to that solitary existence had lost some of its appeal, and a kitten wasn't the solution. It was Prudence's fault. If he hadn't met her, he would still be perfectly happy with his own company. Though he couldn't regret having met her.

He leant his head back against the wall, closing his eyes, enjoying the sun on his face, and allowed himself to relive yesterday's kiss. Everything about it had astonished him, not least the fact that it had happened at all. The events which had culminated in his expulsion from the army had not emasculated him, but he was accustomed to suppressing desire. Yesterday, he had embraced it—and Prudence—losing himself utterly in the moment, in the taste of her and the feel of her, in the unexpected ardency of her response. Back in the old days, he'd always avoided getting entangled with innocents, and he'd known that Prudence had no experience even before he kissed her for the first time, but it hadn't stopped him. At the time, it had seemed inevitable, the culmination of a chain of events that had started when she'd stormed into the bathroom.

Was it only four days ago? Circumstances had conspired to allow them to spend a great deal of time alone. Was that it? Too much time in too close proximity? Yes, but the point was that the more time he spent with her, the more time he wanted to spend. He had been lonely, but it had taken Prudence to make him realise that. And she too, he guessed, had been too much alone.

He ought to get back to his paperwork but, as he got to his feet, instead of making for the door in the wall, he began to walk around the perimeter of the garden, trying to work out what each of the beds had been used for, weeding and pruning, planting and staking in his head as he progressed. It was about four times bigger than his plot at Lavrio, though the Greek weather gave him three growing seasons in a year, so the yield would not be too much higher. It would take weeks of work to get this soil back into any sort of state worth planting in. That spot over there would be perfect for three, maybe even six olive trees. It was too cold to grow a vine in this climate, but if he planted the roots outside cultivating the plant itself in the glasshouse, it just might work.

Not that he was thinking of doing any such thing. Irked, Dominic abandoned his daydream. What was the point in wasting precious time on a garden that wasn't even his? It was time to stop procrastinating and get back to the task in hand. Wade his way through those papers. Turn his mind to working out how the devil he was to rid himself of the burden of his inheritance. And then get back to Greece and his own garden.

Yet his feet slowed further as he approached the kitchen door. He didn't want to go back inside. It was fanciful of him, he knew that, but he couldn't help but feel the ghosts of generations of Thorburns were watching him, an upstart living in their stately home, wanting him gone. He wished he could oblige them. His beard itched. He needed a shave and a haircut. And while he was on the subject of his appearance, he desperately needed some new clothes. Maybe what he needed was a trip to London. It would allow him to spruce himself up a bit, and while he was in town he could poke Doncaster with a stick. Dominic grinned. Now that was something to look forward to.

Chapter Seven

Dominic's note informed Prudence that he had gone to London on business and would be away all day. She was surprised, for he had made no mention of having any such plan and couldn't help but wonder if he was avoiding her. She told herself she was being foolish but, as the day progressed, she managed to convince herself that he had been so shocked by her behaviour in the fernery he had run away to avoid facing her.

The day was hot and humid, the sun struggling to burn away the cloud, and Prudence's mood plummeted. She wished she had not been so diligent yesterday, in completing all the invitation cards for the fête. Clement, who was usually delighted when she offered her services as his scribe, today asked her if she was not feeling quite the thing. She claimed a headache, but after half an hour fitfully lying on her bed, her mind churning, got up again.

The afternoon post brought another letter from Mercy, not much more than a brief note to accompany a photograph which had been taken to mark her birthday, doubtless at her husband's insistence. Mercy was leaning on the ubiquitous pillar in the classic pose, wearing evening dress. Cream moiré silk woven with vertical mauve stripes and trimmed with velvet, she had written, for she understood Prudence's interest in fashion. There was bobbin lace at the neckline, silk-fringed tassels on the short, puffed sleeves and on the bodice, and a Swiss belt with tasselled lappets stiffened with whalebone. Which, Mercy wrote, made her feel as if she were wearing a set of curtains. The gown was, like the photograph, clearly her husband's choice. Mercy's taste was similar to Prudence's, preferring simpler attire, but this gown was doubtless the height of fashion and had likely cost a small fortune, both of which mattered to His Lordship more than whether it suited his wife, who was so beautiful she didn't need adorning. Prudence gazed at Mercy's flawless face, but there was no trace of the misery she knew lay beneath the perfect surface. Mercy had an inscrutable expression that almost never varied from photograph, to *carte de visite*, to photograph, but that did not prevent her husband having her image captured and recaptured. To document for posterity that he had married the most beautiful woman in England, Prudence thought sadly, or perhaps, more charitably, to compensate for the absence of photographs of any progeny.

She was sliding the stiff card back in between the protective papers when the doorbell rang, and a few minutes later Lizzie appeared at the parlour door.

'A telegram has arrived, Miss Carstairs.'

'My brother is in his study.'

'It's for you, miss.'

Surprised and a little apprehensive, Prudence opened the telegram.

BEG YOUR COMPANY FROM 10 TO-MORROW.
YOUR PRIVACY GUARANTEED. APOLO-GIES SHORT NOTICE.
HAY AND SUNSHINE ETC.
D.

Prudence woke early the next day, her stomach fluttering with butterflies. She decided to take breakfast in her room, startling Lizzie by having the range lit and the kettle boiled when she arrived for work. She drank all of her tea but ate only half a slice of bread and butter. By the time she was near to finishing her toilette, she was a jumble of excitement and trepidation. What had Dominic's enigmatic message meant? What manner of outing could possibly guarantee her privacy? Where were they going? And why? Without any clue, she dressed for the weather, with a summer gown of pale green with cream stripes, made high to the neck as usual. Over this, she donned an olive-green jacket fitted tightly to the waist with wide sleeves and a short peplum. Her hat was of the newly fashionable shape with a higher crown than the bonnets she customarily wore, designed to be worn further back on the head. She had adapted it by adding a veil to the narrow brim, which she now pulled forward, then studied herself closely in the mirror. Did the veil proclaim her need to keep her face hidden? She pushed it back, but even with her hair artfully arranged, the scarring on her lip was horribly obvious, and she was rearranging it when the bell rang.

Prudence rushed downstairs, calling to Lizzie that she would attend to the door, hoping that it had not woken Clement, who habitually slept late. At first, she thought the man standing on the step was a stranger. His hair was cropped and he was clean-shaven, revealing a very determined jaw with a small scar in the cleft of his chin. He was dressed in a double-breasted frock coat of dark blue wool, with trousers and a waistcoat of pale grey, a pristine white shirt and stock, and highly polished black shoes. He was wearing gloves and he was even carrying a hat. The effect was to make him look austerely handsome and rather intimidating.

'Dominic?'

'Is it such a transformation?'

'Yes,' Prudence said simply. 'You look completely different.'

He rubbed his jaw self-consciously. 'I haven't been without a beard since—for a long time. The barber told me I was going to be very unfashionable.'

More likely he would set a trend, Prudence thought, eyeing the vision before her, which made her so very conscious of her own defects. 'I thought you were going to London on business.'

'You told me to spruce myself up, remember.'

'You have certainly succeeded.' The clothes were expensive and understated, precisely to her taste, and he wore them quite unselfconsciously.

He looked, in fact, what he refused to acknowledge he was, a titled gentleman with a natural authority. Not that he would welcome such a compliment. 'You look even less like a clerk now,' Prudence said.

Dominic, however, cared as little for his appearance now as he had previously, and simply shrugged. 'I saw Doncaster. He offered me a glass of Madeira. The last time, I got a cup of dusty tea. Progress, I think. Shall we go?'

'Where?' Prudence asked, closing the door behind her.

'Ah, I'm afraid you are going to have to be patient. I'm sorry about the short notice, but I was afraid the weather would break and wreck my plans.'

'So that's what the telegram meant. We are making hay while the sun shines. But where?'

'The train station first of all,' he said. 'I promise you need not worry,' he added when she stopped short. 'I have taken every precaution to ensure that our privacy is guaranteed, and you will be safe from prying eyes.'

'But how can you, Dominic? I can't travel on a train full of strangers gawping at me.'

'Trust me, Prudence.' When she nodded, he

took her hand, tucking it into his arm, and she allowed him to urge her on.

The station stood on the outskirts of the village, with one platform serving both southern- and northern-bound trains.

'There's no train here, and there's no one waiting. What are we—?'

'Ah, perfectly on time,' Dominic said, as a steam engine appeared in the distance. 'Come on.'

The engine drew into the station, belching steam.

'There's only one carriage.'

'That must be ours, then.'

'What do you mean?'

'You'll see,' he said, nudging her in the direction of the carriage, where the conductor had opened the door. 'All aboard, Miss Carstairs. In you get.'

She climbed up the two narrow steps and after a moment's conferring with the conductor, Dominic followed. The carriage was richly decorated, with thick blue carpeting on the floor, a quilted ceiling, and blue and gold curtains. A large sofa upholstered in blue and gold took up most of one side, which was flanked by two other chairs. On the opposite side stood a narrow dining table and two chairs.

'This looks fit for the Queen,' Prudence said, staring around her in astonishment.

The train whistle blew and it began to pull out of the station, forcing her to take a seat. Dominic sat down beside her, immediately taking off his hat and gloves. 'Do you like it?'

'It's ridiculously ostentatious but I love it. How on earth did you manage to organise it, and where are we going?'

Dominic grinned. 'I finally found a good use for a very small portion of the funds that Doncaster forced on me. Would you like some breakfast? I'll have the conductor serve it now, and then you can be comfortable.'

As he spoke, he pulled a bell cord which was set into the carriage roof, and almost immediately the conductor appeared with a trolley, spreading a white cloth on which he laid two place settings, silver pots of tea and coffee, a bowl of strawberries, peaches and apricots, bread, butter, jam and honey, a platter of cold ham and finally a fragrant dish of eggs.

'Madam?' Dominic held out a chair for her. 'He won't come back unless I pull the bell to summon him.'

'Thank you. This is a wonderful treat.'

'Oh, we are barely started.'

He had gone to so much trouble to make her feel at ease, she could not possibly be so churlish as to sit at the table with her veil on, never mind the fact that she would not be able to eat any of the tempting food laid out before her. It ought to be simply a relief to take off her veil, but she couldn't help feeling, as she did so, that gesture was more significant than removing a little scrap of fabric. Dominic, however, simply smiled at her as she sat down, her face naked, making a show of pouring his own coffee and drinking the first cup straight away, as he usually did, giving her ample time to settle and pour her own tea. It was so strange, eating such delicious food and drinking tea as the world rushed by, the dishes moving very slightly when the train took a bend, but it was also a relief, knowing they were cocooned from the world, and as they progressed, excitement quashed her fears and she concentrated on making the most of the privacy he had gone to such trouble to obtain for her. She ate some fruit and drank two cups of tea, while Dominic took some ham and eggs.

'Should I have retained the beard?' he asked, catching her studying him.

'No, it's not that. I've never taken breakfast with a man other than Clement before,' she confessed. 'Oh, goodness, I didn't mean…that sounded… I simply meant that this is all very cosy.' Though what she meant was intimate.

'What did you tell your brother?'

'I led Clement to believe that I was spending the day with Mrs Botheroyd, writing invitations to the village fête. Mrs Botheroyd is the vicar's wife.'

'Why can't she write her own invitations?'

'Because she has far more important things to occupy her, while I have an endless amount of time on my hands to help her with her good works. Though I don't mind, not really. At least not very much. And it's true, I do have too much time on my hands.'

Dominic pushed his cup aside and reached across the table. 'Such very talented hands,' he said. 'It seems to me a great pity that the Hawthorn Wheel is to be your only legacy. You are wasting your talent, hiding away in that backwater.'

'Isn't that what you're going to do?' Stung, she pushed his hand away. 'As soon as you have rid yourself of the inheritance you don't actually want, you're going to race back to your little cottage and spend the rest of your life tending your sheep…'

'Goats.'

'Goats, sheep, cows—what difference does it make?'

'Quite a lot, if you happen to be a goat, sheep or cow in search of a mate. I am choosing to go back to the life that I have made my own,' Dominic said evenly. 'You are running away from the chance of having a different life.'

'You don't even know that I want a different life.'

'So you'll be perfectly happy keeping house for your brother, embroidering his slippers and making patsywork rugs, will you?'

Prudence glared. 'Peggywork.'

'It sounds like the name of a character from Dickens. Madge Peggywork, the proud owner of one tooth and a kind heart, who makes a living from baking biscuits from sawdust.'

'Hypatia Peggywork,' Prudence countered. 'She has three teeth and an iron constitution from making her living as a tosher.'

'I'm almost afraid to ask what a tosher is.'

'Then I will tell you merely that it involves sewers and sieves.'

He laughed. 'I should have guessed it would involve plumbing.'

'Dominic, if this trip is your attempt to persuade me that I can make a life away from the village, I must tell you that I have tried to brave the world, but people's reactions are always the same.' She shuddered. 'I have to accept that it will never change. Unfortunately, you are, in my experience, quite unique.'

'A compliment I would return if it didn't sound so back-handed. Shall we retire to the sofa?'

Dominic stood up and Prudence was in the process of getting to her feet when the train hit a bend, making her stagger against him. His arms went around her, and for a moment they stood entwined, and she knew from the change in his expression that he was thinking, exactly as she was, of the fernery. His hands slid up her arms. She leant in towards him, lifting her face. And then the train jolted again, forcing them both onto the safety of the sofa, and she had to concentrate on trying to rearrange her crinoline very quickly, lest any of the hoops were crushed out of shape.

'We should be there in about twenty minutes,' Dominic said, consulting his watch. 'There are…er…facilities, through that door, though it might be safer for you to wait until we have come to a stop. The convenience is of the traditional sort. I'm sorry to have to disappoint you, but I'm afraid not even the most luxurious of railway carriages comes equipped with modern plumbing.'

Prudence heaved a theatrical sigh. 'It would have made the day perfect too.'

'I shall do my best to make it up to you. Do you want to know where it is I'm taking you?'

'I've only asked three times already.'

'We're going to Bognor Regis. I considered Margate, and Worthing too, but I'm told that Bognor Regis is not nearly so popular with day-trippers, perhaps because the railway line was only completed recently.'

'We're going to the seaside.' Instinctively, her hand went to her face.

'Better than that, we're going to our own private beach, which is ours for the day.'

'You've hired a beach?'

'You said you had never been to the seaside, and the weather really is rather fine. When I was in London yesterday, amid all the smoke and the stench, I kept thinking how wonderful it would be to go for a swim under a blue sky, and Doncaster made some chance remark about shares in a private railway, and I asked him if one could hire a carriage such as this and…' Dominic broke off sheepishly. 'I thought I'd surprise you, but perhaps I should have asked first. I assumed…'

'You assumed perfectly correctly. I'm not— Have you actually hired a beach?'

His face broke into a beaming smile. 'I have. Can you believe that such a thing is possible? It belongs to some aristocrat who uses it for a week every August. Doncaster's wife's brother handles the man's business or something like that—I don't know the ins and outs of it. That man has a finger in every pie.' His expression darkened temporarily. 'Too deep in too many pies, if you ask me.'

'Do you think he's a crook?'

'No, though I reckon he sails close to the wind. I meant that he takes much more of a cut from the business than is warranted. My only experience of such matters was a stint standing in for a quartermaster, but it's been plain to me, almost from the outset, that my predecessors kept a very loose hold on the reins when it came to business. Doubtless they thought it beneath them. If it were my money though, I'd take much better care of it.'

He never missed an opportunity to distance himself from them, Prudence noted.

'I'm woefully ignorant of military matters. I don't know what a quartermaster does.'

'Stores. Supplies. Pay. It's the custom for them to be commissioned from the ranks, so it's not the most prestigious of appointments. Not a post for a gentleman, probably because it smacks of trade. I stepped in when our man contracted the Crimean fever, and I was recovering from a flesh wound in the shoulder. As one who had worked his way up the ranks, it was no skin off my nose to take on the role, and, besides, if I hadn't our men would probably have gone even hungrier than they were.'

'There was a great deal of comment in *The Times* regarding problems with supplies,' Prudence said warily, for this was the most information he had so far volunteered about his time in the army.

'I met Russell once—the reporter? At Sebastopol. I think he was instrumental in setting up the railway there. There was a line running from the harbour at Balaclava to the frontline. They built it in weeks, towards the end of the war. It was hailed as a triumph of technology, bringing guns and supplies in and taking our wounded out, the advantage we needed to finally put an end to the conflict. I didn't see much evidence of it helping,' he said sardonically, turning towards her, 'but it gave those in charge something to crow about.'

'You were there, at Sebastopol? Throughout the siege? Oh, Dominic, that must have been—'

'I don't know why I mentioned it,' he said, interrupting her. 'Probably because, until I came back to England, it was the last time I was on a train. They don't have railways in Greece. Anyway, we're here to have an enjoyable day out and I think that's the train slowing. We must be nearly there.' He fished his watch out, making a point of consulting it. 'Bang on time.'

Chapter Eight

⸎

There was no station building, and no platform either at the terminus. Prudence, her veil carefully back in place, stepped lightly onto the ground, handling her billowing crinoline with admirable aplomb. The carriage Dominic had hired was a four-wheeled covered vehicle with one rather mangy horse attached, the musty, cramped interior smelling of pipe tobacco.

'A bit of a comedown, I'm afraid,' he said as he helped Prudence in, 'but I believe our beach is not above a mile away.'

'Are you planning on going for a swim?'

'I rather hoped to persuade you to come into the water with me.'

'Very amusing.'

He couldn't see her face properly through her veil, but she obviously thought he was joking.

Deciding to postpone that battle until he had established the lie of the land, Dominic contented himself, as she did, with looking at his first sight of a traditional English seaside town.

Travelling past several quiet residential streets, they drove along a wide thoroughfare lined with shops, and surprisingly quickly reached the seafront. Several very genteel-looking hotels faced onto the wide esplanade. The beach shelved steeply down, a mixture of sand and shingle, with wooden breakwaters at regular intervals and a few small boats beached high up on the foreshore. Despite the fact that it was the middle of the week, there were a significant number of visitors, strolling along the promenade that ran along the top of the beach, resting on the benches, leaning on the railings and perched on the sea wall. Small children paddled in the shallows. A clutch of brightly painted bathing huts, each mounted on a platform with four large wheels, stood at the water's edge, with a couple wheeled into the sea, though the bathers, if they had braved the waters, were hidden from view.

As the carriage continued along the esplanade, the beach became less crowded and the way narrowed until they were bumping along a road that was not much more than a track, drawing to a stop at a high wall.

'This must be it,' Dominic said, opening the door and jumping down. 'Let me make sure the entrance has been unlocked.' He was not at all convinced that it would be, the arrangements had been made in such a hurry, but Doncaster had obviously seen the need to impress him. The handle of the wooden door turned. Instructing the driver to return in four hours, he helped Prudence down.

'I am so excited,' she said. 'I can't believe you have managed to lay all this on just for me.'

'I simply issued the instructions, to be fair,' he said. 'Doncaster has his uses.'

'But it must have cost you a fortune.'

An eyewatering amount, truth be told. 'Let's see if you think it's worth it.' He pulled open the door and let her precede him, then stepped through.

'Oh, Dominic.' Prudence pushed back her veil impatiently, gazing around her wide-eyed. 'This is wonderful.'

The beach was a perfect crescent bounded by a high stone wall. A narrow, fenced path formed the perimeter, and beyond it could be seen the associated mansion, shuttered and rather ugly.

The beach was flatter here, and the shingle had given way to golden sand. Two beach huts stood ready at the water's edge, painted in pale green and white stripes.

'They match my gown!'

'It's a good omen,' Dominic said.

'I am not going into the sea,' Prudence said. 'You're teasing me, aren't you?'

'There is a costume in the hut. What's stopping you?'

'I can't swim.'

'I can. I won't let you drown.'

'No.' She backed away from him, the sparkle fading from her eyes. 'No, Dominic, I can't.'

'You don't have to do anything you don't want to,' he said, puzzled. 'If you want to take a paddle...'

'Oh, I'd like that.'

'Then you shall paddle.'

Two chairs had been set out invitingly on the sand under the shade of a large parasol. A hamper containing their lunch stood under a table, with a bottle of champagne in an ice bucket, though the ice had nearly all melted. There were some advantages, Dominic thought, watching Prudence's face light up, to spending money, especially when it wasn't his.

The sun was actually warm today, and there was no breeze. The sea was more green than blue, the wavelets of the still retreating tide sparkling on the sand. 'I can't sit here dressed to the nines. Would you mind if I made myself more comfortable?' he asked.

'Of course I wouldn't. Compared to your usual attire, I'm not surprised you are finding those clothes constricting.'

'Nothing to the constraints of full dress uniform, I promise you.'

'What regiment were you in? I don't know why, but I can't imagine you rigged out in one of those preposterous Hussar uniforms.'

'You're damned—dashed right. Cardigan and his ilk would never have countenanced someone like me among his officers. "A man must be born a gentleman first",' he quoted scathingly, shrugging himself out of his jacket and hanging it over the back of his chair.

'Would it have made such a difference to your career, if your name had been Thorburn and not Caldwell?'

He had a sudden, horrible flashback to that morning. The mist had not lifted. It was freezing cold, and his men were a ragged-looking lot, standing in formation, forced to watch his humiliation unfold. One of his medals had clung stubbornly to his tunic when the row was roughly ripped off. He had unpinned it himself and handed it to his Colonel while his men looked on in shocked silence. The bastard who had accused him had been the son of a viscount. An earl trumped a viscount, so it would have made a world of difference.

'Dominic?'

He had wound his necktie tightly around his fist, so tightly that the stitches were straining. He opened his fist, dropping the ruined garment onto the sand, unable to think of a single innocuous remark to explain his lengthy silence.

Prudence picked the tie up, shaking it out and draping it over his coat. 'Why don't you take your waistcoat off too? If you'll turn your back, I'm planning to take off my shoes and stockings.'

He did as she suggested, slowly unbuttoning the grey silk waistcoat, momentarily distracted by the rustling behind him, recalling the glimpse he'd had of her lacy petticoat one of the first times he'd seen her. Prudence, he was willing to wager, would not wear plain woollen stockings. Silk, he reckoned, tied with pale green garters to match her gown.

'You can turn round now.'

She was sitting down, her feet hidden from sight under her gown. 'I can feel the sand between my toes. It's much colder than I expected, but lovely.'

'I'll take a leaf from your book, if you don't mind,' Dominic said, sitting down beside her to unlace his shoes, pulling off his stockings with some relief. She was looking studiously at the sea. Were bare feet indecent? He'd never thought so before. The thought of Prudence's dainty bare feet curled into the sand under that cage she wore was certainly rousing indecent thoughts in him. Better than those other thoughts. He leant back, stretching his own feet out in front of him and dug them into the cool sand. Five years, and he still burned with shame every time he thought of that day, though he had done nothing wrong, save tell the truth.

He turned his face to the side, unsurprised to discover that Prudence was studying him. He smiled faintly, reaching for her hand. 'Yes,' Dominic said. 'The answer to your question is yes. It most likely would have made a difference if my name had been Thorburn and not Caldwell. Which is proof, as if I needed any more, that I'm right to want nothing to do with the name, or the class it represents or any of it. I'm my own man, and I intend to stay that way.'

'A name doesn't change who you are. You are still Dominic, whether you are Caldwell or Thorburn or Smith.'

'Do you think so? Would you be the same person if your name wasn't Prudence?'

'I don't even know if my name…'

'What?' He leant over, for she had turned away from him, removing her hand from his clasp. 'You don't even know what, about your name?'

'Whether it suits me. You told me yourself that I was badly named.'

'But that isn't what you were about to say.'

'No, it wasn't. Are you really going for a swim?'

Recognising his own evasive tactics, Dominic conceded defeat. 'Yes. And I'd really like you to come with me but, since you are adamant you won't,' he added hastily, 'then why don't we both go for a paddle?'

Dominic offered his hand to help Prudence out of the chair and she accepted it gratefully. Crinolines were not designed to be worn on these low chairs, which were comfortable enough to sit on, but incredibly difficult to get back out of. Crinolines were not particularly suitable for paddling in either, she thought wryly as a rogue wavelet washed over her feet and soaked the hem of her gown and petticoat before she could lift either.

'Oh! That was unbelievably cold,' she said, hastily adjusting the various skirts of her gown as another wave approached.

'You're going to ruin that dress,' Dominic said.

Her feet and her ankles were under the water but her calves were now exposed, and if she went any further into the sea she'd be showing a great deal more leg, or her gown would indeed be ruined. 'I'll have to come out,' Prudence said, backing up several steps.

'You've barely gone in. Don't you like it?'

The sand was rough on her soles, the water smooth on her skin, and the feel of the little waves rippling over her was delightful. The waters were quite clear. She could see the sand shelving down and the wavelets giving way to a very slight swell, which would caress her skin. The sun baked her head and face, but the cold of the sea on her toes was such a delightful contrast and the air was so salty, unlike anything she had breathed before. Prudence closed her eyes, lifting her face to the sun, her skin tightening and tingling with the salt and the heat. It was such a novelty to expose her face to the sun. She could feel her skin drinking it in.

'I love it,' she said, smiling, opening her eyes to find Dominic smiling at her. 'I already completely understand why you like to swim. It must feel so...so liberating.'

He laughed, putting his arm around her waist to steady her as another ripple made the sand around her feet shift, and she leant gratefully against him. 'It stops you thinking,' he said. 'Your mind empties, and it's only you and the sea and the sun. The sea holds you, but you have to push back against it too, to stop from drifting. There's a rhythm as your body and your breathing and your mind work together with the sea.' He laughed again, softly this time. 'That sounds fanciful, I know.'

'It sounds magical,' Prudence said, looking longingly again at the water.

'I know you can't swim, but you could easily float. You'd be safe with me.'

'I'm not afraid of drowning.'

'Then what?'

His arms were around her waist, holding her

in the shelter of his body, the pair of them facing out to sea. The gentleness in his voice brought a lump to her throat. He would not be disgusted by her, she knew that, but still she felt she would be diminished in his eyes, more flawed than he realised, and what Dominic thought mattered a great deal to her, much more than it should.

'Prudence?'

She turned around to face him, trying to find the words to explain.

'Are there more?' he asked, gently touching her cheek. 'Is that what it is?'

She nodded. 'One more,' she said, touching her shoulder, 'from here, down my back.'

'Unless you are planning on swimming without a suit…'

'Dominic! This is England, not Greece.'

'In fact, I am given to understand that there are still some bold men who insist on swimming *au naturel* in Margate, much to the horror of the other day-trippers, but if you insist on wearing a suit…it is a very modest suit, I imagine, Prudence, and it should go without saying that I won't think any differently of you.'

'I know it's true, but I never… I hardly look at it myself,' she confessed, her cheeks burning. 'I know you think I'm being foolish.'

'I don't think that at all. You didn't have to tell me. You could simply have pretended that you didn't want to swim, that it was too cold, or that you were worried you might drown, or get eaten by a shark—No,' he added hastily, 'there are no sharks here. But you didn't say any of these things, Prudence, you told me the truth. I think…'

'I am *not* extraordinary.'

'I think that you are very brave, and I am honoured that you were honest with me.'

'Oh.' She blinked furiously. 'Well, then. Thank you.'

'It's the truth.'

'I know you think so.'

'Prickly Prudence.'

'Debonair Dominic.'

'Oh, no, surely you can do better than that.'

'Dashing?'

'Dear God, no.'

'Different,' Prudence said. 'Distracting,' she added when he smiled.

'Distracted, when you look at me like that,' he said, smoothing his hand down her arm, making her shiver. 'I am going to go for a swim now, and break with my own tradition by wearing a suit, but I am *not* going to push that machine into the water. The sun is quite strong, I'd advise you to sit under the parasol or you'll burn.'

He made no other effort to persuade her to join him, for which she was immensely grateful, but as Prudence sat on the canvas chair under the parasol she began to question her decision. The water looked so tempting. Dominic had made such an enormous effort to make her feel comfortable. When was she likely to get such an opportunity again?

He had disappeared into the bathing machine to change. After a few minutes she heard the door at the front of the machine creak open, but she didn't see him until he had waded out beyond the hut and the water was at the top of his legs. His bathing suit was dark grey, wool or flannel, she could not be sure from this distance, with short sleeves, the fabric darkening and clinging to him as he waded steadily into the water. Prudence walked across the sands to the water's edge, shading her eyes with her hand. The suit was loose on him, no more indecent than a shirt. If hers was similar, then her neck would be exposed but nothing more.

Dominic stopped wading and stood quite still for a moment. And then he dived into the sea.

He was under the water for what felt like a very long time. She held her breath and was beginning to panic when he finally emerged, quite a long way from the shore, and began to swim. She watched him, his arms beating a steady rhythm, his legs making only the gentlest of splashes. It was such a physical activity, and surprisingly graceful. He must be very fit.

She envied Dominic the way he was so at ease with his body. His clothes didn't really matter to him, and that meant whatever he wore, he looked like himself. He would never look like a clerk, he would never be mistaken for an effete aristocrat or even a land labourer, and she had never seriously believed he was a vagrant. He was Dominic, and if he was anything, he was a soldier. It was in his stance, in the way he expected to be obeyed, in the way he didn't like to be challenged. This morning, when he'd appeared on the doorstep looking so radically different, it had not taken her too long to realise he hadn't changed at all.

She had never been comfortable with her body or her face. Her clothes mattered to her because they were a distraction from both, but they were also a statement, not about her taste but about her position in life. She took care not to wear anything ostentatious. She wore muted colours and kept to simple lines. The only part of her clothing that reflected her inner self was her undergarments, and no one ever saw those.

Dominic was swimming parallel to the shore now. Droplets of seawater sparkled in an arc as his arms moved, and his head moved from side to side as he breathed, his hair glinting blueblack. Everything about today spoke of his understanding of her. He didn't believe she should hide away from the world, but that was what she chose to do, and so he had created a secret world, hidden away just for her. A world where she could swim safely, yet she hadn't even taken the first step. She was being churlish and selfish, and she was insulting him too, by underestimating him. Such a little risk it was to take, to expose herself to him, when the rewards could be so high.

As Dominic reached the edge of the little bay and turned around, Prudence made her way determinedly towards the other bathing box. The steps were wooden slats set into a ramp. The door opened outwards, almost knocking her off balance. Inside, it was nothing much more than an empty box with a few pegs on the wall. It smelled rather fishy, not unpleasant, but not exactly a place she'd choose to spend a lot of time in. Her crinoline brushed both sides. The floor was gritty with sand. She took the suit from its peg and examined it. It consisted of a pair of bloomers and a tunic, both in dark blue flannel. The bloomers were extremely wide, gathered at the ankle and waist, which left great folds of fabric, she presumed to disguise the shape of her legs, though she couldn't help wonder about the weight of it, once it absorbed some seawater. The tunic was short-sleeved and full-skirted, buttoning up the front and trimmed with two bands of blue ribbon which looked very elegant, but would only add to the overall drag. An outfit with considerably less fabric and without unnecessary ornamentation would be entirely more practical. Then again, how many women actually went swimming wearing such clothes? Perhaps they went no deeper than the knees?

With a great deal of difficulty, she removed her gown and her crinoline, folding it flat and balancing it against the wall. Did one wear undergarments with a bathing costume? Impractical, yes, but it seemed quite indecent not to wear anything. There was no mirror, but her fingers told her that the scar on her shoulder could be seen, and would be revealed to a greater degree the moment her tunic got wet.

She was committed now. She would not let herself down and, more importantly, she wanted to prove her faith in Dominic, who had shown such faith in her. So she opened the other door of the bathing hut and ventured onto the first step. The tide had come in and was lapping against the wheels, and she reckoned it would be at least over her knees when she reached the bottom of the ladder. Dominic was still quite far out, floating on his back, too far for her to see his face.

Her heart was pounding as she stepped gingerly into the water, struggling not to lose her balance, for there was no handrail. It was much colder than she remembered and, just as she'd predicted, the bloomers of her costume became leaden and saturated, the material cold and dank on her legs, making her shiver. The last step brought her thigh-deep and gasping, clinging to the steps in order to keep herself upright, for the sand seemed to be shifting beneath her feet. She was growing accustomed to the cold now, and the slow creep of the water up her clothing, well ahead of her actual immersion. Taking a deep breath, she let go of the ladder, steadied herself, and decided to venture further.

It was terrifying and exhilarating. The sun felt hotter on her bare head and so very strange on her neck and shoulders. The bathing costume was horrible, considerably hindering her progress, but the sensation of the water enveloping her, gently nudging her along, was like nothing she had ever felt before. Brushing her hair out of her face, she tasted salty water and felt the sting of the salt in her eyes. She was waist deep when she became conscious of Dominic, standing just a few yards away.

'You were right,' Prudence said, smiling triumphantly. 'It is elemental. Did you enjoy your swim?'

'Very much, though I found the suit a hindrance.'

'Mine is made with enough fabric to construct a ballgown. If I fall, I doubt I'll be able to get myself back up again.'

'Have you had enough, or do you want to try to float?'

'Could I? Won't my suit drag me down?'

Dominic shook his head. 'The water will support you, and I will too.'

'How? Do I have to go deeper?'

He shook his head, holding out his hand. 'Stand next to me, and lie down, it's that simple.'

Prudence laughed. 'It can't be.'

'Try it.'

She took his hand and edged closer to him, concentrating hard on not overbalancing. The water crept up past her waist, making her gasp, and the skirts of her costume became tangled between her legs, but she was determined now to prove herself.

'Ready?' he asked, and she nodded. He put his arm across her shoulders. 'Now lie back slowly, and I'll put my other arm under you, to hold you. Go on, I promise you'll float.'

She did as he asked her, gasping as the water enveloped her, struggling to keep her head up, until he told her not to, her legs paddling frantically, until he hooked his other arm under her knees and lifted her so that she was splayed in the water, her hair soaked, her eyes dazzled by the sun, rigid with fear. And then, suddenly, she was floating. 'It works!'

'Close your eyes,' Dominic said. 'Relax. Don't think about it. I have you.'

She did as he bid her. Sunspots danced behind her lids. The sea lapped around her, creeping into her ears, splashing her face. Her bathing costume floated around her like weeds. She was weightless, cocooned, tingling all over, elated.

And as she lay, lost in a dreamlike trance, slowly, increasingly conscious of the man holding her. Of the strength of his arms. Bare arms. Separated from her skin by one layer of wet flannel. Of the way the water swayed her body towards his, the bump of her thigh against his torso, the brush of her fingers against his taut belly. She opened her eyes, at first dazzled by the sunshine. His suit buttoned up the front as hers did. It clung to his body, the peaks of his nipples, the dip of his navel, the smattering of hair at his chest where the neckline had stretched. Was her suit as revealing?

Prudence kicked her legs in an effort to stand and Dominic released her immediately, but she stumbled, flailing for him, and he caught her, steadied her.

'I told you, I had you.'

She was standing on his toes, her skirts tangled around his legs, and she was pressed against his chest. She looked up, their eyes met, and she forgot that she was cold, or that her suit was clinging to her, or that her situation at this precise moment in time was far beyond scandalous. She forgot everything save for the urgent, desperate need to taste his lips on hers. She said his name. She might have. Or he might have said hers. And then their mouths met.

Hot mouths and tongues. Cold hands. Salty skin. Burning sun. And the sea, insistently forcing them closer. This time, she needed no coaxing to open her mouth. They kissed deeply, and desperately, as if the first kisses had been centuries before, and as if these might be their last kisses. She pressed herself against him, not knowing what she was doing, letting her body guide her, her mind lost in relishing every single sensation he was rousing in her, relishing the dragging ache inside her, the throbbing of her nipples pressed against the wall of his chest, the shallow harshness of his breath. His hands on her bottom and the small of her back and her waist, sliding up, brushing the side of her breasts, making her nipples ache in a very different way. And then a wave caught them, knocking them both off balance, and when she was finally on her feet again the water came up almost to her chest.

'The tide is coming in,' Dominic said, putting out a protective arm as another wave hit her. 'We'd better go in.'

He waded ashore, keeping just behind her, standing waist deep as she clambered back into the bathing hut. It was several minutes before

Prudence could catch her breath. This was a very different kind of floating. It was only when she struggled to get out of the dank, clinging tunic that her fingertips brushed the scar on her shoulder. He must have seen it as he'd followed her in from the sea. He must have touched it when he was kissing her. But she hadn't noticed. And it hadn't made any difference.

Prudence had fallen asleep, still clutching the remnants of her champagne. Dominic leant over and carefully removed the glass, draining its contents. The carriage would be arriving in about half an hour, to take them back for their train. He wished, absurdly, that they could remain here for ever.

What was wrong with him? He set the glass down and got up to adjust the parasol to keep Prudence's face in the shade. Her nose and cheeks were flushed with the sun. How often did she have the opportunity to expose her skin to the elements? Every day since he was a young man and the weather had begun to shape his day, first as a soldier and more recently on his smallholding, he had surveyed the sky, turned his face towards the sun, gauging the weather and planning his day accordingly. This simple act, the small pleasures of the wind on her face or now the sun warming her skin, were denied Prudence on a daily basis. A nun in a cloister led a less sheltered existence, in some ways, than she did. She must resent the restraints placed upon her, but she accepted them. It wasn't fair!

Her hair, usually so carefully arranged, was a tangle of wispy tendrils gently ruffled by the breeze which had got up with the changing of the tide. One little pale foot peeped out from below her gown. It was covered in sand. He wanted to kneel down and brush it clean. He would roll her stocking back on for her, up over her slim ankle, her calf, her knee, and the soft flesh of her thigh, and...

Dominic swore under his breath. What the devil was he thinking? He tipped the last of the champagne into Prudence's glass and stalked down to the water's edge. The problem with Prudence was that there came a point in her company when he stopped thinking and gave in to the desire that was beginning to plague him. He had not planned today with the expectation of being rewarded with kisses. He had simply wanted to give Prudence something no one else had, or would think of, because he had realised, sitting through Doncaster's procrastinating, that he could. His reward was her expression when she'd boarded the train, when she'd seen the beach for the first time, when she'd dipped her toes in the water for the first time, and when she'd surrendered to the pleasure of floating. He'd been responsible for that excitement in her eyes, the triumph when she'd overcome her fears and the bliss of surrendering to the sea, that feeling he shared, that he'd wanted to share with her—and that he'd never even tried to put into words before either. That was part of her allure, the way she managed to extract his feelings and thoughts from him, because he'd been so alone with them for so long. Though the downside of that was that feelings and thoughts he didn't want to express also came tumbling out before he could prevent them.

He'd been too long alone, Dominic told himself, draining the glass, and she was too...extraordinary. If she had not been Prudence but some other woman, then he'd have no problem keeping his thoughts and his hands to himself. Truth be told—and it was time to admit that—his feelings for her frightened him. He'd known her less than a week, but she'd already proved far too much of a distraction. Was that it? He was using his interest in her to avoid concentrating on the business of his inheritance. What did he plan to do with it all? Doncaster had asked him despairingly yesterday. He'd played the haughty, how-dare-you-question-me? card quite successfully, but the man was in the right of it.

A wave rippled over his bare feet, soaking the hem of his trousers. Time to go. Prudence, awake now, was bent over her foot, putting on her shoes, having put her own stockings on without his help. 'I fell asleep,' she said, smiling uncertainly up at him. 'I hope I didn't snore.'

He held his hand out to help her up. 'So loudly I have a headache.'

She laughed. 'Too much champagne and too much sunshine.'

'One can never have enough of either.'

'Dominic, I have had the most perfect day.' She took him by surprise, kissing him softly on the mouth. 'Thank you. I'll never forget it.'

He wanted to pull her into his arms again. He wanted to kiss her sunburnt nose and taste the salt on her lips, to have her arms around him and her head on his shoulder, and to hold her. And then what? Time for a serious dose of reality, Dominic decided. He lifted her hand to his lips, kissing her knuckles. 'My pleasure,' he said. He'd begin tomorrow.

Chapter Nine

Yesterday had been perfect, Prudence thought as she passed through the gates of the Manor the next morning. Almost too perfect. She had never felt so carefree as on the beach and in the water, so unencumbered—if one discounted that ridiculous bathing costume. And when they had kissed! But as the Manor came into view, remembered delight gave way to the nagging doubt which had plagued her since she'd woken up very early this morning. Though she knew she and Dominic had no future together, she was afraid that her heart was taking no account of this unavoidable reality.

They had met under extraordinary circumstances. He was the first man to have seen past her disfigurement, the first man to think her something very far from the Poor Prudence most people saw. Spending so much time together, in such close proximity, had heightened their feelings, and Dominic was an extremely attractive and intriguing man. It was inevitable that she might persuade herself she was falling in love, but it was vital that she understood that her feelings were illusory. Unless she wanted to end up nursing a broken heart when Dominic left, it was long past time for a dose of reality. Today, she was determined to return to the role of helpmeet he had first offered her, and equally determined to stick to it.

The front door was open. Prudence hung her bonnet up on the hook beside Dominic's greatcoat, but when she went in search of him in the kitchen it was empty. The dregs in the coffee pot were still warm though. Too restless to sit and wait for him, she decided to take a walk to the fernery, but a streak of ginger crossing the path to the walled garden made her change her mind, and she followed Frank through the gate.

Dominic was digging in the south-facing bed. He was dressed in clothes that he had obviously brought with him from Greece, a pair of loose-fitting trousers made from what looked like flour sacks, with a rough cambric shirt, open at the neck, showing off his deeply tanned throat.

The sleeves of the shirt were pushed up to reveal his sinewy forearms. The pale shadow of his shaved beard had already disappeared after yesterday's exposure to the sun and sweat made his shirt cling to his chest and his back. A fierce gust of primal desire made her stop in her tracks to catch her breath and by the time she looked again, Dominic had spotted her and had stuck the spade in the ground, making his way onto the path to greet her.

'This place looks as if it's not been worked in years,' he said.

'It hasn't. As I mentioned before, the old Earl lost interest and neglected to maintain the house and grounds.'

'It seems a shame to me that his son didn't prioritise restoring the kitchen garden. A man can't dine off ferns. Not that I'll be eating any of this produce. The chances are that by the time any of this is ready I'll be back in Greece.'

'Then why bother?'

He wiped his face then his hands with his handkerchief. 'I find it helps me relax. How are you after yesterday? No sunburn?'

Prudence shook her head, wishing for once that she had put her bonnet back on, not to hide her face but her thoughts. 'What are you planting?'

'Lettuce. Carrots. Marrow and cucumbers. I've no idea if they will grow outside here, they flourish in the sun on my farm, but they never did well in the Crimea.'

'You had a garden during the war?'

'A number of my men did. Sometimes it was the only fresh food they had. The French fared much better. They remembered what Napoleon said about an army marching on its stomach. Shall we take a leaf from Frank's book and go and sit in the shade? I want to talk to you.'

'I want to talk to you too,' she said, wondering from his somewhat cool greeting if he had been thinking the same as she. She ought to be relieved if that was the case, but it was with a sense of dread that she sat carefully down on the bench. 'Are you missing Lavrio? Is that why you are in the garden?'

'Digging helps me think. What is it that you wanted to say to me?'

Now she had her opening, she hesitated, reluctant to put an end to something that was rare and precious. Which was precisely why she had to speak out. 'Yesterday,' she began, 'it was wonderful.' She was forced to stop again, for tears had welled up in her eyes. 'You thought of everything, Dominic, and I'll never forget it, but I know… I think it's time that we concentrated on the reason you are here. You made it clear from the moment that we first met, that your first and only ambition was to reject your inheritance and return home. I have been distracting you from that task.'

'You have been the most delightful distraction,' Dominic said, reaching for her hand, then changing his mind, 'but yesterday made me realise that I am beginning to want—to care—to feel what I have no right to feel for you. It would be very wrong of me to continue to behave in a way that would encourage you to believe…'

'Dominic, I don't. I swear, I have no expectations, you have not led me astray and I know you never would.'

This time he did touch her hand, though only fleetingly. 'You have no idea how much that means to me, but I wanted to, yesterday. I mean I wanted more—I wanted to make love to you, and though I would not risk—not ever—but I wanted to, and that is a warning sign I dare not ignore. I don't want to hurt you, Prudence.'

'I am determined you won't.'

He laughed grimly. 'I meant yesterday to be

special for you. I didn't count on it meaning so much to me too.'

And she had not counted on him being so frank. It was painfully bittersweet, to hear her own thoughts and feelings reflected back. To have Dominic care deeply for her, even for a few days, a few weeks, would be…foolish beyond compare. To be forced to say goodbye then, would make of her a very, very pathetic Prudence. She smiled valiantly. 'At least I now understand why you love the sea so much. How did the English version compare?'

'Colder, not so salty, and more tide to battle with, but I enjoyed it. Whether I'd enjoy it quite so much in the depths of winter, however, is another question. You should learn to swim. You have a natural affinity for the water.'

'I'd have to come up with a more practical design for a bathing costume.'

'You know my thoughts on the subject. To swim unencumbered by any costume, there is nothing like it.'

She could imagine it now. The cold caress of the water on her skin, the sense of being at one with the elements, exposed but free. And Dominic by her side. The warmth of his flesh against hers when he held her, making her conscious of every part of their bodies that touched, the water between them heated, while around them it remained cold. The touch of his lips on hers, the taste of him. The need to taste him again was so overpowering, it was almost impossible to ignore. And he was holding her hands now. And she could see from his expression that he was thinking the same. All she had to do was move one inch closer, maybe two.

'I can't,' Prudence blurted out. 'Learn to swim, I mean.'

Dominic blinked, looked down at their clasped hands as if they belonged to someone else, then let her go. 'Why not?'

'You know why not.'

'You don't have to lock yourself away here, Prudence. You deserve a better life. You are talented and brave and witty and clever and, yes, I'm going to say it again, quite extraordinary. If you would stop hiding yourself away…'

'I could be the main attraction at Bartholomew Fair. Yesterday didn't change anything, not in that sense. You are uniquely blind to my scars.'

'Your scars don't define you.'

'They should not, but they do.' She was once again on the brink of tears, and took a moment to compose herself, gazing down at her lap, her hands tightly clasped. 'What I choose to do or not do with my life when you have returned to Greece is none of your concern.'

'You're right, of course,' he said firmly. 'There is no more to be said. I should get back to my planting.'

She got to her feet, shaking out her skirts, extremely reluctant to leave, though she knew that was what she ought to do. 'I was thinking perhaps I could give you a tour of the house before I go. I would feel I had done something practical to assist you and, in any event, it would remind us both of why you are here.'

He hesitated for a moment, then shrugged. 'Perceptive Prudence,' he said wryly.

The idea was a sound one, Dominic concluded, but not without risk. There was no escaping the fact that the opportunity to spend a little more time with Prudence had been a factor in his agreeing to it. But he also needed to remind himself why he had put himself through the pain and effort of establishing his entitlement to be here. And to prove to himself that he was right to reject it all. This was his chance to refocus and regain his perspective, provided he did not let Prudence distract him.

To watch Prudence blossom yesterday, to see her delight in what should be simple pleasures— a train journey, a trip to the beach, a paddle— had, he decided, accentuated his own feelings. Today he would rein them in. Wonderful as the notion was, of spending the next few months creating other such perfect days, it would be misguided. He was already entranced by her. She was occupying his thoughts unduly. They were already in thrall to each other. A perfect storm of circumstances had brought them together and kept them here, secluded from the world, free to enjoy each other's company in a way that no other situation would allow. It was inevitable that they would become fascinated, smitten—whatever the right word was! Yesterday had added to that enchantment, another private day out of time. When he had held her, kissed her, touched her, aching with desire and longing, it was not his own needs which drove him but the need to please her. And afterwards, as she lay sleeping, so vulnerable and so lovely, what he'd wanted was to keep her safe, and to find a way to make her happy.

It was not possible and, as she had pointed out, none of his concern. He might think that this secluded life she led was not good enough for her, but that was her choice. Though as he'd watched her earlier, making her elegant way across the walled garden, knowing she had hung her bonnet on the peg in the hallway beside his greatcoat, he had been ridiculously pleased by her trust in him and her comfort in the surroundings. You see, he'd wanted to tell her, this is but the first step. Though the next steps were for her to take alone—or not take at all.

As they made their way back to the Manor they were both quiet, their ease in each other's company strained, and it became more strained as they progressed through the rooms. Even the steam heating system failed to animate Prudence. Until today, Dominic had shuttled between the bathroom and the bedroom and the kitchen, avoiding the dining room and the drawing room and the library and the morning room and the state bedchambers and their plethora of furnishings and tapestries. What struck him now was the sheer volume of *things* that served no purpose save to scream of old money, of tradition and good taste. Though Doncaster had assured him that the most valuable of the silver and jewellery was in safe keeping, it seemed to Dominic that the Manor was still awash with valuables, incontrovertible evidence of a line of Thorburns going back beyond the Earldom into history. To his relief, he felt no interest in that history, no connection whatsoever with the heritage he was set upon destroying, a line that would end with him.

'This is the gallery,' Prudence said as they reached what he would have called the attics. 'It's where the family portraits are hung.'

Generations of Thorburns stared haughtily down from the walls. Each austere image confirmed what Dominic had known in his bones. His blood was not theirs. He stopped in front of the final two. The Fifth Earl, who had given him away. And the Sixth Earl, whose premature death had forced him to return to England. The two men had been very alike, though they had chosen to be portrayed very differently. The Fifth Earl stood on some mystical hill created by the artist to allow the sitter to proudly survey what was presumably his estate, with Hawthorn Manor in the background. The lands had been gradually sold off in parcels by Doncaster and his predecessor. The portrait of the Sixth Earl showed him standing in front of the foundations of the fernery. It must have been not long after he had inherited, so perhaps three or four years ago.

'We are nothing like,' he said to Prudence,

conscious that she was slanting him worried glances. 'I can see nothing of myself in either of them. It simply confirms what I thought. That man did not sire me.'

'But Jeremy must at the very least be your half-brother. Don't you feel anything?'

She seemed anxious, though he couldn't understand why, and so for her sake he looked again. 'What are you imagining I might feel? I didn't know him, and I never will now. I cannot imagine we'd have had anything in common.'

'You both had an affinity with plants.'

He smiled faintly at that. 'And he is responsible for commissioning the only item in the Manor I'll regret leaving.'

'If you mean the Hawthorn Wheel, you could easily afford to have it shipped to Lavrio, if you truly are that fond of it.'

It hadn't occurred to him, and the idea had instant appeal, until he imagined himself being reminded every day of its creator. 'Water is scarce enough there,' Dominic said. 'Besides, the fernery would be incomplete without it.'

He turned away, pulling the Holland cover from what he'd assumed was a table, discovering to his surprise that it was a billiard table. He set the balls out, took up a cue and executed a few shots. The surface was perfectly even, the table better quality than any he had ever played on.

'Do you like to play?' Prudence asked.

He grinned, his mood lightening. 'Every spare moment I had, back in the day. I was unbeatable.' His smile faded. 'Though it would probably have been better if I'd lost gracefully every now and then. It's bad form to trounce a superior officer. There was one in particular, I ought to have let him win the third frame to save face, apparently. Perhaps I would have, if he hadn't been such a poor loser.' He hit another ball. 'Perhaps not. I'm a stubborn ba— I'm stubborn. I play by the rules. It's a problem of mine. Have you ever played?'

'Good heavens no. Jeremy would never have let a woman near his precious table. He was afraid I might rip the cloth.'

'The words of a man afraid he might be out-played,' Dominic said, rolling his eyes. 'I don't know how many times I've heard it. Do you want to try?'

'Really?' Prudence took the cue he offered. 'What do I do?'

'Stop holding the cue as if it were a loaded gun. Here, let me show you.' He placed her left hand on the table, then stood behind her to line up the shot. Her crinoline billowed out behind her as she leant over, forcing him to stand to one side, leaning over her shoulder. 'Drop your elbow. You don't push the ball, you strike it.'

Her hair tickled his chin. His hand brushed the side of her breast as he demonstrated the cueing action, and he felt her inhale sharply as the cue made contact with the white ball at an angle completely different from the shot he had lined up, sending the red ball flying into the pocket. She did not move, and he didn't want to move. He wanted her to turn around in his arms. He wanted to kiss her. He *ached* with longing.

'Well done.' He let her go.

She set the cue down and stood up. Her cheeks were flushed. 'Beginner's luck,' she said, brushing an imaginary speck from the immaculate baize. 'Will you keep this table?'

'I don't have the room. My cottage is not much bigger than your precious bathroom.'

'You could build yourself a bigger house.'

'I am happy with the house I have. It's mine. I thought you understood.'

'I'm trying to.'

'That man,' he said, pointing at the Fifth Earl's portrait, 'did his best to write me out of the family history. I'm glad he did. If he had not, I'd have been harnessed to the Thorburn plough, a second son with no purpose save to step in and sire the next generation if the first son failed. At least I was spared that. Fate, in the form of a train crash, brought me back into the Thorburn orbit. I couldn't have that hanging over me indefinitely.'

'So you came back here to write the Thorburns out of your history, once and for all. To do to them what they did to you?'

'To wipe the slate clean.'

'So that you can make a fresh start?'

'So that the fresh start I made can be permanent. Can't you see, I've found my place in the world and I am content there. These men,' Dominic said, allowing his disgust to show as he swept his arm around the room, 'with their rank and privilege, their power to order the world as they wish it, and to trample on those who dare to disagree—that is not me.' He turned away, taken aback by his vehemence. 'It's really that simple.'

'You would still be you, Dominic. Only wealthier. And with more influence,' Prudence said, frowning. 'Influence you could use to do good.'

'I would be a member of a club I don't want to join.'

'Isn't the army a club, with rank and privilege?'

His mood darkened. 'Precisely the reason I'm no longer a member.'

'But you were happy there for many years. Successful too. Why did you leave?'

'Are there any more rooms? What's over here?'

Without waiting for her, he strode over to the end of the gallery, taking the left-hand of two doors, finding himself in a small octagonal room, with windows looking out over the full sweep of the gardens. A most ingenious shelf was fitted all the way round, with sets of drawers positioned underneath it at regular intervals and a chair set on wheels to allow the person working there to move around depending on the time of day and the light.

'This was where Jeremy worked,' Prudence said, following him in. 'My turret is on the opposite side. Dominic, I didn't expect you to... I intended to warn you about the portrait.'

A small fireplace occupied the only solid wall, and over it hung a painting. It depicted a young woman, seated on a rustic bench with a spaniel beside her. Both the woman and the dog looked blissfully happy, she gazing outwards, the dog gazing adoringly at her. She was simply dressed in a white high-waisted gown with short sleeves and a very low neckline which made the most of her alabaster flesh. Her face was quite lovely, heart-shaped with a rosebud mouth and a pair of brilliantly sparkling deep blue eyes, topped with a tumble of wild raven-black curls.

He knew, without reading it, what name the brass plaque would bear, but he forced himself to read it anyway. *Monica, Fifth Countess of Bannatyne.*

'I'm sorry,' Prudence said, 'I should have warned you.'

He was completely unprepared for the shock of seeing her. He tried to speak and could not, so he tried to shrug. Every emotion he had failed to feel looking at the portraits of his half-brother and his reputed father now surged through him. This was the woman who had given birth to him. Who had died giving birth to him. His eyes were the same colour as hers. His hair the exact same colour. A lump rose in his throat. Tears smarted in his eyes. She looked so young and so vibrant and so happy, yet only a few years later she was dead.

Dominic cursed under his breath. It was *pathetic* of him to be feeling this, he was a grown man.

'Jeremy found the portrait in the attic after his father died. It had obviously been there for many years,' Prudence said, slipping her hand into his.

He tried to drag his gaze away, but he could not. 'Proof,' he said, his voice raw, 'that I am not his son, no matter what the law says, thank God.'

'She is very beautiful. Her eyes are the exact same colour as yours, and her hair too.'

And the tilt of her chin, he thought, mesmerised. A wave of grief threatened to engulf him. Had she ever held him, or had death taken her before she knew she had a son? Was he dragged, squealing from her arms? Did she give him up willingly? Had she died cursing him, or cursing her lover, or screaming in agony, or had she embraced death as a release from her cares? Would she have loved him? Or would she have hated him, the proof of her infidelity and, if she had lived, her road to ruin?

He had been lucky. Prudence was right. He had been very, very lucky. Here, before him, was the true victim. What must it have been like for her, to carry him inside her, knowing that she would not be permitted to keep him? Had she plotted her escape or resigned herself to losing him? What kind of choice was it? Keep her bastard brat and live as an outcast, or give him away, remain shackled to a man she could not have loved and who would never let her forget that she had wronged him. Whatever she chose, if she had been permitted a choice, she would have been miserable. Ruined and shamed.

'If you persist with this course of action, you will be ruined and shamed.'

He reeled backwards, for the familiar voice was so clear it was as if his Colonel was in the room with him.

'You meant well, Caldwell, but it would have been better for you if you had left him to finish his business and minded your own.'

'Dominic?'

With a huge effort, he banished the memory. The cases were not the same, but the parallels were painfully easy to draw. Here was all the confirmation he needed that the course he had set himself was the right one. 'What do you think would have happened, if she had lived?'

Prudence shrank at his harsh tone. 'I don't know. It may not have changed anything.'

'You don't think that the Earl might have allowed her to keep me, do you?'

'Oh, Dominic, if you had been a girl, or a third son...'

'But I was a cuckoo in the nest, and a second

son, far too dangerous to keep. Besides, she had broken her vows. Doubtless he wanted to punish her.'

'I am sure she would not have surrendered you willingly, Dominic.'

'It doesn't matter,' he said. 'What she wanted, how she felt, what she thought, wouldn't have mattered. All that mattered was what *he* wanted. She was his wife. I was not his son, but we were both his property, both his to dispose of. He could even rewrite our history.'

'Rank and privilege,' she said, her face white.

'Exactly. The power to order the world as you want it.'

'And to trample on those who dare to disagree. Is that what happened to you?'

'Yes.'

'Will you tell me?'

He had never spoken of it, but he nodded. 'I need to. I want you to know the whole wretched story.'

Prudence took his hand, gently urging him out of the room. 'I think we might need some coffee.'

Chapter Ten

⌒◯⌒

Prudence had seen Dominic brew enough pots of his strong, bitter coffee to be able to say with some confidence that she would make it instead. That he did not demur spoke volumes of the turmoil going on in his head. She pretended to bustle about, watching him anxiously as he sat at the table, staring down at his clasped hands. She had no idea what he was going to tell her, but finally, she guessed, she would learn the real reason for his isolated life in Greece.

She set the pot down in front of him with a cup and saucer, and took her habitual chair opposite, with her back to the light. Though it felt like a long time since she had worried about exposing her face to him, it was still only a matter of days. Far too few for her to be worrying about the depth of her feelings for him, she told herself automatically, but *her* feelings right now were not important. Dominic had poured a cup of coffee and drunk the scalding brew in one. His hand wasn't shaking as he poured the second cup, but his knuckles were white as he gripped the coffee pot. Was he about to confess to a crime? She couldn't believe he was a criminal, but what, really, did she know of his past?

He threw back the second cup of coffee then pushed the pot away with an air of finality. 'I didn't leave the army,' he said. 'I was dishonourably discharged.'

'*Dis*honourably? I don't believe it!'

'I don't think I believed it would happen either, but it did, just after the siege at Sebastopol ended.' He stared down at his hands again, frowning deeply. 'You can't imagine the conditions during that siege. It went on for more than a year. The early part of fifty-five was the worst. It was so cold at night, and the men were so inadequately clothed. The snow would melt during the day and their boots would get soaked in the wet mud. Then the temperature would plummet and their boots would freeze, so they'd cut off their boots to ease the agony they were suffering, and then—no new boots were forthcoming, and in some cases gangrene would set in, and they'd lose their feet. When the rains came, the tents were useless and they'd have to wallow in the mud like pigs, the sick and wounded together with those who could still hold a gun. They were starving, freezing and exhausted, but they continued to serve their country and obey orders.'

Dominic pushed his chair back, stretching out his legs. 'By comparison, the officers lived a life of luxury. I'm not saying we didn't suffer, but there were some—Cardigan, Raglan and their ilk—there were dinner parties on a yacht, picnics with their wives, champagne and smoked salmon, while the men were gagging on broth made from rank meat.

'Lord Cardigan was hailed as a hero after the Charge of the Light Brigade.

'Cardigan's commanding officer was Lord Lucan, his brother-in-law. The pair of them loathed each other. Whether Lucan was responsible for the fiasco of the charge or Cardigan or both, it was Captain Nolan, of inferior bloodstock, and conveniently too dead to dispute the facts, who was made the scapegoat,' Dominic said savagely. 'By the end of that year, Cardigan's precious troops were marginally worse fed than their horses. I had nothing to do with Cardigan and his ilk, I mention him only because he was typical of those in charge. Well-born, well-connected, arrogant, and in the main useless. I thought myself fortunate that my own colonel was at least competent. I rather naively assumed that meant he was also a man of principle.' He paused for a moment then shook his head. 'No, that's unfair of me. He had principles; they just didn't chime with mine.'

Dominic stared down at his hands again, gathering his thoughts or lost in the past, and Prudence poured her own tea. She still had no idea where his story was heading.

'The long and short of it is that by the end of the siege in September fifty-five, discipline was breaking down and the men increasingly had little faith in their commanding officers. Those of us who had direct contact with the men, as opposed to sending out incomprehensible commands from remote observation points, had a hard time of it to keep them in line. There were cases of looting, violation of women.' Dominic swallowed hard, his mouth thinning. 'Unfortunately, there are always incidents like these when war has gone on too long and men have been away too long. It's dealt with harshly when it is discovered.'

Prudence pushed her cup away, for the tea had

brewed too long and was bitter. 'When you say violation, do you mean rape?'

'I do.'

She felt sick. 'One of your men?'

'No, not one of my men.'

'I won't believe you if you tell me that you…'

He swooped on her hand, squeezing her fingers so tightly that it hurt. 'Thank you.' He picked up the coffee pot again, his hand shaking as the dregs sloshed into his cup, grimacing when he swallowed it. 'I was patrolling in the burnt-out ruins of the town. I heard her cry out. It was a moan. Or a groan. Muffled. Not a scream. As if she was already—as if she knew it was useless to protest.' Dominic closed his eyes, his hands clasped painfully tight. 'He had her against a wall. I could see matters had gone far but not—not too far. I called out his name. He told me to mind my own business. Couldn't I see that she wanted it? he said. And he actually turned back to…' He broke off, covering his face, swearing viciously.

Prudence, struck dumb with horror, forced herself to sit quite still, waiting for him to regain control, sensing that if she went to comfort him he would be unable to continue, and that he needed to.

After a moment he sat up, his expression strained but determined. 'She didn't say a word. That's what got to me. She simply wanted it to be over. So I grabbed him by the shoulder and pulled him off her, and I punched him. He couldn't believe it. It would have been funny, the look on his face if it was not…but it wasn't funny. I caught him on the jaw. I felt it crack. He went down and lay there cursing me and threatening me, but I paid no heed. The girl ran off into the night. I'd only have put the fear of God in her if I'd gone after her offering to escort her home.'

'Was there any chance at all that you could have been mistaken? That the woman…'

'No,' Dominic said grimly. 'The look on her face was one of resigned terror. There was no way on earth I could have been mistaken, nor ever forget it either. That one of our own was taking advantage of an innocent women amid the bloodshed and suffering affecting both sides on a daily basis sickened me. It still sickens me.'

'You saved her, Dominic.'

'Yes, I did, but I shouldn't have had to. To abuse the very people whose lives we were there to protect was unforgivable. That poor woman would see every man in uniform as a potential rapist after that experience.' He dug his knuckles into his eyes, his throat working. 'It happens, in wartime. Blood lust, they call it. It happens, and it's dealt with, but that night for me was the last straw. I went back to my quarters, trying to decide how best to report what I'd witnessed, but by the time I arrived the decision was made for me. I was placed under arrest.'

'What? What on earth for?'

'Striking a superior officer. A Lieutenant Colonel, to be precise.'

'An officer? The man who…it was an officer?'

'An officer and a gentleman, with enough sense of entitlement to think he could do what he damn well liked, without consequences,' Dominic said viciously. 'From a far more prestigious regiment than mine, what's more, who also happened to be the son of a viscount. As you can imagine, when I informed my own Colonel of what actually happened, he was appalled.'

'I should blooming well hope he was! Dear heavens, I don't know why it should be so much worse, that the man was an officer.'

'Because he was ultimately in charge of discipline! Because he should be setting an example!

That's why. And do you know what my Colonel advised me to do?'

Prudence, shocked into silence, shook her head mutely.

'He told me to put up and shut up. Accept the charges. Take my medicine and forget the whole thing. I would have been demoted, but the war wasn't quite over, so I still had a chance to prove myself. I had an impeccable record. My men were loyal. I'd get over it.'

'*Did* you consider it? No, no, of course you didn't. Do you want me to make more coffee?' Prudence asked, desperate to help. 'Or shall I fetch you a brandy?'

'Both. In a moment. I'm almost done.' With a valiant effort, Dominic pulled himself together. 'I was determined not to let him get away with it, as you've already guessed. I can't really explain it, but what I saw that night, it broke something inside me. It had been a long war, and a bloody one, and there had been so much unnecessary suffering. More men died of exposure and starvation and fever than of their wounds, I reckon. But it was that woman, her mute suffering, his indifference, that's what made me say enough is enough.'

Dominic raked his hair, his feelings writ large

on his face. 'I filed a counter-charge. My Colonel held onto it for a week, trying to persuade me to change my mind. The siege had come to an end, and the end of the war was nigh too. Why destroy my career, when all I had to do was stay silent, rescind the accusation? But I wouldn't do it. I couldn't let him get away with it. I'm a stubborn ba— I'm stubborn.'

'And you play by the rules,' Prudence said, recalling his earlier words. 'So the counter-charge was filed, and the Lieutenant Colonel denied it?'

'Worse than that, he said it was me. He said that he'd caught me attempting to force myself on the woman, that I'd lashed out at him when he intervened. That, until I accused him, he had decided not to speak out, knowing that it would ruin my career, but he couldn't have his name blackened and so he told the truth.'

Prudence was stupefied. She knew the outcome, but still, stupidly, she'd hoped to be told differently. 'What about the woman you saved? If you had found her, she could have spoken up for you.'

'There was no chance, and no point. Even if I had found her, he'd have turned the tables on her, accused her of lying, or taking a bribe. I didn't want to drag her into it and publicly shame her, which is what would have happened.'

'So it was his word against yours?'

'I had no chance. "If you persist with this course of action, you will be ruined and shamed." That's what my Colonel said to me. "You meant well, Caldwell, but it would have been better for you if you had left him to finish his business and minded your own."'

'No! That is vile. It would hardly have been better for the poor woman.'

'At that point, my Colonel's primary concern was for the reputation of his regiment. That's what he really meant. I should have looked the other way and spared all of them, myself included. My trial was a foregone conclusion. It came down to the word of an inferior officer with no connections against his superior in rank and privilege.'

Dominic pushed back his chair and put the kettle back onto the range to boil. 'A dishonourable discharge of an officer is a relatively rare event. They make a point of publicly humiliating you,' he said, keeping his back to her as he waited for the kettle to boil. 'I was frog-marched out into a courtyard in front of my entire regiment. My epaulettes were ripped from my shoulders, my medals were torn from my chest and my sword was broken. It was freezing cold, and misty. My men were a right ragged lot, standing in formation, forced to watch. One of my medals got tangled in my tunic and I had to unpin it myself and hand it to my Colonel. He looked sick as a dog.'

He flung himself around, grabbing the empty coffee pot from the table, his face tight with anger. 'He *knew* the whole thing was a charade being played out to preserve face and tradition. And everyone knew, they all did, that the man who had accused me was a liar and a seducer. How many other women had he violated? I kept asking myself that. How many more victims had there been—and how many more would there be?'

'None, surely none,' Prudence said. 'Not after you had denounced him.'

'They condoned what he did. I don't suppose he'd have been popular in the mess, but he wasn't punished, wasn't stripped of his reputation, wasn't shamed and written out of army history as I was. And they all connived in it, the men he shared a mess with. Closed ranks and maintained a conspiracy of silence. All my commendations, all the years of service, gone, because I refused to play their game.'

Prudence got up, slipping her arms around his waist and resting her head on his back. 'You proved yourself an honourable man, a man of principle, and a very brave one. It must have been very tempting to back down and save yourself.'

'It wasn't. I never considered it. I knew I was in the right, but I ruined myself.' He twisted around in her embrace, putting his hands on her shoulders. 'And I didn't do my regiment much good either.'

'You saved that poor woman.' Prudence shuddered. 'You prevented her from being violated, and you spared her the trial too.'

'I did save her.' Dominic heaved a sigh, shaking his head. 'But the one who committed the crime got away with it. He may have been shunned for a while, but men of that ilk always bounce back. Look at Lord Cardigan, promoted to Lieutenant-General, appointed colonel of the Hussars. Mud doesn't stick to those people.'

'If you had been the son of an earl, would it have made a difference?'

'If I had been *raised* as the son of an earl, I'd have been taught to play the game.'

He let her go, and she went to fetch the brandy, pouring them both a glass while Dominic poured another cup of thick, viscous coffee. 'I don't believe you would have walked away,' she said. 'You would still have tried to save that woman.'

'I'd like to think so, but I don't know that.'

'I do,' Prudence said vehemently. 'I am sure of it.' She was shaken to the core by what he had told her, but his actions at every point had been unsurprising, almost predictable—or at least to her. Dominic, however, seemed unconvinced, so she asked him what happened next.

'I sailed to Greece. I wanted—I needed to get away from the army, from a world that seemed to me to value position and power above everything.' He tipped some of his brandy into his coffee cup, swirled it about and drank it, grimacing. 'I hadn't intended to make Greece my home. I went initially because there was a ship heading there and because, from what I'd heard, it was a country where you could live a quiet, simple life. I wandered around a bit until I settled in Lavrio.'

'And then you read in the newspaper about Jeremy's death.'

'I can't explain the effect it had on me, Prudence, as if the tentacles of the world I had exiled myself from were reaching out to embrace me. I know it's fanciful, and I know that the chances of anyone ever confronting me as the heir to the Bannatyne estate were almost nil, but *I* knew, and until I'd put an end to it I also knew I'd never be able to feel that my life was completely my own.'

His shoulders slumped as he reached across the table for her hand. Prudence twined her fingers tightly in his, not wanting to let go. He was so very brave, and so very stubborn. 'What was it that you saw in your mother's portrait today that affected you so much?' she asked.

'I have always assumed that I was not the Earl's son and now I'm more convinced than ever that I am right, but I'd never before considered the situation from her point of view. I'd never asked myself any of the questions that came into my head today. What would have happened to her if she had lived? She would have been shamed. She would be the one to pay the price.'

'Like the woman you've just told me about, if you had not intervened?'

'Exactly. The circumstances were not the same. I know my mother was not entirely innocent, I know that she in all likelihood broke her wedding vows, but if she'd lived she'd have been forced to surrender me, or she'd have been forced to live in exile somewhere and, which-ever of those, the choice would not be hers. Her husband, perhaps even the man who was her lover, would have conspired to save face, to tell history their way. It was a reminder to me that I want no part of this kind of world.'

'Are you really going to live alone in a cot-tage for the rest of your life?'

'Yes. Probably. Unlike my mother, I am for-tunate enough to have a choice in the matter.' Dominic threw back his brandy. 'But until I rid myself of all this, I can't think about the future.'

Prudence stared into the amber liquid in her almost untouched glass. 'I wonder who your fa-ther was?'

'I don't. Whoever he is or was has no bear-ing on my life. I've no way of finding out, and I'm not interested in trying. I've enough to do, putting the past to bed, without digging up yet more skeletons to lay to rest.'

'Do you know, I agree with you on that. Let sleeping dogs lie is what I think.'

'Are there any skeletons lurking in the re-spectable Carstairs cupboard?'

'Oh, no. Not that I'm aware of. I'm sure there are not.' Flustered, Prudence took a gulp of brandy, coughing as it burned its way down her throat. 'Will you keep the portrait of your mother?' she asked, thinking to divert him. 'If I had such a thing I would treasure it.'

'What do you mean?'

'I meant it is a very valuable portrait,' Prudence floundered. 'It's by Thomas Lawrence. He was one of the most famous artists of his time.'

'I've never heard of him. Don't you have one—a portrait of your mother, I mean?'

'Clement has one. It hangs in the drawing room.'

'Isn't it a good likeness?'

'It is very good, but I don't see...'

'It's an odd remark for you to make, that's all, if you do have a portrait. Do you look like her?'

Prudence tried not to panic. He was simply being curious, that was all, but now was most certainly not the time to dig into her history. She pushed her chair back and began to stack the cups and saucers. 'No, but Mercy is very like her.'

'So you take after your father?'

'I...I suppose so.'

He followed her into the scullery. 'What happened to you, Prudence?' Dominic lightly touched the scar on her cheek. 'It's not a cut, but a tear. And on your back,' he said, his fingers feathering over the exact spot, 'it looks as if something heavy fell on you. Was it an accident?'

She shook her head, catching his hand between hers and pressing a kiss to his knuckles as the emotions of the morning caught up with her. 'Thank you.'

'What for?'

'Everything. Confiding in me. Explaining. And for trusting me.' She kissed his hand again. 'That can't have been easy.'

'I wanted to tell you. I wanted you to understand.'

'I do.' She kissed him again, ignoring the niggle of her conscience that reminded her that she had not been as open with him. There was no point, for she couldn't answer his questions and, besides, like him, she felt it was best to let sleeping dogs lie. 'What will you do now?' she asked.

'Start to sell up. Get one of Doncaster's real clerks to come here and make an inventory. Think about how best to dispose of the proceeds.'

'You won't need my help.' It was a statement, not a question. They had already agreed as much, but saying it made their parting unbearably imminent. 'How long, do you think, before you return to Greece?'

'Weeks rather than months, if I can appoint someone trustworthy to oversee matters. This is the nineteenth century. A telegram will eventually reach me, even in Lavrio.'

'Will you be happy, spending the next thirty years or more slowly desiccating in the sun in the company of a few goats?'

'It's my choice. You have choices too, Prudence.'

He was wrong. He didn't see that her choices were limited in a way his were not, but she did wonder, for the first time, if they were as limited as she had assumed. 'I'll think about it.'

'Dearest Prudence, I look forward to reading of your fame in *The Times*, when Her Majesty commissions a water feature for Windsor Castle.'

'Water spouting from a set of bagpipes should win her heart.'

'I think you might be onto something.'

He slid his arms around her, pulling her closer. She put her arms around his neck, pressing herself against him, careless of her crinoline billowing out behind her, crushed against the heavy scullery stone sink. She burrowed her face in the open neck of his shirt, pressing her lips to the warm skin, breathing in his scent.

'Prudence.'

The way he said her name sent a frisson of desire down her back, made her lift her face, more than ready for his kiss. Their lips clung for one long moment and then they kissed feverishly, desperately. She curled her fingers into the silky softness of his hair and he pulled her tighter against him, and their kisses became more urgent. His hands stroked her neck, her back, and he groaned with frustration as her crinoline prevented him going further. Their tongues touched, stroked, thrust, and their kisses became frantic. She instinctively arched against him, her hands sliding down his back, under his coat, cupping the tense muscles of his buttocks, making him groan with desire, his hands finding the swell of her breasts, making her nipples peak, aching for his touch, once again frustrated by her layers of undergarments.

She wanted more. This was not enough. She wanted what they had had yesterday, their bodies melded to each other, but without even a layer of flannel bathing costume between them. She wanted to feel her skin on his, to feel his hands on her, touching her, bringing this throbbing, aching desire to a conclusion. She wanted more.

It was Dominic who broke the kiss finally, wrenching his mouth from hers, breathing hard and fast, his eyes glazed, his cheeks slashes of colour, his hands on her shoulders clinging as if he might drown if he let go. She burrowed her face into his neck again, her own breathing equally harsh, her heart beating wildly, everything about her racing, braced, tingling, on edge.

And slowly they both came back to earth. The tap in the sink was dripping. Her hair had come loose and was falling down her back. Her neatly buttoned blouse was awry. Dominic's cropped hair was standing up in little tufts. His shirt was torn slightly at the neck. She was well beyond embarrassment. Her body was still humming with anticipation, and it would be so very easy to give in to it, to lift her face to his again for one last kiss.

But it wouldn't be enough, and there could not be more. Prudence carefully disentangled herself and made her way up to the hallway, where she tried to adjust her clothing into a semblance of its usual neatness. Her hair was bundled up under her bonnet when Dominic joined her and she took the front door key from her pocket, setting it down on the hall table with a heavy heart. They both knew the significance of the gesture.

She couldn't speak. He was similarly silent. One last fierce embrace, his arms tight around her, and then he set her free. She made for the door and closed it behind her, hurrying down the driveway until she reached the gatepost, where she stopped and looked back at the Manor. Tears dripped down her face. She made no attempt to stop them. One advantage of a bonnet and veil was that she was free to cry without embarrassment.

Chapter Eleven

It was two weeks since Prudence had last seen Dominic or been to Hawthorn Manor. She had spent a great deal of time in the kitchen helping Lizzie make strawberry jam, rhubarb compote and bottled raspberries for the village fête, and received a polite note from Mrs Botheroyd in return, informing her that the produce would be most welcome. She had written a long letter to Mercy excluding almost all of her actual news and declining to ask her sister any of her anxious questions. She had reorganised Clement's filing and dealt with a mound of his outstanding correspondence. And, in desperation, she had worked her way through every back copy of *The Builder*, clipping articles she wished to keep in a new scrapbook.

Today was the village fête, and Clement had

reluctantly attended to show his face, leaving her alone with her thoughts. The weather was muggy and overcast, headache weather. Her high-necked blouse irked her. She was bored and irritable, and though the last thing she wished was to be stared at and muttered about if she made an appearance in her veil at the fête, the fact that she had not even been invited riled her. 'Especially since I spent a whole day writing the blasted invitations,' she muttered to herself, heading to the empty kitchen to make herself a cup of tea.

She was the only person in the village who wouldn't be there. Save for Dominic. What was he doing? She didn't even know if he was still at the Manor. Had he been joined by one of Doncaster's clerks, or had he gone to London? She set the kettle onto the range and took out the tea caddy, telling herself for the umpteenth time that his whereabouts were none of her business. They had said their farewells. But she couldn't bring herself to believe that she'd never see him again.

'Oh, excellent, just what I need,' Clement said, coming in through the kitchen door and making her jump. 'I bought strawberry jam and bottled raspberries. Where shall I put them?'

Prudence opened the larder. 'With the others that Lizzie and I made?'

He surveyed the shelf containing identical jars with comical dismay. 'I did the same last year, didn't I?'

'Never mind. Shall I bring your tea up to the study?'

'Will you join me? I think we ought to have a chat.'

'That sounds ominous.'

'Not at all,' he replied entirely unconvincingly, setting down the jars. 'Shall I take the tea tray up while you wait for the kettle to boil?'

She followed him up the stairs a few moments later and found him behind his desk, frowning over a letter. 'From Mercy,' he said. 'She's off to Baden-Baden next month again and won't have time to fit in a visit here.'

'Harry won't spare her,' Prudence said, pouring the tea and sitting down on the chair across from him. 'It's not that she doesn't want to see us.'

'Does she confide in you, Prue? I'm not asking you to tell me what she says, but I worry that she's not happy.'

'I don't think she is, though she doesn't say, not in her letters. If she would pay us a visit, if only for a few days, perhaps I could persuade her to talk.'

'It's a shame you can't go up to town.'

'You could go.'

He baulked. 'She wouldn't want to talk to me and, besides, *he'd* be there, and I can't stick him.' Clement set the letter down. 'It's not Mercy I wanted to talk to you about,' he said, looking decidedly awkward. 'The vicar's wife accosted me at the fête.'

Prudence's heart sank. 'Mrs Botheroyd is very well named. I expect she suggested that you put an end to my visits to the Manor, for fear that my particular disadvantages might have made me easy prey to Mr Caldwell's overtures.'

'She said nothing of the sort,' Clement said, quite taken aback. 'Good grief, Prue, never say she said that to you.'

'Something similar,' she confessed, regretting that she had spoken.

'Presumptuous woman. Though she means well,' her brother added hastily.

'What did she say then, if it was not to warn you of my imminent seduction?'

'It's hardly imminent.' Clement took up his cup of tea, realised he had already drunk it and set it down again. 'Especially now your visits have ceased.' Seeing that she was quite speechless, he smiled crookedly. 'Come on, Prue, you know me well enough. I see a great more than I let on.'

'Yes, I have—we have agreed—I won't be going back to the Manor while Dom—while Mr Caldwell is in residence. I don't even know if he still is in residence.'

'Yes, he's still there.' Clement poured himself another cup of tea and topped up her cup. 'Who is he, Prue? He's not a clerk, I've known that from the beginning.'

'He's the Earl. Jeremy's brother. Half-brother. Though he won't be claiming the title. It's a long story.'

'More like a very tall tale! Jeremy didn't have a brother. What on earth? The man has been spinning you yarns, Prudence.'

'No, I assure you, he is who he claims to be.'

'Good Lord. I can barely believe it. I'd very much like to hear this long story.'

'I don't see why not. I know you won't let it go any further.'

'Well,' Clement said half an hour later, 'that is a tale that our Mrs Botheroyd would love to hear. How extraordinary. And there's no chance of him remaining here in England, you're certain of that?'

'Absolutely. He's set on returning to Greece.'

'I see. And you, Prue, am I permitted to ask how you feel about that? I know it's none of my business, you're a grown woman, but I'm your brother and I love you, and I don't want to see you hurt.'

'Oh, Clement, you don't need to worry on that score, I promise.'

He studied her through narrowed eyes for a moment, then gave a sigh of relief. 'You've no idea how many times I've wanted to ask you that question over the last couple of weeks,' he said wryly. 'But that remark you threw at me hit home. "You are treating me like a child," you said, and I was miffed, but when I thought about it I saw you were right. I've a tendency to be overprotective, I see that.'

'It's not your fault—well, not wholly. I should speak out for myself more. I've become too accustomed to being Poor Prudence, I think.'

'I've never thought of you in that way.'

'No, but you do try to spare me—and I'm grateful, Clement, but I've been thinking perhaps I ought to try to go about a bit more in the world—with my veil, I mean. In fact, I was wondering if perhaps I might take a trip to London for the day and visit Mercy.'

'On the train? Are you sure? Not that you could not, of course, but—it's a big step, Prue.'

'You could come with me?'

'I could.' Clement nodded. 'I am very glad we had this chat.'

'I'll let you get back to your books.'

'Yes, I've lost the better part of the day. Did you say this Caldwell—Thorburn?—has a cottage in Lavrio? That's Laurium, isn't it, or Thorikos? I believe the ancient workings of the mines can still be viewed. I wonder if he's familiar with them. It would be fascinating to hear from someone who's seen them first-hand, so to speak. Perhaps I'll pay him a call. But first, shall we arrange to pay a call on our sister?'

'You'll come with me!'

'Sooner rather than later, I think. What about the day after tomorrow? I believe she's in town. Let's send her a telegram, and we'll just have to hope that she can find a time to see us when that husband of hers is out.'

It had been fifteen days since Dominic had last seen Prudence. He checked his watch. Fifteen days and four hours. Not that he was counting. He was seated in the turret room, flicking through the pages of her designs. Her imagination seemed to know no bounds. The drawings looked so utterly different from anything he had seen and impossible to execute, yet each one was accompanied by detailed plans and notes to make the impossible possible. She had been far too modest in claiming the Hawthorn Wheel to be the work of an engineer. He missed her. The long days were proving difficult to fill, despite his having applied himself so diligently that he had read and mostly digested all of Doncaster's papers. What to do next was the question.

He had no final figure regarding what the estate was worth, but it was going to be one of those numbers that was too large to comprehend. He was going to have to work hard to dispose of it all, but how?

What he'd spent on their day at the seaside had seemed to him a small fortune, but it was a drop in the ocean—ha! He had bought Prudence freedom for the day. If he could purchase her freedom for the rest of her life, it would be money well spent. He wanted her to have a different life, a better life, a life where she was not forced to hide from the world, and he had probably hammered that point home far too hard already. Of course, Prudence wanted the same for herself, but she saw what he was reluctant to admit—her scars made it impossible. He was choosing to hide out in Lavrio. She had no choice but to hide out here.

Not that he was *hiding out*. He was exiling himself from the world. A very different thing. Was it exile, or was abdicating a more accurate description? He had arrived in Greece feeling powerless, furious, ashamed, thwarted, defeated. If he chose to, as Prudence had pointed out, he could wield a great deal of influence now. He could use it to do good. But the fact remained, he'd have to join a club he didn't want to join to do that. Money was power though, wasn't it? He couldn't change the world, he didn't want to rub shoulders with those he'd rejected in the vain hope of making them see the error of their ways, but if he spent wisely he could ease some of the suffering they caused.

He had no idea how, or even who these name-less sufferers might be. Women. Children. It was a start though, something for him to focus his mind on, and when it was done he could return to Lavrio and pick up where he'd left off.

Could he do that, as if nothing had changed? Wasn't that the point of him being here, to ensure that nothing did change? On a practical level, he would miss the convenience of the range when he returned to Greece, and the hot water it provided. He could fit his cottage into the bathroom that Prudence had created, and which he had become inordinately fond of. One thing he was not looking forward to was a return to his home's very basic facilities. Would Prudence be able to design a bathroom for his cottage which was fed from the well? He was being fanciful, he'd never be able to afford the solution, even if it was practical.

He missed her. He went out to the gallery, setting up the billiards table and beginning a game, but his mind wasn't on it. He went into the other turret room and gazed at the portrait of his mother. He would take it with him when he left, his one memento, a reminder of who he was, and who he was not.

There was a stack of papers to be returned to Doncaster. Some of the assets he had acquired seemed very dubious. The properties in London, in particular, where the rental income seemed quite disproportionate to the value. He need not concern himself with it since he was going to sell it all anyway, but it niggled at him. If he took the train up to London tomorrow, he could take a look at them before he paid an unannounced call on Doncaster. It would give him something constructive to do.

How to begin his new, temporary career as a philanthropist was a thornier issue. He could commission one or two of Prudence's designs. Dominic closed the notebook and put it back in the drawer. He wasn't ready to let go of it yet.

Chapter Twelve

Prudence dressed with nervous care for her trip to London, Mercy having telegrammed back immediately saying that the timing was most fortuitous and she would be delighted to receive her. She wore a gown of grey patterned with a narrow teal-blue stripe, with bugle beading around the wide sleeves and high collar. The hem of her skirt was decorated with a geometric pattern of stiff black braid, designed to keep it from trailing through the filth of the city streets. As usual, the design was her own, adapted from a more elaborate creation in the *English Woman's Domestic Magazine*. A short jacket, grey gloves and a hat with a grey veil completed her toilette. She twisted around in front of the mirror in her bedroom, and eventually concluded that the result would meet with Mercy's approval.

Clement was waiting for her in the hall, adjusting the angle of his hat. 'You look very elegant.'

He was, as ever, dressed with an understated sophistication, sharing both her and Mercy's horror of ostentation and, like Mercy, needing none. 'You look very handsome,' Prudence said, making a final adjustment to her veil. 'When I am in your company I can be at ease, for everyone is too dazzled by you to look at me.'

'You are being ridiculous, Prue. Shall we?'

It had rained in the night, but the road to the railway station was already steaming in the muggy sunshine. Prudence was trying very hard to concentrate on the upcoming, much anticipated meeting with her sister, but as they approached the station it was inevitable that her mind turned to the last trip she had made. It had been seventeen days now since she had seen Dominic. Her designs were still in the turret room at the Manor, providing her with an excuse to call. He could have sent them to her or handed them in, but he had not. He knew they were there. Perhaps he was hoping that she might...

'Perfect timing,' Clement said as they reached the station. 'I'll go and purchase our tickets. Will you be all right alone for a moment—yes, of course you will.'

Alone on the platform, she smiled to herself beneath her veil. Clement was trying so very hard not to be protective. Was she nervous? Yes, but only a little. Provided that she kept her veil on, she had no reason to worry. Dominic had been right to encourage her to have the courage to venture out more. Perhaps this really was the first step towards a different future.

The train slowed, belching steam, and Clement reappeared, waving tickets. A cluster of men jumped into the third-class carriage next to the engine before it had come to a stop. The first-class carriages at the rear of the train, furthest from the locomotive, were very quiet. They found an empty compartment and were settled in opposite each other, the train pulling out of the station, when the door was wrenched open and a man threw himself into the carriage.

'I do beg your pardon, I— Prudence?'

'Dominic! What on earth…?'

'Prudence.' He sank onto the seat beside her, smiling in disbelief. 'This is the last place I expected to meet you.'

She laughed. 'Are you surprised?'

'And delighted.'

He was dressed in the double-breasted frock coat of dark blue wool which he had worn for their trip to the seaside, but his trousers and waistcoat were black. As ever, he was carrying his hat, and had already started to take off his gloves. His hair had grown a little, she thought, and his face was not quite so deeply tanned. She had missed him so much.

'Mr Caldwell. This is an unexpected pleasure.'

'Oh!' Prudence jerked back in her seat, blushing wildly under her veil. 'Clement. Dominic. Mr Caldwell, I should say—you remember my brother.'

'Carstairs.' Dominic stood up, offering his hand, impressively unflustered. 'How do you do?'

'Very well, I believe,' Clement said, shaking his hand. 'And you?'

'Well enough.'

'We are off to visit Mercy,' Prudence said as Dominic sat back down beside her. 'It was my idea, though she can only spare us this morning, which is why we have caught such an early train. We gave her very little notice, and her husband has plans for this afternoon which apparently could not be changed.'

'Not even for you?'

'Armstrong prefers our sister not to break engagements,' Clement said.

'Lord Armstrong,' Prudence added when Dominic looked enquiringly. 'Mercy's husband.'

'Is he related to Major George Armstrong?'

'Harry's younger brother. Do you know him, Mr Caldwell?'

'I've come across him. A man with a very inflated opinion of himself,' Dominic said, his tone making it clear that he did not share it. 'Your sister married into high society.'

'Mercy is very beautiful, and the Carstairs family are very well-connected.'

'I had no idea.'

'My brother is quite a catch,' Prudence teased, 'but he has never met a woman he loves more than his history books.'

'Nor one who can make rugs and embroider slippers as well as his sister,' Dominic said, smiling at her.

'Make rugs and embroider slippers? Prudence, do you mean? I don't believe she has ever done such a thing in her life.'

'It's a little joke we share, Clement,' Prudence said, colouring under her veil.

They were silent for a few moments as the

train drew into a station, but when they set off again Dominic turned back to her, frowning. 'A man like Lord Armstrong won't spend all his time in London, surely. He will have a country estate. Why don't you visit your sister there?'

'We prefer to have our sister at home with us, when she has the chance,' Clement said.

'The truth is that Lord Armstrong prefers me not to visit, Dominic.'

'Why not?'

'The man is a pompous—'

'He can't bear to look at me,' Prudence interrupted her brother.

'Prue!'

She had shocked Clement with her bluntness, but she had said nothing he didn't already know. 'You know it's true,' Prudence said. 'He thinks my deformity puts people off their food. You heard him say it at the wedding breakfast, even though everyone pretended they hadn't.'

'He's Mercy's husband. She was mortified. It would only have made matters worse if I had said something.'

'At the time, but Mercy's not here now. Please, Clement, I'd rather you didn't pretend, it makes me feel worse, not better.'

Her brother flushed. 'I've never forgiven him,'

he said tersely. 'It sticks in my throat to make polite conversation with him, if you must have it.'

'Why doesn't your sister have a word with him?' Dominic asked. 'Surely she doesn't permit him to keep you from her?'

'If I thought it would make Mercy happy, I would put up with her husband's shuddering and grimacing every time he saw me, whether I was wearing my veil or not. But the one time I did visit her in the country she was miserable, on tenterhooks, trying to protect me from him. So it's easier…'

'For you to be denied each other's company than to force an arrogant, ignorant peer to overcome his vile prejudices?'

'Because it would be Prue who would suffer. I won't deny I share your views on the man, though I do believe they are better not voiced,' Clement said. 'I would not have described Armstrong in quite such terms, but you have him to a tee.'

'His brother is the same. They all are.'

'Well, it's my sister who concerns me,' Prudence said. 'If today is a success, then I plan to make more visits to town.'

'Bravo.' Dominic smiled warmly at her. She smiled back, wishing that she did not have her veil on, and only Clement's self-conscious clearing of his throat made her drag her gaze away.

'What will you do with the rest of your day, if your sister can spare you only the morning?' he asked her.

'Clement doesn't like London. We'll come home.'

'There is an International Exhibition in Kensington, which I believe displays all the wonders of the modern world.'

'I have read of it. They have a machine which makes ice, and an analytical engine, a machine which can calculate, would you believe?'

'What, are we to replace all the office clerks with machinery now?'

Prudence chuckled. 'Perhaps one day.'

'Would you care to visit it?'

'Oh, no, I can't.' Her hand went automatically to her veil. 'Though perhaps—but Clement isn't interested in the modern world.'

'I am though. I could escort you.'

'Would you? But your business…'

'Can wait.'

'Clement, would you mind?'

'Clearly I am superfluous. In fact, if I'd known that you were going to London today, Caldwell, you could have spared me the journey.'

'But you want to see Mercy.'

'I do, but frankly, Prue, I think it would be better for me to leave the pair of you alone, provided she has managed to rid herself of her husband. I'll escort you, say hello, and then come back for you at noon. If you are really considering this Exhibition—are you absolutely sure, my dear?'

'I think so. Yes, if Dominic was serious about escorting me?'

'My business is likely to take me until about one.'

'Then I will escort my sister to the entrance of the Exhibition, and we will meet you there. Now,' Clement said, 'that is enough of the modern world. My sister has been telling me a little of your family history, Mr Caldwell. You must not think she betrayed your trust too easily, but I rather pushed her on the subject. You seemed such a very unlikely clerk.'

Dominic grimaced. 'So Prudence told me, the first day we met.'

'I must tell you, Mr Caldwell—I presume that is how you prefer to be addressed?—I am very interested in the little village where you make your home. Have you visited the ancient mines there?'

'Several times.'

Prudence listened with some surprise as Dominic and Clement entered into a detailed discussion of various ruins and ancient sites on the Attic peninsula. The train drew into another station, and they were joined in the carriage by an elderly man of the cloth and a sulky young boy, obviously in his charge. As the train filled, drawing nearer and nearer to London, she began to fret, several times checking her veil. By the time they halted on the viaduct just outside the station to allow the conductor to check the tickets, which required him to walk on the track between compartments as they had no connecting doors, she could easily have been tempted to take the first train home again.

'You will be absolutely fine,' Dominic leant over to whisper in her ear, his hand pressing hers as they slowly set off again for the last few yards of the journey and the other passengers were intent on collecting their belongings. 'I am very proud of you.'

Clouds of steam obscured the view from the window as they came into Waterloo Station, the brakes screeching and squealing. Doors were flung open and passengers began to leap down onto the platform before the locomotive drew to a halt. Their fellow travelling companions nodded a polite good morning, then Dominic got to his feet, holding the carriage door open for her, and Prudence descended, followed by Clement. The other passengers streamed past her, a swarm of people hastening purposefully to the station exit. Porters sprinted by with laden trolleys, shouting warning cries to clear their paths. The air was chokingly thick from the trains, which continued to arrive and depart with frightening speed, spewing smoke into the enclosed space, making her eyes sting, making her grateful for her veil.

The noise and the bustle, the sheer numbers of people from every station in life, the polluted sky, the roaring and panting locomotives, the crush of humanity kept her rooted to the spot. Dominic's hand on her arm made her jump. 'So many people,' she said, and then had to repeat as he leant in closer to hear her. 'And all of them in such a hurry.'

'Eager to make themselves seem important, most of them,' he answered, pulling her closer.

The tide was abating a little now. No one, Prudence realised, had been the least bit interested in her. As she checked her veil, her spirits lifted. 'So many people,' she said, this time marvelling. 'It's exciting. As if something is just about to happen. Something important.'

Dominic smiled, taking her arm and nudging her into motion. 'It has. Prudence Carstairs has arrived in town. Your brother has gone ahead to procure a hackney at the stand outside. Mind your purse. Pickpockets and thieves prey on the unwary. I shall see you at the Exhibition at one.'

Chapter Thirteen

The Armstrong family town house faced onto Cavendish Square. Prudence and Clement were admitted by one of the liveried servants before they had a chance to knock on the door. A huge clock ticked loudly in the reception hallway, and the portraits of the various Armstrong ancestors gazed sternly down as they followed the footman up the stairs to the drawing room on the first floor where they were informed that Lady Armstrong would join them shortly.

It was an oppressive room decorated in the latest style, the walls covered with a dark red and gold patterned paper. Matching red velvet drapes braided with gold framed the three windows, the light and the London dirt excluded by the voile which covered the glass. The sofas which faced each other across the fireplace were similarly upholstered in red and gold, as were the numerous gilded chairs that were scattered around the room, all of them looking far too flimsy to be practical. Prudence counted eight tables, the surfaces covered with porcelain ornaments, glass vases and pierced silver boxes. More Armstrong ancestors peered down at her from their gilded frames, and over the mantel was Lord Henry, the diplomat and revered father of the current marquis, whose name he bore. His hooded eyes beneath bushy brows seemed to follow her as she wandered around the room, wondering how her sister could bear such clutter.

'Prudence, and Clement too. I am so sorry to keep you waiting. There was an urgent matter which my lord wished me to attend to.' Mercy crossed the room and embraced her lightly. 'What a lovely surprise this is. How are you both? You look very elegant, Prue. Shall we sit down? I've asked them to bring tea.'

'I won't stay,' Clement said. 'I have some business to attend to, but I'll come back at noon and collect Prue. She is headed to the Great Exhibition, would you believe?'

'Really? My goodness, Prudence, that is a... that is excellent. Must you go, Clement? My lord is out and won't be back for a while yet.'

'No, I'll leave you two to have a good chat. Prue has been anxious about you. I'll be back in town soon.' Clement gave Mercy a hug and made his escape.

'Does our brother prefer the British Museum to our company?' Mercy asked.

'Do you truly want me to answer that question?'

Mercy smiled faintly. 'Probably best not to.' She ushered Prudence to a sofa and sat down gracefully opposite. 'I am delighted to see you. It was such a surprise to receive the telegram. What has made you decide to spread your wings?'

'I decided it was time. And I've been worried about you, Mercy. You say so little in your letters.'

'There's very little to say, unless you wish me to bore you with a list of my engagements. I'm perfectly fine.'

'You look as lovely as ever.'

'I look terrible. I have had the most dreadful headache for days. I hate being in town at this time of year, but my lord wished…and then I required some new gowns for our trip to Baden-Baden, and of course I'm very glad of the opportunity to see you, for I don't know when I will next—I wonder what's happened to the tea.'

'Mercy, there's no rush.'

'No. I don't suppose…though I am afraid that I have only until noon at the latest for I am required… I am so sorry that I can't spare you any longer. You know I would if I could.'

'Of course I do. I gave you so very little notice, I'm relieved that you were available at all.'

'I didn't tell him you were coming, Prudence.'

'Thank you.'

'I *hate* the way he treats you. You know that, don't you?'

'I do know that, I promise.'

'And I hate that we hardly ever see each other.'

'That is as much my fault as…that's partly my fault, Mercy. I have been too timid about travelling to town. After today, I plan to make more regular trips. We'll be able to see more of each other, if you can…'

'Lie to Harry about where I'm going and who I am seeing? I shall. If you are brave enough to come here, then I will be brave enough to make the most of it.'

There was an awkward silence. Mercy had said more than enough already to make Prudence's blood boil, but what was the use in saying so? They both understood the situation. Mercy was choosing to endure it.

'He is every bit as unhappy as I,' her sister said now, as if reading her thoughts. 'There is nothing to be said.'

'Then we won't say anything more,' Prudence agreed reluctantly. 'That is a lovely gown.'

'Do you think so?' Mercy smoothed the silk pleats of her skirts. 'Harry said that the colour made me look like a ghost.'

'It perfectly matches your eyes,' Prudence said, her hackles rising. 'You could wear a sack and still look lovely.'

Mercy, to her relief, laughed. She was an extraordinarily beautiful woman, with silver-blonde hair and almond-shaped eyes of blue-grey. Her skin was quite flawless, her nose straight, her lips full and sensuous and her chin prettily pointed. She had been the toast of the town in her first Season and, fifteen years later, remained one of London's most accredited beauties. A fact which made her husband loathsomely possessive rather than proud.

A servant arrived with the tea. The silver pot, sugar bowl and cream jug were set out on the table with the burr walnut tea caddy. The spirit stove was lit and the kettle was placed upon it.

On another little table, the service of delicate porcelain patterned with forget-me-nots was laid out.

'There,' Mercy said when the servant left, 'now you may be comfortable.'

It was their long-standing signal for Prudence to put back her veil, but though the phrase had been uttered by Mercy many times in the past, it was Dominic's use of almost exactly the same words that she recalled, from their first train journey together. She carefully pushed the netting back, wondering if she dared confide in her sister, and was watching Mercy begin the ritual of tea-making, warming the pot and carefully measuring the leaves from the caddy with the gilt spoon, when the drawing room door flew open and Prudence hurriedly put her veil back in place.

'That footman of yours is such a self-important prig. Would you believe, he wanted to have me send my card up. I told him you were expecting me, but—oh!' The tall, flame-haired woman stopped on the threshold. 'You *do* have company. I'm so sorry, Mercy. I thought that husband of yours had forbidden…'

'Sarah,' Mercy said, getting up hurriedly, 'this

is my sister. Prudence, this is my friend, Lady Sarah Fitzherbert-Wright.'

The woman, who looked to be about the same age as Prudence, was dressed in an extremely stylish emerald-green walking dress trimmed with navy-blue braid. A jaunty little hat with a feather in it was perched on her head. With deep-set blue eyes and a sprinkling of freckles across her nose, which she had made no attempt to disguise with powder, she was not a classic beauty, but her smile was the kind which was reflected in her eyes, giving her countenance a warmth and vivaciousness that made Prudence take an immediate liking to her.

'How do you do?' she said, extending her hand. 'Mercy and I were supposed to be taking a walk in the park this morning, which is why I've burst in on you. I do apologise.'

'I forgot to cancel,' Mercy said. 'Prudence sent me a telegram yesterday telling me that she was coming up to town.'

'And of course a sister takes precedence over a friend. May I stay for tea instead, if I am not in the way? Mercy has spoken of you, Miss Carstairs, and I must confess to being curious to meet you. Mercy told me all about the fountain you designed for the Earl of Bannatyne. I wish I could see it.'

'It is the most magical construction, Sarah. You would love it.'

'Why haven't you asked her to design one for you—? Oh, no, don't answer that.' Sarah rolled her eyes. 'It's rather too modern for His Lordship. Honestly, Mercy, you must feel like you're living in a mausoleum.' Sarah took a seat beside Prudence. 'Look at this room! Armstrong spent a small fortune on redecoration and the effect is monstrous, don't you think? All it lacks is a throne.'

'You should see what he's planning to do to our country pile,' Mercy said, wrinkling her nose.

'Let me guess, he's taking Windsor Castle as his model for cosy and comfortable,' Lady Sarah said, accepting a cup of tea. 'Have you nothing to offer a poor starving soul to eat? Don't tell me you're on another reducing diet.'

'I have gained half an inch around my waist.'

'Really? Don't tell me Harry has finally succeeded in…'

'No, no, it's not that,' Mercy said, colouring painfully.

'I'm sorry.' Sarah leant over to pat her hand.

'Perhaps the waters at Baden-Baden will help this year.'

'They haven't helped the last five years I've taken them, and I'll be thirty-six next month.'

'My mother was almost forty when she had me. I was her first and only,' Lady Sarah said with a rueful smile, turning to Prudence again. 'She left me with a huge fortune and a determination never to put myself through what she did, in having me. My determination to remain free and single is one of the many reasons that Lord High-and-Mighty Harry Armstrong loathes me. The main one being that he thinks I'm an unhealthy influence on Mercy. The feeling is entirely mutual too. I believe that's something you and I have in common?'

'Let us not waste what time we have on discussing my husband,' Mercy said.

'You're absolutely right, it is a waste of time. Will you not put up your veil, Miss Carstairs, and take your tea? Mercy has told me about your disfigurement, and I assure you I am not at all squeamish.'

'Sarah!'

'I beg your pardon, ought I not to have mentioned it? But how is she to take her tea?'

'Messily,' Prudence said. 'It's fine, Mercy,

your friend is right. I feel ridiculous sitting here in my veil.'

'But you always wear it in company.'

'Perhaps it's time I changed. When the company is right.' Though she still felt extremely self-conscious putting the veil back. Lady Sarah, however, neither shuddered nor looked away.

'It must have been quite a horrific accident,' she said matter-of-factly. 'You were a child, I believe? You were fortunate to have survived. A wound like that, if it had become infected, could easily have killed you.'

'I never thought of that,' Prudence said, taken aback.

'One of my mother's many good causes was visiting a home for soldiers. She used to take me with her—following Her Majesty's example, during the Crimea, when Her Majesty still fulfilled her public duties. Some of the sights I saw there, I assure you, have remained with me ever since, and I was older than the little princesses Queen Victoria had with her. Your scar is ugly, there is no denying it, but I've seen worse.'

'A man—a soldier who fought in the Crimean—told me something very similar.'

'It's worse for you though, in a sense, isn't it? It's not a battle scar. A woman in our society must be flawless—or whatever version of flawless happens to be *à la mode*. I look forward to the day when red hair will be fashionable, though I reckon I'll be at least seventy by then. Do people stare?'

'Sarah,' Mercy intervened again, 'you are embarrassing my sister.'

'Am I? I beg pardon, Miss Carstairs, but it seems to me that if I pretended there was nothing unusual about your face and made no comment at all, then you might think I'm feeling sorry for you, and being pitied is simply the worst thing, isn't it?'

'It is,' Prudence said, startled and grateful, 'though I can't imagine anyone pitying you.'

'Ha! I'm thirty years old and single. As far as Society is concerned, that is reason enough. I am looking forward to the day when I reach forty and not even the most desperate fortune hunter or widower with nine motherless brats will consider me worth taking on.'

'Sarah,' Mercy said with a fond smile, 'likes to shock.'

'No, I like to speak my mind, another reason why your husband loathes me. Sorry,' Lady Sarah added contritely, 'I promise I won't say another word about him. So do tell us, Miss

Carstairs, what brings you to town. Did you come by train? Did you travel alone?'

'I came with our brother, Clement.'

'Where is he now?'

'At the British Museum, but he is returning to take Prudence to the International Exhibition, so you may meet him then, if you stay.'

'The scholar.' Lady Sarah grimaced. 'Almost as exciting a prospect as a visit to the International Exhibition. It is a very odd mixture, Miss Carstairs. Mostly machines which do very worthy but rather tedious things, and art, which I fear is almost as worthy and tedious.'

'You forget, Sarah, that my sister has an interest in engineering. Though Clement—I must say, Prudence, I'm surprised you have persuaded him to accompany you.'

'I have not.'

'You can't go alone!'

'I'm not going alone. In fact, I'll be accompanied by a…a new acquaintance.'

'The soldier? How did you come to meet a soldier? You have made no mention of him in your letters.'

'He's not a soldier. Not any more.'

'Prudence, you are looking very mysterious. Who is this man? Where did you meet him?'

This morning she'd had no notion of sharing any of her history with Dominic, but meeting him on the train had made her realise how very much she had missed him. Absence had not made her heart grow fonder, it had allowed her to gain a strict hold over her heart, but that meant, surely, that they could see each other again without risk? If he hadn't thought so too, he would not have suggested their outing this afternoon. Besides, it wouldn't be fair to keep from Mercy the limited amount that Clement already knew, would it?

'I met him at Hawthorn Manor,' she said. 'He is the new owner.'

'I cannot believe it,' Mercy exclaimed for the twentieth time in half an hour. 'What an absolutely extraordinary tale. I still don't understand why he is so determined to remain incognito.'

'And adamant he will not avail himself of the title,' Lady Sarah said. 'And determined to give away all his money. I give a great deal of my own away, but not all of it. I am sure there is more to this tale than Miss Carstairs has told us.'

'I'm afraid I cannot say more than I have already done, without betraying his confidence.'

'Aha! So there is more.'

'He has taken you into his confidence then?' Mercy said. 'Are you sure he can be trusted, Prudence? That he is who he claims to be?'

'I promise, Mercy, there is no doubt about either.'

'And Clement has met him. If he is reassured—though it is so very odd. And odder of you, Prudence, if you don't mind my saying, to have befriended him.'

'He is not a stray dog, Mercy.'

'Don't be so touchy, you know exactly what I mean. What has come over you—making friends with strangers, coming to town to visit me, and next you are off to a public exhibition?'

'I've decided that I want to do more with my life.'

'And I'm delighted to hear it. You are so clever and so brave and so talented, but this is such a sudden change. Are you sure?'

'It's not sudden. I have long been thinking—but I've not had the courage to act until now.'

'And has this stranger been instrumental in your change of heart?'

'He has made me look at myself in a new light, that's all.'

'If this new light means that I will see more

of you, then I am very happy, but are you sure you are not at risk of being in thrall to this man?'

'I am not going to lose my heart to a man who is set on living in a cottage in the wilds of Greece.'

'I am glad to hear it. Keep your heart to yourself, Prudence, that's my advice.'

The silence following this sad little remark was broken by Lady Sarah. 'Tell us, Miss Carstairs, what is this Earl who doesn't wish to be an earl like?' she asked. 'I mean as a man? Is he attractive? Why is he single, do you think, at the age of thirty-five?'

'Perhaps he prefers his independence, as you do,' Mercy retorted, relieved by the change in subject.

'*Is* he attractive?' Lady Sarah persisted.

'Sarah,' Mercy interjected, 'you should not ask such personal questions.'

'Why not? Miss Carstairs strikes me as someone who is not afraid to have an opinion.'

'I'll take that as a compliment,' Prudence said, slightly taken aback. 'In fact, I do think he's attractive.'

'Prudence!'

'He's not handsome, and he can be extremely

forbidding, but when he smiles, he is—yes, he is very attractive.'

'And has he a fine pair of shoulders?' Lady Sarah asked.

'He has,' Prudence said, relishing Mercy's shocked countenance. 'Indeed, he has a most admirable physique. And he is very tanned. From swimming in the Aegean, so he tells me.'

'How much of his tan have you seen?' Lady Sarah asked, her eyes wide.

'For shame, Sarah,' Mercy exclaimed, 'you go too far.'

'Always,' Lady Sarah agreed promptly. 'It is my modus operandi. I am notorious for it, though I do think—'

The door opened, and Mercy's dresser made an apologetic entrance. 'My lady. You wished to be reminded...'

'Yes, yes. I will be with you in a moment,' Mercy said, getting to her feet. 'I am so sorry, Prudence, but I'm going to have to leave you. My lord wishes me to have a new *carte de visite* made. I am to meet him at the photographer's studio and must change.'

'You've only just had your photograph taken,' Lady Sarah said.

'He didn't like it.' Mercy held out her hand to Prudence. 'You will be careful, won't you?'

'I am perfectly capable of looking after myself, Mercy.'

'I know, I know, I am sure you are. I wish I could come with you this afternoon, just to reassure myself—but now I'm putting your back up and you're going to tell me that you can look after yourself.'

'I can. Stop fretting about the time,' Prudence said, for she could see that Mercy was already on edge.

'I'm so sorry, I really must dash. Will you come back to town to visit me soon? It has been so good to see you.'

'I will try. I promise. Perhaps when you return from Baden-Baden...'

'We'll be in the country then.'

'But you'll be back in London for the Season.'

'If there is a Season. They say that Her Majesty is likely to remain in deep mourning for at least another year. I feel so sorry for the royal princesses.' The clock on the mantel chimed the quarter hour and Mercy jumped. 'I really must go.'

'Write to me,' Prudence said, embracing her. 'And please look after yourself.'

Mercy froze, as she always did at even the lightest of touches. 'I am perfectly fine,' she said, slipping free. 'Perfectly.'

'And if she says it often enough, we will believe her,' Lady Sarah said as the door closed. 'Poor Mercy, if anyone deserves a child it is her.'

'She seems so horribly fragile. And she is far too thin. Perhaps the spa will help,' Prudence said sadly.

'You don't really believe that, do you? What makes me so angry,' Lady Sarah said, dropping her flippant manner, 'is that *he* blames her, when the chances are that it's just as likely to be he who is lacking.'

'Do you think so?'

'I would *like* to think so, though from what I can gather, he makes his contribution to the undertaking on a painfully regular basis,' Lady Sarah said. 'If you understand my meaning.'

'Poor Mercy,' Prudence said, horrified, and sadly all too easily able to imagine her stoic sister silently enduring his ministrations.

'Poor Mercy, indeed,' Lady Sarah said. 'My late mother painted a very vivid picture for me of conception and birth, both of which filled me with horror. She wished to spare me, Miss Carstairs, the shock that she had on her wedding night, you see. She wished me to be prepared. I suppose that was partly what was behind her insisting on my company at the lying-in hospital too, another of her pet causes. Her methods were very effective. I am not prepared to subject myself to such…such degradation.'

'Are you serious?'

'Why, yes, I am, and if ever I waver in my resolve, I only need look at poor Mercy. She dreads doing her marital duty.'

'Because her husband is loathsome,' Prudence said with feeling. 'But it is different if there is a mutual attraction—or so I would imagine,' she added hurriedly.

'Have you imagined it, with your mysterious Earl? Oh, my goodness, has he taken liberties?'

'No, he has not,' Prudence said, for it was true that Dominic had done nothing she didn't wish him to do. 'I must go,' she added, forestalling another question. 'Clement will be here in a moment.'

'I shall come down with you and meet this crusty scholar brother of yours. What were your parents thinking, naming the poor man Clement? He was more or less condemned at birth to remain a confirmed bachelor.'

Prudence giggled, adjusting her veil and pulling on her gloves. 'Poor Clement.'

'Clement, Mercy and Prudence. Honestly, it makes you sound like a clutch of orphans named by a particularly zealous workhouse,' Lady Sarah said, following her down the stairs, nodding her thanks to the footman, who opened the door.

'I doubt very much that was our father's intention,' Prudence said wryly. 'But you may see for yourself how well my brother is named,' she added, seeing him standing at the foot of the steps. 'Clement, allow me to introduce you to Mercy's friend, Lady Sarah Fitzherbert-Wright. Lady Sarah, may I present my brother, Clement Carstairs.'

She had expected Lady Sarah to be confounded, but she had not expected a similar reaction from her brother, who looked quite thunderstruck.

'Good heavens,' Lady Sarah said, the first to recover herself, 'you are not at all what I was expecting.'

'Lady Sarah.' Clement, to Prudence's astonishment, executed a flourishing bow. 'Your servant. It is a pleasure.'

'Is it? My goodness, dare I say that I hope

so? You don't look like a man who is married to his books.'

Clement laughed. 'I have been a most diligent spouse, and have earned the day off,' he quipped. *Quipped?* Prudence thought, observing the pair of them with astonishment. Her brother's jokes were usually in Latin or Greek. If she didn't know him better, she might think him smitten. Was Cupid lurking in a nearby window, firing arrows? Should that be Eros in his case?

Lady Sarah had taken a flesh wound too, by the looks of her. She was all but simpering. 'Poor Mr Carstairs, that doesn't sound like much of a day off, if you have spent the morning in the British Museum. What are your plans for the rest of the day?'

I'm off on the first train home, I'm keen to get back to my books, Prudence predicted.

'That is for you to decide, Lady Sarah,' her brother said instead. 'I could be entirely at your disposal if you wish it.'

'Do you know, I rather think I do,' Lady Sarah said coyly, fluttering her long lashes. 'We could go for a walk, if Miss Carstairs has no objection.'

'Prue!' Clement blushed scarlet. 'I forgot all about you. Damn…dash it! I am so sorry, Lady Sarah. I have promised to escort my sister to the

Great Exhibition. If you would be so kind as to wait an hour…'

'I can do better than that. How would it be, Miss Carstairs, if I lend you my carriage and, in return, you will lend me your brother? You will be quite safe with my groom.'

'You are very good, Lady Sarah, but I think my sister may wish…'

'Your sister is perfectly happy to accept Lady Sarah's kind offer,' Prudence interrupted, highly amused.

She half expected Clement to demur, but instead he beamed. 'A private carriage is much better than a hackney. You'll enjoy the ride.'

'Then that is settled and, with perfect timing, here is my carriage,' Lady Sarah said as an extremely smart town coach appeared from the mews. 'Here you are, Miss Carstairs, my coachman will look after you.'

'Thank you. You are very kind,' Prudence said.

'I hope I didn't offend you earlier. I have rather taken to you. If you do decide to spend more time in town, you would be very welcome to stay with me.'

'That's very generous.'

'I mean it, I'm not simply being polite,' Lady

Sarah said, pressing her hand. 'I am obliged to remain in town for the summer, for I have handed my country house over to a distant cousin, and she has five children. Five, and each one takes after its father, poor little mites.'

'Perhaps you should join Mercy in Baden-Baden? The waters might cure your aversion to men.'

Lady Sarah gave a trill of laughter. 'It will take more than a few glasses of chalky water to do that, though I must confess your brother… How you must have laughed up your sleeve when I called him a crusty scholar. Now you had better go. It's not far to Kensington from here, but the traffic is appalling even at this time of day. You'd be quicker walking, to be honest, but you will be a great deal safer in my carriage. I wish I could meet your lost Earl, he sounds intriguing, but I must settle instead for your Adonis of a brother. Enjoy the Great Exhibition, Miss Carstairs.'

Chapter Fourteen

❧

The International Exhibition of Industry and Art was sited in South Kensington. The building was constructed largely of cast iron, behind a brick façade studded with arched windows. Flags flew over the triple-arched entrance and two massive glass domes towered above the whole, the highest ever built, Dominic had read in the catalogue. The building was the design of Captain Fowke of the Royal Engineers, which explained its marked resemblance to a barracks, he thought sourly.

Dominic had arranged to meet Prudence at the front entrance but, noting that all carriages were dropping their passengers off at the corner, he made his way over there to wait. He was looking out for a hackney, but he spotted her instantly, drawing up in an open carriage pulled by two magnificent high-stepping greys, which he assumed her sister had lent her. He watched her descend, veil firmly in place, and waited for her to notice him.

'Dominic! What do you think of my carriage?'

'It's very grand. Does it belong to your sister? How was your visit—was she pleased to see you?' he asked, helping her down.

'Mercy was very pleased to see me and delighted to hear that I plan to make my visits more regular. She had a friend visiting but, even so, I took my veil off. I'm not going to make a habit of it, but in certain circumstances... I am glad I did today. Lady Sarah was very matter-of-fact. In that sense, she reminded me of you. This is her carriage. I left her taking Clement for a walk.'

Dominic laughed. 'On a lead?'

'Metaphorically, yes. He was utterly smitten. Not that I think anything will come of it. Clement is far too set in his ways, and Lady Sarah is a committed spinster.'

'That is not a term I'm familiar with.'

'Nor I, but I rather like it. Perhaps I'll adopt it for myself.'

Was she teasing? He wished he could see her face. He didn't want to think of her with another man, but he didn't want to imagine her leading a lonely life either. As she had been before he'd arrived? Her future, Dominic reminded himself, was none of his business.

'You're very quiet,' Prudence said. 'Are you regretting offering to be my escort?'

'No, not at all. It's been more than two weeks since we saw each other. Plenty of time for us to have taken stock, view the situation more rationally.'

'Is that what you have done?'

Was he imagining the disappointment in her voice? He really wished he could see her face. 'Absolutely,' Dominic said, inwardly grimacing at his bracing tone. 'I've made excellent use of my time too. I now know what I have to dispose of, and this morning I set Doncaster the task of putting that in train.'

'So you'll be able to return to Greece soon then.'

He could sense the effort she was making to sound pleased for him. He wanted to tell her how much he had missed her, but that would set the pair of them back to square one.

'I haven't made any plans yet,' Dominic said. 'I have been thinking a great deal about what use

I can put the money to. I have some ideas, but I'd very much like to hear your thoughts.'

'My thoughts?'

'It was you who pointed out that I was opting out rather than doing something constructive. Since I told you what transpired in the Crimea, I've been thinking that I'd like to find a way to make some sort of amends. Not to the poor woman who I managed to save, but to those I didn't—the powerless and the put-upon.'

'Dominic, that is—that's a wonderful idea.' Prudence pressed his arm. Her voice was tearful now. 'I don't know exactly what you mean by that…'

'Nor do I. Will you help me?'

She nodded several times. 'I would be honoured. Lady Sarah—Mercy's friend, who lent me the carriage—she may be able to advise us. She spoke of her mother's charity work, a lying-in hospital—I think she may at least be able to point us in the right direction.'

'I knew I could rely on you.'

'Predictable Prudence,' she said wryly.

He wanted to kiss her. 'Perfect Prudence,' he said, satisfying himself with tucking her hand into his arm. 'And, before you deny it, you are perfect to me. Shall we go in?'

She looked around her, seeming to notice the crowds for the first time. 'I hadn't expected it to be so busy.'

'Don't be nervous. No one is interested in us; they are all concerned with getting the best view of Mr Babbage's counting machine.'

She checked her veil and nodded. 'Then let us go and see what all the fuss is about.'

They joined the queue and were soon admitted. Prudence chose the eastern dome as their starting point, for *The Builder* magazine said this was where the best view was to be had of the Palace of Art and Industry. The vista was indeed breathtaking, with the glass dome soaring above it illuminating the interior. The galleries, three storeys high, were like the transepts of a church.

Dominic had acquired a layout guide and had already mapped out a plan which included all of the exhibits she had most wanted to see, including the counting machine. She was less interested in the locomotives and weaving machines, but the ice-maker fascinated her, and the goods from Mr Morris's company were quite extraordinary.

She thoroughly enjoyed herself but, after three

hours, her feet were sore, she was hot and thirsty and in dire need of the facilities. They were back in the main atrium, and she was fairly certain that they were over there to the left. Prudence was trying to work out how to politely excuse herself when Dominic swore under his breath.

'What is it?'

He was staring at the plaque which declared that the exhibition had been opened by His Royal Highness Prince George, Duke of Cambridge.

'Her Majesty was in mourning for Prince Albert,' Prudence said. 'Prince George is her cousin.'

'And Commander in Chief of the Armed forces. He was in charge of a division in the Crimea. Thank God, he took ill and was sent home before he could do too much damage.'

'You've met him?'

'He is the epitome of all that is wrong with the army. A colonel at eighteen. A major-general at twenty-six. Do you think he had the least idea of how to command troops?' Dominic asked her savagely. 'If he had his way, there would be no such thing as an officer who earns his rank. Class will out, according to George, and there's nothing that a good flogging of an upstart won't cure. And do you know what's the worst of it?'

Prudence shook her head helplessly.

'The army are trying to change things. End the tradition of purchasing commissions and ban flogging. They're trying to push through better barracks for the men, to learn from the lessons of the bloodbath that was the Crimea. And guess who is planting his big fat royal backside in the way of every change?'

'Prince George?'

'Precisely.'

'He must have an extremely large royal backside if he is trying to oppose Miss Nightingale's reforms,' Prudence said.

To her relief, he gave a shout of laughter. 'I always felt sorry for his horse.'

'Dominic, if you sat in the House of Lords, which you are entitled to do, then you could speak up for reform.'

'I would certainly be one of the few who knew what they were talking about.'

'A voice of experience has surely more chance of holding sway too? Just imagine…'

He turned on his heel. 'That's all it is, a pipe-dream. Have you seen enough? Or shall we go and take a look at the paintings?'

'I am rather in need of some respite,' Prudence

said, sacrificing her dignity for necessity. 'If you will excuse me.'

'I'll wait here.'

She tried to walk slowly but, with her goal in sight, she felt her feet move faster. Back in 1851, when the Great Exhibition opened, the penny toilets had caused a sensation but since then, thank goodness, no public exhibition would be without such a facility.

There was no one else in the ladies' retiring room. She was so hot it was a relief to run cold water over her hands. She was considering lifting her veil to dab her cheeks too, when two ladies dressed in the height of fashion entered, heads together, giggling. Prudence hurried out. She would give a great deal for a cup of tea but lifting her veil before each sip drew too much attention. There was nothing for it but to wait until she was home.

'I was thinking you might like a cup of tea,' Dominic said when she re-joined him at the foot of the stairs leading to one of the upper galleries. 'You won't want to sit in the tearoom, but if I could organise a tray to be brought to a secluded corner of the garden?'

'That's a wonderful idea. I would— Oh!' A hand grabbed her hat and yanked it off her head, and a gust of gleeful childish laughter followed. She looked instinctively up, to see that a little boy had leant over the stair rail and was waving her hat in the air. 'Give that back at once!'

The boy's face crumpled. His laughter turned to a scream. 'Mu-u-u-mmy!'

Dominic swore, grabbing at the child, who screamed louder.

'Mummy, Mummy, look at that lady's face!'

He dropped the hat, and Prudence snatched at it, tugging at Dominic's sleeve at the same time. 'Leave it, please, I beg you.'

But it was too late. A crowd had gathered around them. On the stairs, a woman came rushing up. 'Don't look, Frederick.' She pulled her child towards her, burying his head into her skirts, where he continued to wail, struggling to be free. 'For goodness' sake, sir, cover your wife up. She is frightening my son.'

'*You* are frightening your son, madam.'

A well-dressed man in a top hat and morning dress appeared at the woman's side. 'I say, what on earth is going on?'

'Dominic!' Prudence said in a low voice, trying frantically to pull her veil down. 'I beg you, please don't make a scene.'

'Are you threatening my wife, sir? What did

you say to her to upset her? And my son too. I demand that you apologise at once.'

'It is your wife who should apologise. Your son—'

'Dominic! Please.' Prudence grabbed his arm. 'Let us go.'

'Just one minute, sir. I demand to know...'

Dominic took a step towards the man, who paled. 'Now, look, if there's been a misunderstanding...' he stuttered.

'What you need to understand is that your wife is rude, and your son is a brat.'

Prudence fled. Outside, Dominic caught up with her as she stood uncertainly to the side of the crowds still queuing to get in, tears flooding her cheeks, her knees shaking. 'I want to go home.'

He took her arm, pulling her close to his side. 'Prudence, you can't go anywhere in this state.'

'I want to go home, Dominic. Now!'

'Then that is exactly what we will do. Leave it to me.'

Shocked to the core and furious, Dominic managed to bundle her into a hackney cab and get her to the train station. Once there, a little largesse soon secured them a private waiting room while a private railway carriage was arranged. He was beginning to realise that money could get you most things. Focusing on Prudence's needs kept his own fury at bay, but only just. She had kept a painfully tight leash on herself in the carriage, sitting rigid and silent, her hands gripped tightly together, only the occasional muffled sob betraying her emotion. He knew better than to touch her, simply keeping her within his protective arm as he made his arrangements.

Now that they were alone in the waiting room, he locked the door and gently encouraged her to sit down in the settle by the empty grate, pulling a table over beside it. The little windowless room stank of tobacco smoke. The tea he poured into the thick white china cup looked strong enough to stand a spoon in. He added two lumps of sugar and stirred in the milk. Then he put back her veil and handed her the cup, putting both her hands around it, sitting down beside her to help her take a sip.

'They've promised me a carriage in about an hour,' he said.

Prudence stared at him blankly. Her eyes were wide with unshed tears, her face ashen.

'Drink your tea.'

'There's sugar in it.'

'For shock. Drink it, please.'

She took another sip, making a face, then set the cup back down on the table. The tears brimmed over, dripping down her cheeks.

'Try not to think about it,' Dominic said, but it was too late.

Her breathing became ragged, her face crumpled and a huge sob escaped her. She dropped her face into her hands, her shoulders heaving with the effort she was making to regain her self-control, but when another sob escaped she gave in, and wailed.

Dominic watched, his heart wrenched, feeling utterly helpless in the face of such raw grief. 'I'm so sorry,' he said, trying to put his arms around her.

'I told you how it would be,' she wailed, pushing him away. 'You saw that little boy's face. He thought I was a monster.'

'He didn't, Prudence. If his mother hadn't made such a fuss…'

'"Cover your wife up. She is frightening my son." That's what she said. The words are imprinted on my brain. I am not fit to be seen. Harry Armstrong is right, I put people off their food.'

'Prudence, you know that's not true. Only this

morning you were saying that you weren't going to let that titled upstart dictate…'

'This morning I was deluding myself. I wanted to prove that I could face the world. I can't even show my face in the village. Why I ever thought for a moment that I could face the crowds in London—what a fool I've been.'

'But you did face them, and you were enjoying yourself.'

'From behind a veil, until that child exposed me. Then everyone was staring and pointing, and I was a…a freak show.'

'Prudence! Don't speak of yourself in that way.'

'Look at me, Dominic, look at my face. And *you* know there's worse too, here,' she said, jabbing viciously at her shoulder. '"Your scars don't define you," you said to me once. I tried very hard to believe you, but you were wrong.' She dropped her head into her hands again. 'I should have known better.'

Sick to his stomach, he put his arm around her again. She didn't move, but she didn't push him away. 'I look at you and I don't see a scar, I see your face. I simply see you, Prudence. I wish that everyone else could too.'

She heaved a sigh and sat up, her face blotchy

with tears as she rummaged for her handkerchief. She blew her nose and scrubbed at her eyes. 'I'm so angry with myself. If I'd had the presence of mind simply to put my hat back on. Or if I'd pinned it more securely. Or if I hadn't stood so close to the stairs.'

'I shouldn't have allowed myself to get involved with those horrible people. I should have listened to your pleas. None of this is your fault, Prudence.'

'I subjected you to the most embarrassing ordeal and then promptly had hysterics. And now I've put you to the expense of hiring a private carriage.'

'It's nothing. I'm sorry it's taking a while.'

'I'm sorry that I made such an exhibition of myself.' Prudence grimaced. 'At the Exhibition.'

'I'm angry with myself for not taking better care of you, and I'm furious at dear little Frederick's parents for making such a fuss and having absolutely no concern for your feelings. They ruined your day.'

'And I ruined yours.' Prudence's mouth wobbled. 'I'm so sorry.'

Dominic prised her sodden handkerchief from her hands and replaced it with his own. 'Please stop apologising.'

'You don't see it, Dominic. I don't know why, but you don't. My face repulses people. When Mercy's husband said it put people off their wedding breakfast, he was right.'

Dominic's hands clenched into fists. 'It sounds to me as if the world would be a better place without Mercy's husband.'

'I agree with you, though not for the same reasons. My sister is very unhappy. At least I can call my life my own, even if I do have to live it through a veil.' Prudence folded Dominic's handkerchief up into a very small square. 'I'll wash this for you.'

'This is just a setback.'

'It's the final straw,' she said, dabbing frantically as another tear coursed down her cheek. 'I wish I hadn't tried. I wish I hadn't invested so much hope in today. I wasn't exactly happy, but I was content before...'

'Before I came on the scene?'

'Yes! No! Before I began to dream there could be more! Before Jeremy asked me to help with his house. Before he commissioned the Hawthorn Wheel. I don't even think I was content, never mind happy, now that I think about it, and I should have been. I am fortunate. I've always known how fortunate I am. Look at me, Dominic! Can you imagine how much worse this would have been when I was a little child. Not much more than a baby. Most people would have thought me better off dead. But not my parents.'

'I would hope not!'

'You don't understand.'

'What don't I...?'

A sharp rap at the door made them both jump. 'Your carriage is ready, Mr Caldwell. Five minutes, sir, if you please.'

Chapter Fifteen

To her mortification, Prudence's knees started shaking so much when she got to her feet that she would have fallen back onto the settle if Dominic hadn't caught her. Her fingers shook as she adjusted her hat and veil carefully in the mirror over the empty fireplace, aware of him studiously looking away. Her face was covered in blotches, her eyes rimmed red. As they made their way through the crowds to the platform where their carriage had been coupled to the back of the four o'clock train, she was intensely grateful for Dominic's arm and the protective bulk of him.

'Not quite so luxurious as our last carriage,' he said, pulling the blinds of the windows down as the conductor slammed the door shut and almost immediately they began to clank and screech out of the station.

Two long divans faced each other along the length of the carriage, upholstered in tobacco-coloured silk. A brown and blue patterned carpet covered the floor, and more brown fabric had been used to cover what was left of the walls and the ceiling. The effect would have been rather depressing if Prudence's spirits had not already been at rock bottom. She added guilt and gratitude to her shame and embarrassment and anger. Dominic had once again gone to a great deal of trouble and expense on her behalf.

'Thank you,' she said as he took the seat opposite her. 'In all honesty, I'm not sure that I could have braved a public carriage.'

'Fortunately, that's one thing you don't have to worry about.'

She tried to smile, but her mouth refused to co-operate. 'You want to know what I meant, don't you, when I said that you didn't understand.'

'Only if you want to tell me.'

She was loath to remove her veil. The way she felt right now, she would prefer never to remove it again, not even in the bath, but she forced herself to lift it. 'I'm afraid crying plays havoc with my complexion,' she said with another wobbly attempt at a smile.

'It doesn't do much for my state of mind either, to witness it.'

'I haven't any more tears left,' she said, already feeling considerably calmer. 'I don't know why I haven't told you before. I'm pitiful enough, in the eyes of most people. If they knew the truth, they'd think me pathetic. I know you're different, that you don't think me Poor Prudence—at least not until today.'

'The only thing that ever makes me annoyed with you is when you refer to yourself in that way.'

'I know, but you can't deny, Dominic, that everyone else thinks so.'

'Your brother and sister don't.'

'No.' Perhaps it was because she was worn out, or perhaps now was simply the right time, but Prudence had no hesitation in what she said next. 'Clement isn't my real brother, and Mercy isn't my real sister. I'm adopted.'

Her confession shocked him so much that his jaw dropped, but Prudence felt simply relieved. 'I know next to nothing of the circumstances of my birth. As far as I am concerned, the people I called Mama and Papa were my parents, and they always treated me as one of their own. Mercy and Clement are not related to me in any way, but that has never affected our relationship.'

'Your brother loves you. That is very clear,' Dominic said, looking quite stunned.

'I've been very lucky, to have such a loving family. I never forget that.'

'No. I can see—thinking back—you have been quite vehement on the subject. You'll admit, it's a very odd coincidence that both of us—good grief, no wonder you always got on your high horse at my lack of gratitude.'

'We have both been very fortunate.'

He moved to sit by her side, taking her hand. 'I do know that now, I promise you. My adoptive parents did their duty by me. I was housed and fed and clothed and schooled. Not loved, but looked after very well, and it pains me, thinking back now with fresh eyes, to think of how ungrateful I may have been. When I found the papers after my father—adoptive father—after he died, I thought—that explains it, that's why I had never felt that I truly belonged. Your experience is very different, with the Carstairs family.'

'I never doubted that I was born one of them, until they told me I was not.'

'When was that, Prue?'

She smiled faintly at his use of her pet name, relishing the comfort of his hand twined with hers. 'It was Mercy's eighteenth birthday. I was fourteen.' She wished fleetingly that Dominic could magically produce a tot of brandy to sustain her. After all these years, the memory could still overpower her.

'Growing up, my parents, my brother and sister, were very protective of me. Not in a way I noticed. I didn't go to school. Mama dressed my hair so that it covered my cheek. Looking back, my few friends were carefully selected and carefully instructed. I knew that my scar made me different, but I had no idea that it made me repulsive. No, don't shake your head, Dominic. After today, you can't doubt that I'm right.'

He lifted her hand to his, pressing a fervent kiss to her fingertips, but he did not dispute what she said. 'So you had a happy childhood, then?'

'I did.' Prudence met his eyes, briefly smiling, before bracing herself to continue. 'Mercy was making her debut that Season, and we all knew she would be the toast of the town, that this would very likely be her last birthday before she married. We had a party, she invited two of her school friends, who I'd met before. I had a new gown and I was anxious to show it off, so I came down early to the drawing room. They were already there, the two of them, and I heard my name being used. You know what they say—that eavesdroppers never hear good of themselves?

'"Such a pity, poor soul." That is how they referred to me. They weren't vindictive, they were simply being honest, thinking themselves alone, but I heard enough, more than enough.' Her voice wobbled, but she was determined to finish without crying. 'I ran back up to my room and looked at myself in the mirror, and it was like seeing someone else. And once you see yourself the way others see you, Dominic, you can't un-see it. I remembered lots of times when Mama or Mercy had whisked me away from someone, and I realised that Mama's keeping me at home and teaching me herself wasn't because she didn't want to part with me, it was because she wanted to protect me. Because she loved me, Dominic. You see, that's what mattered—what still matters the most.

'Mama came looking for me, to ask why I hadn't joined the party, and that's when I asked her what was wrong with my face and my back. What had happened to me. Mama was very upset. I was her daughter, and that's all that mattered, she said, over and over. Fate brought me to her. She fell in love with me the moment she set eyes on me. And my imperfections,' Prudence said, touching her cheek, 'only made her love me more. And that's how I discovered that I was adopted.'

'So the accident—if it was an accident—happened before she adopted you?'

'Yes.'

'Is that truly all you know? You must have asked again, once you had recovered from the shock.'

'Mama got so upset, the one time I did ask. She said the circumstances were tragic and it was best for all concerned not to dwell on it. I felt it would be disloyal and ungrateful if I persisted in pressing her on the subject.'

'You never tried to discover for yourself where you come from after your parents died, I take it?'

Prudence shook her head, choosing her words carefully. 'I wasn't wanted, probably because of how I look. I can't be certain of that, but it's highly likely. I was taken in by a family who wanted and loved me. I have no more interest in finding out about those who rejected me than you do. Whoever gave me away, whatever the circumstances, they won't want me turning up like a bad penny.'

'Let sleeping dogs lie,' he said wryly. 'I remember you using that phrase.'

'I'm so sorry that today turned out this way, and I'm extremely grateful that you have gone to such an effort to get me home safely, Dominic. I've learnt a salutary lesson.'

'Don't give up, Prudence.'

'I'm being realistic, that's all. I'd forgotten how fortunate I am. Talking to you has been a timely reminder. I shall count my blessings more carefully in future.'

'Prudence, this is a setback, that's all.'

'It's not, Dominic. I am sorry, I simply can't live up to your expectations of me. I will always be a social pariah. It's better to accept that now, once and for all. I will disappoint Mercy, for I promised that today would be the first visit of many—but she'll understand. And Clement too. He always thought it was too big a risk, and he was right.'

The train had begun to slow. 'I think this is our stop,' Dominic said, raising one of the blinds.

Prudence pulled her veil back down with relief. She was on the verge of tears once more, but she would not feel sorry for herself, and she would not let Dominic see what this was costing her. All she had to do was get herself home and lock herself in her room.

'Ready?'

It made her heart ache, to see him so apprehensive on her behalf. 'I'm perfectly fine now,' she lied, pulling on her gloves and getting to her feet. The train was busy. She was aware of the interested gazes of several people as she and Dominic descended onto the platform and waited for the small crowd to subside.

'We will be the talk of the village,' she said as they made their way out of the station. 'A lawyer's clerk and a recluse descending from a private carriage at this little stop is not exactly commonplace.'

'I am sure they will come up with a hundred reasons, and I personally couldn't give a damn, but I do think the lawyer's clerk story is wearing just a little thin, don't you?'

'Are you thinking of letting the truth be known?'

'I don't know. If I am to remain here for a while—but that's for another day.'

'I forgot! I have been so selfish. You wanted to talk to me about disposing of the proceeds of the estate.'

'There's plenty of time.'

'Aren't you in a rush to get back to Greece?'

'Prudence, in all truth I haven't even thought about it in weeks,' Dominic said, looking rather startled by this admission. 'The only thing on my mind right now is to get you home safely. You must be exhausted.'

'It has been a long day,' she said, thinking wearily of how brightly and optimistically she had set out. 'I confess, I am glad to be home. London doesn't suit me, it is far too noisy and dirty. I am a country woman at heart.' They had reached the path leading to the front door, and she stopped. 'Thank you for everything, Dominic. I won't ask you in. I *am* exhausted. Goodbye.'

She turned without waiting for his answer, anxious to reach the sanctuary of her room, for despite all her resolutions tears were once again stinging her eyes. Clement's hat was not on the peg. Thankful for very small mercies, Prudence ran up the stairs and locked her bedroom door.

She slept, but her dreams were vivid and troubled and for long periods of the light summer night she lay trapped in a nightmarish state between sleeping and wakefulness, her mind churning and her heart racing. She was on a beach, barefoot, her feet sinking deeper into the sand with every step she took, and behind her the sea was forming into one huge wave about to break over her. She was in the fernery and the Hawthorn Wheel was spouting water from all the wrong places, but every time she fixed one leak another sprang. She was on a train but she had lost her ticket and her purse, and she couldn't remember where she was going and she couldn't open the carriage door each time the train pulled into a station. She was running a bath but the taps dissolved when she tried to turn them off.

Prudence jerked awake, bathed in sweat, her head thumping. It was very early, but the night had already given way to a hazy dawn. She dragged herself from her tangled sheets and pulled the curtains further apart, opening the window to the fresh air. Her dreams were already forgotten, leaving her with a sense of acute anxiety, of something pressingly urgent that she must do if only she could remember what it was.

Outside, a cockerel crowed and the dawn chorus began. The blackbirds were particularly loud this morning. Clement hadn't returned until late last night. He couldn't possibly have spent the whole day in Lady Sarah's company, could he?

She had never seriously considered the possibility of her brother marrying. What would happen to her if he did? The notion of him marrying a woman like Lady Sarah was preposterous, for he was a man who needed order and calm and books and, besides, Lady Sarah was a committed spinster.

As was Prudence. Her heart sank. She'd joked about it yesterday, but it was true. Save that it wasn't. She had no more tears, but a sob caught her breath all the same. She was in love with Dominic.

She could admit it now that she had proved once and for all that it was futile. She had been falling in love with him almost from the moment she'd set eyes on him. The weeks they had spent apart hadn't extinguished her feelings, merely suppressed them. When he'd appeared in the railway carriage yesterday, her stupid heart had leapt, and every one of the dire warnings she'd delivered to herself when they were apart was forgotten.

It was inevitable, she supposed. He was the first man who had ever looked at her and seen past her scars. No, more than that. He saw her scars as part of her, that was what it was, and no one had ever done that. She touched her cheek, tracing the line down to her lip, marvelling that she had managed to fool herself into believing that her feelings were transient. She loved him. There was utter certainty in her head and her heart about that, and no regrets either. There was no future for them, she had never been so foolish as to consider there could be, but to know love was more than she had ever expected.

She loved him. For a moment she allowed herself to savour this thought. To recall the kisses they had shared. The intimate moments. The way he looked at her. The way he listened to her. The way he had bared his soul to her. And she to him, yesterday. She loved him so much.

Outside, the cockerel crowed again, and Prudence snapped out of her daydream. Time to return to reality. She loved Dominic. He cared for her but he was not in love with her and, even if he was, they had absolutely no future together. All the dreams he had urged her to dream were dust after yesterday. There was no point in her railing against the injustice of her disfigurement or resenting the impact it had on her life. She had to resign herself to a future locked away from the world, and she had to remember what she'd said so vehemently to Dominic yesterday. She was lucky.

But she had also learnt her limitations. She had tried to live up to his expectations. She had dared to dream. She had been desperate to offer Mercy support and solace. And she had been determined to prove to herself that there might be the possibility of a future beyond the boundaries of this house, this village. Beyond her veil. She had failed spectacularly. She'd made a public spectacle of herself, and she had broken down in front of Dominic. She would not risk any of that again. He had been so gentle and understanding, but it was his eagerness for her to try again that bolstered her resolve. She didn't want to prove that he was mistaken, that she was not the woman he believed her to be, nor ever could be. It was time for her to retreat to the safety of the world she had inhabited before she'd met him.

Dominic stood in the turret room. It was raining outside. It wasn't proper rain, not like the rare summer downpours in Greece, which made the sky black, which bounced off the hard-baked earth forming huge pools, and which ended as suddenly as they began, leaving the earth steaming and the sky bright blue. The sky here was watery grey, the sun still weakly shining as if it was cloaked in gauze. The rain fell so softly, floating down as if it couldn't quite be bothered to land, and it would do the garden absolutely no good whatsoever.

He turned his attention away from the grey landscape to the portrait of his mother. What would she think if she could see him here? Would she be pleased or horrified? He had no idea. The more salient question, and the one which had prevented him from sleeping, was what he thought he was playing at. He left the room and set up the billiard table. The idea of returning to Lavrio had been so fixed in his mind he had not questioned it, until Prudence had. His cottage had been his haven. His sanctuary. He couldn't imagine returning to his sedentary life, where the only important decision to be made was whether to go for a swim in the morning or the evening.

He missed the red ball completely and abandoned his game to wander morosely round the room and the gallery of aristocrats. He wasn't one of them and never would be, but that didn't mean he had to hide himself away. There was a great deal of work to be done here in distributing his ancestors' accumulated wealth, and he wanted to oversee it himself. He wanted to ensure that the money was well spent. He wanted to establish that his choices had been good ones. A return to Lavrio in the near future would be premature. And unappealing. If not impossible.

The decision was made, and it was a huge relief. It changed none of his feelings about the men glaring down at him, nor his determination never to join their ranks, but he would enjoy the irony of using their wealth if not to undermine the world they ruled, but to make it easier for those in their power to endure.

Bounding back downstairs, Dominic brewed a pot of coffee. He was looking forward to talking his plans over with Prudence. He stopped in the act of pouring his first cup. Wasn't that precisely the sort of thing he shouldn't be doing? He frowned, trying to recall what pompous verbiage he'd used to justify their outing to the Exhibition. Something about taking stock and seeing the situation more rationally. He had taken stock and he had thought it all through, and he'd concluded they had been right to maintain a safe distance. And then, at the first opportunity he got, he'd closed it.

And look what had happened! Recalling the scene, Prudence's shame and humiliation, made him furious. She had been so brave and so full of hope for the future, it had been an agony to see her so completely broken. He was still racked with guilt, knowing he was partly to blame. It was unfair, and it was wrong, but a night's reflection had forced him to accept that the stark, unpalatable reality was exactly as she had described. Outside her closest circle, she would always be a social pariah. The world would not see Prudence as he did, and it would be she who suffered if he persisted in suggesting that she try to change that. Prudence wouldn't risk going out in public again and he couldn't blame her. After yesterday, the last thing he would do would be to encourage her.

Yet how she had blossomed, that day they'd spent at the beach. The simple pleasure of the sun on her face, the wind in her hair, of a different perspective and the freedom to enjoy it had shown him a very different, vibrant woman. A sensual woman who relished the elements as he did. He couldn't stomach the idea that she might never be that woman again.

But what was to be done? After yesterday, she would be bound to retreat into herself. They had tacitly agreed that it would be wrong of him to arrange another such day, but that was exactly what she needed, the gift of freedom. If he could design a day that was entirely and uniquely to her taste and not his, a day that would engage her mind and not her body, with no romantic backdrop, then it would be easy for him to keep a leash on his own feelings. That, Dominic decided, had been the mistake he'd made the last time. The combination of the sun, even the English sun, and the sea, even the cold English sea, had worked their sensual magic. This time, it would be different.

His conscience clear and his mind eased, Dominic picked up his coffee cup again and began to plan.

Chapter Sixteen

It was one thing, Prudence quickly realised, to resolve to retreat from the world in the early hours of the morning, alone and melancholy after a traumatic day. It was quite another to have the willpower to retreat from the man she had fallen in love with, but she tried, the task made easier by the fact that the man himself had sent her a note informing her that business had called him back to London.

Clement, blissfully unaware of the traumatic end to her trip, resumed his scholarly pursuits. When she tentatively enquired about his day with Lady Sarah, he informed her that it had been a very pleasant interlude in a tone that made it clear he considered the subject closed. Prudence tried to take a leaf out of his book, but the days passed slowly and she spent far too many hours wondering what Dominic was doing and if he was thinking of her. She wished she could see him, simply to prove to him that she had fully recovered from her embarrassing hysterics, and to prove to herself that she could be in his company without betraying herself.

A week after she had last seen him, he sent a note requesting her assistance in a business matter. She had her chance. But as she arrived at Hawthorn Manor, Prudence was once again struggling to keep her emotions in check. Dominic was waiting for her at the front door, and his face lit up when he saw her, and just for a moment her heart leapt. But by the time she reached him, his smile was tempered and the touch of his hand was fleeting, and by the time she took off her hat and veil she had her own foolish smile under control.

'The weather is holding remarkably well,' Prudence said, cringing inwardly at her overly formal tone. 'How is your garden progressing?'

'Slowly,' he answered. 'Most of my lettuce has been ravaged by snails. They seem to have a voracious appetite.'

'Don't you have snails in Greece?'

He grinned. 'Yes, and they're delicious, cooked in rice and tomatoes.'

'Ugh! Are you teasing me?'

He shook his head. 'You cook them in their shells. They're very small, you have to suck them out.'

'That sounds absolutely disgusting. Please don't tell me you intend a similar fate for the ones in the garden.'

'I thought we'd have them for lunch with a glass of Claret. I've been exploring, and have discovered the wine cellar. I must say, that's one aspect of my inheritance I might hold onto. I am only teasing,' he added. 'English snails are far too big to eat. They'd be chewy. Shall we go up to the turret room?'

He was dressed in grey trousers with a matching waistcoat and a plain white shirt. The clothes were new, but he wore them with casual assurance that no other gentleman would, the sleeves rolled up, showing his tanned forearms, the neck of the shirt open with neither a collar nor tie. His hair was already long enough to flop over his brow, curling slightly at the back. As Prudence followed him up the stairs, she couldn't help but notice how well his trousers fitted and, before she could stop herself, she recalled the taut firmness of his buttocks on her palms when they had kissed in the water, the way he had responded to her touch, the catch of his breath, the arch of his back, the swell of his…

'I've had some photographs taken,' Dominic said, turning around on the top step at the gallery. 'Careful.'

She had almost walked into him. For heaven's sake, what was wrong with her? 'Photographs?' Prudence said. 'Of what?'

'The houses that I currently own in Clerkenwell,' Dominic said. 'Are you feeling unwell?'

'The climb, that's all. So many stairs. And I have rather more clothes on than you. What I mean is, they are much heavier. Did you know that the average woman's toilette weighs between twenty and thirty pounds?'

'That's almost the weight of a trooper's backpack.'

'And yet we are reputed to be the weaker sex.'

'Ha! Tell that to Florence Nightingale and her nurses. Have you sandbags strapped to your waist under that crinoline contraption?'

'My crinoline is a good deal lighter than some, and all crinolines are lighter than the horsehair petticoats they have replaced.'

'Your petticoats don't look as if they weigh much.'

'You shouldn't be looking at my petticoats.'

'I've seen tantalisingly little of them, but what I have seen surprised me, I must admit. Ribbons and lace and ruffles, Prue.' He was teasing her, but the way he was looking at her wasn't wholly teasing.

'I like the contrast,' she said.

'So do I.' He sighed, turning away. 'Though I know that's not the point. I hope you don't mind, but I've appropriated your office.'

'It's your house, Dominic.' And she was not here to flirt with him, Prudence reminded herself, following him into the room.

The photographs were laid out on the circular desk. There were about twenty of them, some taken inside, some outside, of a rundown terrace of houses. Prudence studied them with increasing horror. 'How many people live here?'

Dominic told her how many, and she listened in disbelief as he described the conditions, picking up and scrutinising each of the images. There were no sculleries in any of the houses, no running water and no toilets. There was one standing pipe to provide water to every household that was switched on three days a week. There were three privies. Worse, according to Dominic, the buildings had been so cheaply made that every corner possible had been cut, from inadequate foundations to shoddy roofing. The houses were sinking into the London mud.

'Repairs are carried out only when either one of the residents is injured or the press take heed of their complaints,' Dominic said. 'Maintenance is non-existent. Doncaster had the nerve to inform me that there were considerably worse places to live.'

'I cannot imagine where.'

'Nor I. I've seen poverty in my life, I've seen some appalling living conditions in wartime, but these,' Dominic said, waving at the photographs, 'are right in the heart of London, one of the richest cities in the world. And the inhabitants—my tenants!—are not criminals or wastrels, they're decent, hard-working people. I had no idea, Prue. What I've seen shocked me to the core. And this is only one street. I own several more. And what I own is nothing, a fraction of the thousands of similar places.'

'But who owns them? Why are they not called to account?'

'The owners who profit from them, the lawmakers who aid and abet them, are ultimately one and the same. Men like those out there lining the walls of the gallery. They don't collect the rent themselves, they don't even have their names on the lease, they employ others to do their exploitation, so that by the time the money reaches their well-lined pockets it's neatly pressed and laundered.'

'You exaggerate, surely,' Prudence said, taken aback by his vehemence.

'Unfortunately not. I've done a little digging. I managed to track down a sympathetic journalist, and what he showed me made my blood run cold. To think that in the eyes of the people who live there I am one of the men exploiting them,' he said, picking up a photograph of the whole terrace. 'It makes me sick to my stomach.'

'What will you do, Dominic?'

'Fix the houses up, rebuild if necessary, make them worthy of *The Builder* magazine, and of the people who are my tenants.'

'Yes, but what I meant was, what about the other houses, the ones you don't own?'

'What can I do about those?'

'I don't know. The journalist you spoke to, couldn't he…?'

'No one wants to know, Prue. No one would pay attention to him.'

'They would listen to you, if—'

'No.'

She was silent, knowing it would be pointless and wrong for her to remonstrate. She, who could not venture from her doorstep to the Manor without her veil, was hardly in a position to encourage Dominic into the world of public politics.

Dominic was standing with his back to her, looking out at the walled garden. She joined him, taking his arm to catch his attention. 'You have come a very long way in the last few weeks. You take so much in your stride, I forget sometimes how much you have achieved. Making sense of all those documents, challenging Doncaster— my goodness, the man must be rueing the day you walked into his office.'

Dominic grinned. 'I must admit, it remains one of my cherished memories.'

'And one of his worst nightmares. I wonder that you are still employing him.'

'He's not a crook, and he seems genuinely to have believed he was acting in the best interests of his clients—Jeremy, and his father.' Dominic frowned. 'Which he was if you value profit above all. He needs a strong hand, a bit of discipline. I think I might knock him into shape.'

'Like a raw recruit.'

Dominic laughed gruffly. 'Better the devil

you know, as they say. We're beginning to understand one another.'

'And now you're going to rebuild London together.'

'A few terraces. And I'm hoping that you will help me.'

'I can't help you with this. I'm not an engineer or a builder or even a plumber.'

'No, but we can hire all those, Prue. I want you to use your imagination. Think about how we can make these houses fit for the people who live in them. They have to be practical, not simply attractive façades.'

'But I don't know anything about the people who live there.'

'We can find out. Don't you want to help? I thought…'

'Oh, Dominic, I do. I would love to help, but unlike you I'm rather daunted by the size of the task.'

'You give me too much credit. When I first saw this street, I realised it was a massive undertaking.'

'I think you are extraordinary. You ought to be very proud of yourself. A man who until very recently spent his days tending his goats and his garden.'

'I'm still tending my garden. I'm still me, Prue.'

'Yes, but you're a better, stronger me—I mean you. No, that's not right. You were always impressive. You must have been, Dominic, for your Colonel to make it so difficult for you to do what you did. He would not have done that for a lesser man.'

She expected him to brush her off, or to turn the subject, but after a moment's silence he nodded. 'I suspect I'd had enough of the army by then anyway. I'd joined up so young, I never knew anything else. But I never missed the life once I'd quit it. I'd never experienced living alone. Never had the chance to be alone with my thoughts, and no responsibilities either. Lavrio provided that.'

'You sound as if you have consigned Lavrio to the past.'

'I haven't, not yet. I simply don't think of it, I've too much else on my mind.'

'Such as building a few hundred houses.'

'I can't do more, Prue. You do understand that?'

'You're not going to join their club. I do understand.'

'I wouldn't make any difference anyway,' he

said, sounding oddly unconvinced. 'I'm better spending my time and energy on what is within my power.'

'Then we'd better get our sleeves rolled up and get on with it. Though I see you already have a head start.'

'I cannot accustom myself to long sleeves.'

'You are still maintaining your tan, despite our cold English summer.' She stared at the open neck of his shirt. She should not have mentioned his tan. What was wrong with her? She was in love with him, not in lust. Did the two go together? 'On your arms,' she said, 'and your face. That's what I meant.'

'Not enough swimming to maintain the rest.'

She looked up to find him smiling at her and she knew that, like her, he was remembering. Mesmerised, she stepped closer just as his arm reached for her, sliding around her waist. She must not do this, but she would die if he didn't kiss her. She lifted her hand to touch his cheek, and his eyes fluttered closed.

And then she stepped back, just as he let her go, and the pair of them stared at each other helplessly for a moment before returning their gazes to the walled garden. 'The weather is bound to break some time soon,' Prudence said. 'You should take the train to the coast and go for a swim, make the most of it while you can.'

'Now you come to mention it, I do have plans for another day out, though not to the coast. I was hoping you'd join me.'

'Oh, Dominic, no. I can't.'

'You'd be perfectly safe, Prue, I promise.'

'I don't want you wasting your money on me. Especially not if it means there is less to spend on all this.'

'You won't be robbing my tenants of their own lavatory, I promise. Will you trust me? Let me make it up to you for the last time?'

'That wasn't your fault, and I have always trusted you, you know that.'

'So you'll come, then?'

'I don't know.'

'It's all arranged for the day after tomorrow. Doncaster has pulled out all the stops. Or should I say plugs?'

'Now I am intrigued. Where…?'

'It's a surprise. But one I am absolutely certain you will enjoy, though there will be no… no swimming.'

He didn't mean swimming. He had forgotten himself a moment ago, but not as much as she had. 'I'm glad of that,' Prudence said with a determined smile. 'Swimming gets me into deep water.'

Chapter Seventeen

'We'll have to walk from the station,' Dominic said as the train made the now familiar screeching, squealing stop on the viaduct for the tickets to be collected in the public coaches. 'I'm afraid that a carriage would be impractical where we're going. But it's a very short distance.'

'I am sure I'll be fine,' Prudence said, sounding unconvinced but giving him a tight smile.

She was dressed in the same blue and grey striped gown and jacket that she'd worn on their first trip to London, though the veil she was now adjusting in the mirror at the far end of the carriage had been changed from pale grey to a much darker blue. She was sticking a great number of pins into her hat. Her gloves were dark blue to match, when the last time they too had been grey. As always, she looked poised and elegant. There was something graceful and alluring in the line of her back, accentuated by the tight-fitting bodice of her jacket, the way it curved down to her small waist, made tiny by the voluminous skirts of her gown. Her petticoat today was black, quite plain save for a deep ruffle. Practical, and intriguing. Were her other undergarments matching or contrasting? He had only the haziest idea of what they might be, for it had been a long time since he'd undressed any woman and he had never peeled the layers from someone so very well-dressed. There would be a corset. Drawers? A camisole of some sort? Stockings and garters. How many layers? She had a very neat little bottom under that skirt, that he did know. The perfect size for his hands. And her breasts, he remembered all too well...

The train whistle blew, and Prudence staggered as the carriage began to move again. 'We're almost there.'

Dominic cursed himself for his now aroused state, for allowing himself to indulge in just the sort of musings that he had determined he would not, and most of all for forgetting even for a moment how brave Prudence was being. 'We'll wait until the crowds disperse a bit before we alight,' he said, pulling on his hated gloves and putting on his hat. 'You needn't worry.'

'I will be fine. I am not worried, I'm excited. I can't imagine where we are going, unless you have organised a tour of Mr Bazalgette's sewers. They do offer such a thing, you know. Until such times as they are put into service!"

'I do know, and I actually did consider it, but frankly the thought of walking for miles from one end of a tunnel to another with nothing to see save possibly a few rats did not strike me as a particularly interesting way of spending the day. A tunnel is a tunnel, whether it carries trains or…or waste products.'

'Effluent, I believe is the accepted word in polite society, according to my sister,' Prudence said. 'That any word at all is accepted, I call progress. If not the sewers, then where are we going?'

'The river, first. Ready?' Dominic opened the carriage door and gave her his hand, though she needed no help to descend. The crowds had subsided a little, but he pulled her close and she did not resist, her arm tucked tightly into his. Her courage made him both proud and angry, though to tell her either of those things would be to undermine the efforts she was making. 'We're headed to the Hungerford Stairs,' he said. 'I've hired a steamer.'

Prudence stopped short. 'I've never been on a boat in my life.'

He shouldn't have been surprised, but the constraints of her life were appalling. It was so damned unfair! 'Here's hoping you don't get seasick then.'

She had never been on a steamer, though she was living through the age of steam. Dominic hadn't quite managed to cover up his shock at that admission. Must she continue to deprive herself of so many commonplace experiences? But as they left the station the noise and bustle of the city filled Prudence with excitement. The air was dense and dank, but it was the air of a modern, thriving city full of purpose. She could smell the river before she saw it, a brown churning mass clogged with steamers, barges and skiffs of all shapes and sizes. The narrow passageway they walked down was lined with advertisements for milliners and photographers, for patent medicines, for gin and for porter.

There were a number of piers, each with their own ticket kiosk.

'Cremorne!'

'Lambeth!'

'Chelsea!'

'Westminster!'

The cries came from the various boats, a bewildering number of them arriving and departing, some of them barely stopping, forcing the passengers to leap aboard.

'I'm told it's much busier first thing,' Dominic muttered, 'but I can't imagine how.'

'Mr Caldwell? Welcome aboard the *Downy Thistle*. Mind your step now.'

The skipper, wearing a top hat, was standing on the bridge. He watched as Dominic helped Prudence aboard, then called out something indecipherable. A hand appeared from the hatch giving the thumbs-up sign, and they were away.

The *Downy Thistle* was equipped with a number of wooden benches in the prow, and a small covered cabin aft, where Prudence and Dominic made themselves comfortable out of sight of the skipper and whatever crew lurked below decks, allowing her to put back her veil. The rank stench of the Thames filtered in through the draughty windows, and the river was much choppier than Prudence had ever imagined. Much busier too. She marvelled at the way their paddle steamer cut a swathe through the crowded channel and caught her breath a couple of times as a smaller boat hove into their path.

Seeing the city from the river provided a very different perspective. Not far from their departure point, they passed several grand mansions, their grounds running down to meet the muddy banks. Lighter barges stood three-deep at the wharves, and as they passed under London Bridge with the Tower looming on the left bank, steamers jostled for space with the ocean-going tall-masted ships. They picked up speed after the huge bend that encompassed the Isle of Dogs, and on to Greenwich and the Royal Dockyard, when the river became less congested and rougher.

'Tide must be turning,' Dominic said. 'How are you feeling?'

'Awestruck,' Prudence replied promptly, 'and not at all sick, though I have no idea if this is rough or calm.'

'The worst weather I've ever endured on the water was in the Black Sea. I was stuck on a troop ship for three days, waiting on the weather abating enough for us to land. I learnt then that I wasn't as salty a seadog as I'd thought.' He took his watch out of his pocket to check the time. Closing it, he ran his thumb over the inscription, a habit that Prudence had noticed before. He caught her eye and smiled, surprising her by handing the timepiece to her. 'It was a gift from my men to mark my promotion to Captain.'

She read the inscription, ran her fingers over the various dents and scratches on the case, which was still warm from his body. 'It's seen a lot of action.'

'Too much,' Dominic said, returning it to his pocket. 'I was good at my job; you were right about that. I had forgotten.' He took her hand, made to lift it to his mouth and then changed his mind, pressing her fingers before letting it go. 'We should be there soon.'

'Where?'

'A building which I have been assured will be one of the new wonders of the world, when it is finished, and one which you once told me you'd give your heart to see,' he told her, smiling. 'A palace, in its own way, or perhaps I should say a cathedral. Celebrating...'

'Oh, dear heavens, sewage!' Prudence burst out laughing. 'Dominic, are we by any chance going to sail past one of the new pumping stations?'

'Better than that. We're going to visit it.'

'But I can't, it will be full of workers.'

'It's Saturday. I have arranged for us to have private access.'

'No!' Prudence jumped to her feet, pressing her face to the window. 'Which one is it?'

'Crossness, on the other bank.'

She staggered to the other window, frustrated by the grime, salt and spray on the glass. 'You could not have arranged anything more wonderful. I know you think it's odd...'

'Endearingly odd.'

'You could not have made a better grand gesture. Not that it is a grand gesture,' she added, flustered. 'You simply wanted to give me a little confidence after the fiasco at the Great...'

'Let us never mention that again.'

'Oh, I will happily agree to that. Dominic, I can't believe—have you really—I simply can't believe it.'

He laughed again, shaking his head. 'I hope you're not going to be disappointed. It's a building site, and not due for completion for at least another two years.'

'They are hoping the Queen will open it, if she is out of mourning by then, but we will have been there first.' Prudence beamed. 'How marvellous is that? How lucky am I? Thank you.'

She meant to kiss his cheek, but the boat

turned, lurching its way to the jetty, and he threw his arms around her, and her mouth landed on his. His hands tightened on her waist. She felt him inhale sharply. She broke the kiss immediately. 'Sorry. I meant—it was a thank-you, intended for your cheek. Sorry.'

'Prue?'

Dominic was looking at her as if for the first time. The paddles ceased their pounding, the engine cut to a gentle roar and the skipper could be heard shouting instructions. 'What is it?' she asked, puzzled.

Dominic shook his head. 'Nothing. Looks like we've arrived.'

Crossness Pumping Station was a short walk from the river, enough time for Dominic to recover a little of his composure. The massive exterior of the building looked to be complete. There was a huge central block, disconcertingly in the style of an Italian Renaissance palace, a large central arched doorway surmounted by pillars flanked by windows almost as grand. Rows of arched windows with flanking pillars marched along the second floor. A tall parapet hid the shallow roof. The two wings had been built in a very different style, single storey, much plainer, with pitched roofs of differing heights. A tall, narrow brick chimney towered over everything.

'It looks finished,' Prudence said, echoing his thoughts, 'though I know it can't be.'

'Doncaster has arranged for the plans to be laid out inside. I hope it lives up to your expectations.'

'It has already surpassed them. I didn't imagine it would be so huge. It makes one wonder— actually, I think I'd rather not speculate. I'm glad we're viewing it before it becomes operational.'

Dominic laughed. 'So am I.' He handed her a large key. 'Do you want to do the honours?'

'Your Mr Doncaster is certainly doing his best to redeem himself.' Prudence opened the door and stepped through. 'Oh, my! Oh, my goodness. I know you joked about it being a cathedral, but it really is,' Prudence said, pushing back her veil to gaze up at the ceiling, high above them.

The scale of the interior was so impressive that Dominic put his mental turmoil to one side. 'I think that might be sacrilegious, given what is being worshipped here.'

She laughed, but her attention was wholly taken up by her surroundings.

The promised plans were set out on a table

by the door. Doncaster had indeed earned his stripes, Dominic thought wryly, for without them he would have struggled to make sense of the vast space. One of the four steam-driven engines had been installed, with the flywheel and the beam in place, two pieces of engineering so monumental that they reached almost to the top of the double-height roof. The ornamental cast ironwork that partitioned the pumping station was almost completed, the partitions and iron pillars marking out a large octagon where they stood and reminded him of a mosque he had visited in Constantinople. Miles of pipework was stacked in one corner, waiting to be connected up. The plans showed details of the colour scheme, which was primarily gold and green and would, he reckoned, add to the presumably intended impression that here stood a temple to engineering. There were stairs leading upwards to a floor made of cast iron that looked to be floating over their heads and which he could not believe would hold anyone's weight. Stairs led downwards to the reservoirs, which they would need to light the lamps to view.

Admirable and impressive as it all was, Dominic was more interested in watching Prudence and mulling over the thoughts that occupied him.

While she made her first tour, wandering in a daze between the three components of the building, she said very little, allowing him to indulge himself, wholly entranced by her. It was such a huge relief to finally let go of the hold he had on his feelings, to revel in watching her thoughts flicker across her face and to bask in the satisfaction of knowing he had arranged an outing that was so exactly to her taste, and one that no one else would ever have dreamed of. When she tugged at his arm, pointed some obscure feature out or speculated about another, when she beamed her pleasure at him or gave a little skip of excitement, he thought he would burst with the joy of having made her so happy.

Having completed one circuit, Prudence returned to the plans, studying them in detail, muttering to herself. 'Are you bored?' she asked.

Dominic shook his head. 'Very far from it. There's no rush. Take your time.'

'Thank you. Thank you so much, Dominic. This is a dream come true.'

Which was precisely what he'd wanted. He had also wanted to prove to himself, in surroundings as unromantic as possible, that his feelings for her were transient or shallow, or at the very least that he had them under control. Instead,

when she had fallen into his arms on the steamer
and accidentally kissed him, what he had felt
with complete and utter certainty was that he
loved her.

Bloody hell, he was in love with her!

When had he fallen in love? How could he be
so certain, so suddenly, that it was love? From
the moment they'd met, he had been intrigued
by her and attracted to her. She was extraordinary. He smiled, recalling the many times he'd
told her so, and how resistant she was to agreeing. He loved her strength and her courage in the
face of her vulnerability. He loved her slightly
subversive sense of humour. He loved the way
she embraced challenges, and the way she embraced him! He loved her for her strange ob-
session with plumbing, and for her passionate
belief in progress, and for her thirst for knowledge, and the fact that she willingly confessed
to ignorance. He loved her for her independence,
and her refusal to conform. He loved her because
from the very first she had seen something in
him that he had thought lost. She had helped to
restore him, and she'd made him look afresh at
himself. He loved her for all of those things and
so much more. What was astonishing was not

the suddenness of the revelation but the fact that it had taken him so long!

'I think I have it straight in my head now,' Prudence said. 'I'm going to make another tour. Do you mind?'

'I'll light the lamps. I take it that you want to go down to the reservoirs that will hold the—hold the...'

'Waste product? Who wouldn't?'

She wandered off and he picked up one of the lamps, trying to work out how to light it. He loved her. He had never been in love before but he knew that was what he was feeling, and he knew it would last. There was a permanence to how he felt, a solidity, a sense that at last he'd found the answer. He was in love with Prudence. He was going to be in love with her for the rest of his life.

Did Prudence feel the same? She had never been in love before. He was the first man to kiss her, the first man to see past her scars, she made no secret of either fact. But did she love him? His gut told him that she did, but was that simply wish fulfilment? And even if she did love him, what the devil, Dominic asked himself, was he to do about it?

The question remained unanswered as they

descended the stairs, with the lamps finally lit, to the crypt-like reservoirs. It was dank and cold and there was a smell that might have been wet clay but could have been any number of other things.

'I think I've seen enough,' Prudence said, wrinkling her nose. 'Do you think they will ask Queen Victoria to ceremonially open the sluice gates?'

'With a peg on her nose?'

She giggled. 'You've been very quiet. Admit it, you've been bored.'

'Not in the least, I promise you.' He took her lamp and made sure both of the wicks were extinguished. 'It's been a delight, watching you.'

'No one could have arranged a more thoughtful outing, Dominic. Even my own brother and sister don't know me as well as you do. Thank you.'

She leant in to kiss him, once again aiming for his cheek. He caught her round the waist, pulling her up against him, and their lips met. She made the softest sound, a sigh or a moan, and melted against him.

He stopped thinking and kissed her. She opened her mouth to him without hesitating and kissed him back, and he was lost. The taste of her, the softness of her mouth on his, was so exactly, precisely what he needed. She felt so right. Desire shot through him. He wanted her so much. He wanted her more than he had ever wanted any woman. This woman was the woman he had been waiting for, though he hadn't known it.

Her hands were in his hair, raking through it, urging him to hold her tighter. He staggered backwards, bringing her with him, until his back found something solid. She leant hard against him, her breathing ragged and her mouth clinging to his. He kissed her back deeply, his tongue touching hers, then deeper into her mouth, making him achingly hard, making her moan his name, and the sound of it driving him wilder.

He smoothed his hands over the curve of her spine, feeling her arch against him, groaning at the weight of her against his erection, frustrated by the layers and layers of her clothes. Her crinoline bent at his attempts to caress her bottom. She pushed his coat open, her hands inside sliding down his back, his buttocks, making him tense, driving him wild. He smoothed his hands over her breasts and was frustrated by the boning of her corsets. Her hands were on his chest now, under his waistcoat. He could feel the heat of her skin and he wanted…

He dragged his mouth away. 'Prue, we have to—we can't. Not here.' His chest was heaving.

'I'm sorry. We agreed…'

'I'm not.' He kissed her again, softly. 'I love you, Prue.'

'What did you say?'

'I love you very, very much. I can't fight it any more. I don't want to.'

'Oh, Dominic! I've tried so hard, but I can't fight it either. I love you too.'

He had no idea what the consequences would be, how he would overcome the many, many obstacles which would threaten their future together, but there was only one question at this moment which had to be asked. He took her hand and in the vaulted, unfinished cathedral that would become one of London's first pumping stations, Dominic went down on one knee. 'Will you marry me, Prue?'

The steamer's whistle blew, sparing Prudence the need to answer, which was as well for she was struck utterly dumb. She tried to right her clothes, which were not nearly in as much disarray as Dominic's. She didn't want him to tuck his shirt in, she wanted to slide her hands under it and feel his skin, his back, his chest, feel his muscles tense at her touch. She had never in her life felt so alive.

Dominic loved her. Dominic had asked her to marry him. Dominic loved her! She glanced over at him fastening his waistcoat and her heart gave a little leap. Dominic loved her, and she loved him. But marriage? She couldn't think of anything more wonderful, but that would be impossible, wouldn't it?

The steamer's whistle blew, twice this time, and she pulled her veil down. Hurriedly locking the door behind them, they made their way quickly down to the river, where Captain Binnie gruffly told them to hurry up and come aboard, his engineer casting off almost as soon as Prudence had her feet on the deck.

They sat together under cover on the aft deck. The roar of the engine as the skipper headed back upriver against the tide and the steady drum of the paddles made conversation difficult.

'I didn't know I was going to ask you. I know it's sudden,' Dominic said.

'You can change your mind.'

'I don't want to.'

'You really love me?'

'I really love you.' He kissed her tenderly. 'And you really love me?'

'Oh, yes. I don't doubt that.'

'Then we'll make it work, Prue. We can find a way. You told me the first day you met me that Hawthorn Manor was your haven. We can make it a haven for two.'

'But you can't marry a woman like me. A woman who can't show her face in polite company.'

'I'm not interested in any company except yours. You're the only woman I want, the only woman I will ever want. Think of the days we can have like this one, any number of them.'

'Think of the myriad things I won't be able to do, Dominic.'

'But there will be less of those than there are now. And we'll be together, isn't that the important thing? We could be so happy together.'

'Could we?'

'I think we could.'

He smiled. And then he kissed her. And Prudence thought hazily that perhaps he was right. By the time they descended, dazed with kisses and dizzy with desire from their private railway carriage at the end of the day, she had said yes.

Chapter Eighteen

Prudence fell asleep in a state of bliss. Dominic loved her. It had been such a relief to be able to tell him she loved him. And to hear the words she had never thought to hear returned. He really did love her.

She wrapped her arms around herself and snuggled back into her pillow to relive some of the kisses they had shared yesterday. Kisses that drove them both wild with desire, that ended time and again when they became frustrated by her clothing, or by the train arriving at a station, or when they simply had to stop to breathe, staring dazzled into each other's eyes, smiling and then kissing again. If they were married they could spend their days locked away in Hawthorn Manor making love. They would be everything to each other. They would make the Manor their world, and if they chose to leave it they would do so in their own bubble. Dominic would purchase a railway carriage and together they would travel, cocooned from prying eyes, safe.

Prudence pushed back the sheets. Outside the sun was blazing, the sky a perfect summer blue. Dominic would probably have been up for hours. He would have had his first pot of coffee, then in all likelihood gone out to his garden to pick snails off his salad. If she married him, her life would be transformed beyond anything she had ever dreamed of. Her horizons would be wider, but his would be narrowed considerably. He loved her, of that she had no doubt, but he would be sacrificing a great deal of his freedom if he married her.

She couldn't do it. She loved him far too much to marry him. She couldn't be a burden to him. He didn't see it but everyone else did, she was damaged goods and she always would be. He'd found a purpose in life and she would be a hindrance, not a help, forcing him to live with her in seclusion, making of him the same social pariah that she was. As she took her morning bath, she rehearsed her speech. She dressed carefully in her favourite summer gown of cream cotton sprigged with green flowers. The matching petticoat was green sprinkled with white flowers, and her garters were also green. Dominic would approve. Not that he would have the opportunity to pass judgement because she was going to tell him that they could not get married. Which meant that there would be no more kisses, they would never make love. Never?

Her resolve faltered. The enormity of what she was trying to persuade herself to do deserved much more consideration. She loved Dominic and he loved her. They could make their marriage work if they loved each other enough, couldn't they? If she refused him, she would be giving him up for ever. Or would she? Could they work together as he had suggested, on his housing estate, find a way to become friends? She couldn't imagine it. They had tried to resist each other and failed. It would be torture. They loved each other.

Torn and confused, Prudence decided that the only sensible thing to be done was to see him, to discuss the matter rationally and hope that he could allay her fears as he had done yesterday. Relieved and very eager to see him again, she pulled on her hat and veil and set off without bothering to have any breakfast. It was a beautiful morning. The meadow that had once been the lawn was a swathe of wild grasses going to seed. Butterflies fluttered. Bees droned. Dragonflies hovered. Dominic was intent on acquiring some goats to keep the meadow in check and to provide him with milk for cheese. He had talked of growing olives and a vine too, bringing a little bit of the Mediterranean to the south of England, he'd said, grinning. Hawthorn Manor could hardly be compared to his smallholding in Lavrio, but if he married her he'd be locking himself away from the world here just as effectively.

No, she was exaggerating. The two situations were not comparable. He had a huge portfolio of property to upgrade and rebuild, and that was only the beginning of his plans to dispose of his inherited wealth. He would be needing a great deal of it for himself though, if they married. Days out like yesterday did not come cheap.

'Prudence!' Dominic called from the front door of the Manor and she hurried to meet him. He was dressed in trousers, shirt and waistcoat, his hair damp and his jaw freshly shaved, and his smile made her forget everything except that this was the man she loved, and who loved her.

'I was getting ready to come and call on you,'

he said, sweeping her into his arms. 'This is a lovely surprise.'

All her doubts fled. She pushed back her veil and lifted her face for his kiss and forgot the world. She put her arms around him, relishing the familiarity of his body, the tension in him at her touch, and the way her own body responded to his.

Their gentle good morning kiss deepened in the cool dim light of the stone-flagged hallway, where Prudence yanked her hat off, throwing it in the vague direction of the peg, dropping her gloves on the floor. Their tongues teased and taunted and she tugged at Dominic's waistcoat, their fingers colliding as they both tried to undo the buttons. She ran her hands over his chest, feeling the heat of his skin through the soft linen of his shirt, making him groan, his groan heightening her own pleasure. He smoothed his hand over her back and then her arms, then up her sides, his hands cupping her breasts. Her nipples were hard against her undergarments, but there were too many of them to feel his touch, and she wanted his touch.

'Too many blasted clothes,' Dominic said, as frustrated as she. 'How quickly do you think we can arrange our wedding? I can barely keep my hands off you, but we have waited this long, a few more weeks…'

'I don't want to wait a few more weeks.'

'I wish you wouldn't say that when I'm trying to exercise some restraint.'

'I don't want to exercise restraint. I am thirty-two years old, Dominic. I've waited long enough.' She pulled his face to hers, kissing him deeply. This was what she wanted. This was what she needed. 'I love you,' she said with growing confidence. 'I love you so much, Dominic. Please make love to me.'

'Are you sure?'

Was she sure? She was sure that she wanted this. 'Yes,' Prudence said simply.

'My lovely Prue, I swear I'll be careful,' Dominic whispered confusingly, before pulling her once again into his arms.

They kissed at the foot of the stairs. They kissed on the landing. They kissed at the top of the stairs, and they kissed inside the doorway of Dominic's bedroom, where the bed was neatly made, military style, with sheets tightly tucked, Prudence noticed, before her eyes drifted closed again, and they kissed again.

He threw off his waistcoat. She struggled with

the fastenings at the back of her bodice, her fingers shaking.

'Let me,' he said, turning her around, lifting her hair to kiss the nape of her neck before loosening her gown. The curtains were not drawn. The sunlight was strong. Despite the fact that she knew he had seen the scarring on her shoulder, she tensed as he eased her gown carefully down, letting out a surprised gasp when he deliberately kissed the marks. Trails of butterfly kisses from her nape, along one shoulder and then the other as he pulled the bodice looser, so that her arms were freed, but when he tried to pull her gown off completely, her crinoline defeated him.

'It has to go up,' Prudence said, laughing, embarrassed, disappearing into the folds as they both lifted it over her head. Her hair was coming undone when she emerged, so she pulled the rest of the pins free, shaking it loose.

'You are so lovely,' he said, scattering kisses over her face, her neck, her throat, the tops of her breasts, licking into the valley between them, running his fingers through her hair, stroking her shoulders and her back.

She tugged his shirt free of his trousers, smoothing her hands over his torso. Rough hair.

Warm skin. Muscles tensing at her touch. There was a ridge in his shoulder.

'Bullet,' he muttered, his hands tugging at every lace and fastening he could find. 'Delightful as this petticoat is, Prue, I think we might dispense with it, and the cage beneath, if you tell me…'

'Up,' she said, almost beyond embarrassment now, helping with the tapes and wriggling out of both at once.

'Oh, Prue!'

Any trace of embarrassment was lost as he gazed at her, his desire writ plainly on his face, and spoken eloquently in his kisses. He removed both her camisole and her corsets without any help, leaving her in her chemise and drawers and stockings. His breathing was shallow and fast like her own, but his kisses slowed, his hands gentled on her, cupping her breasts, sucking her nipples through the thin lawn cotton of her last undergarment. She muttered his name, muttered incoherent pleas and gasped as his mouth claimed her nipple again, the chemise gone, his lips warm, rousing her to heights she had not known existed.

His shirt was gone. Her hands roamed wildly over his tanned torso, over his back, then down to the curve of his buttocks, only to encounter the barrier of his trousers.

He steered her towards the bed, kissing her, easing her backwards, his hands on her breasts and then his mouth again. More kisses as they lay together, his hands smoothing over her buttocks, then between her legs, finding the opening in her drawers and sliding a finger gently inside her.

'Dominic,' she said, clutching at his arms, pulling him towards her. 'Dominic!'

'Are you sure?'

'Yes!'

She watched unashamedly as he divested himself of the last of his clothes, her body clamouring for his, though nothing had prepared her for the reality of him, naked and aroused. Her confidence drained and her passion began to wilt.

'Have you changed your mind, Prue? You can...'

'No. I don't know what to do.'

'Stop thinking.'

He kissed her gently. Then their kisses deepened. She could feel his erection pressed against her stomach. More kisses. His hand sliding inside her, stroking her this time, and she stopped thinking. Kissing. Stroking. Kissing. Stroking.

Breathless pleading. And then her climax took her and she was bucking under him and urging him on, because she needed him inside her.

He entered her carefully, but she was beyond caution and utterly in thrall to her passion. Her legs wrapped themselves around his waist and she tilted her buttocks, urging him deeper, surrendering to her instincts. He thrust, and she cried out, tightening around him, and he thrust again, driving deeper, and again, her body matching his, then racing ahead, her second climax ripping through her, drawing a deep, heartfelt groan from him as he followed quickly, pulling himself from her to come with a hoarse cry. Falling onto his back, his chest heaving, he pulled her tight against him for one last, sated kiss.

He had not expected this when he'd woken up this morning, Dominic thought, running his hand down the long, delightful curve of Prudence's back to rest on her equally delightful bottom. She looked up and smiled at him through her tangle of hair, and he kissed her gently on the lips. 'I love you.'

'I love you too. Was that…?'

'Wonderful.' He kissed her. 'Delightful.' Another kiss. 'Perfect.' He kissed her again, and she smiled at him, that slow, sensual smile that never failed to stir him. Not even now! He edged carefully away from her. 'We have plans to make.'

Her face fell. 'There's an awful lot to discuss, Dominic.'

There was. A daunting amount. 'We should get dressed then, because I can't think straight with you naked.' With a supreme effort, he got out of bed, draping a towel around himself. It was still damp from his shower. He'd need another shower now.

'Prue,' he said, as a very appealing idea popped into his head, 'have you ever actually used this shower bath that you're so fond of?'

'Of course I haven't.'

'Would you like to?'

'Now?' She sat up, pulling the sheet over herself. 'Is there enough water?'

'I filled the cistern yesterday, though it might be a good idea to save some of it. Two showers would be a bit of a waste, don't you think?'

'Dominic!'

'Prudence?'

He held out his hand and, to his delight, after a moment she clambered out of the bed, still draped in the sheet, and followed him across the hall to the bathroom. He still half expected her to change her mind, not sure himself what he would do if she did not.

She did not disappoint him.

An hour later, in the kitchen, Dominic poured them both a glass of wine and set out some bread and cheese, reluctantly turning his mind to the practicalities of the situation. Across from him, Prudence set about crumbling her bread, frowning. He reached for her hand. 'I love you.'

'I know.'

'What's wrong, Prue? Do you regret...?'

'Oh, no! I regret absolutely nothing about this morning, I promise you.' She took a large swallow of wine. 'It's not that.'

'What, then?' he asked, disconcerted by her change in mood.

She took another large swallow of wine. 'I'm not sure you truly understand what it would be like to have me as your wife.'

'Prudence, if this is about your scars...'

'Of course it's about my scars! You don't see me as other people do, but you're the only one, Dominic. To everyone else, I'm an object of pity, if not horror, and if I was your wife, people would pity you too. They'd talk about you behind your back. I couldn't bear that.'

'I don't give a damn about what people say about me.'

'But I do, and it would be my fault. I'd hold you back. Just when you are starting to realise how much good you can do, the difference you can make, there I'd be, the poor soul who is so disfigured she has to hide herself away.'

'Stop it!'

'I'd make you unhappy eventually, Dominic. You'd come to resent the sacrifices you had to make on my behalf. You'd hate being pitied and gossiped about. I want to marry you,' she said, looking quite miserable, 'you've no idea how much I want to marry you, but I don't know if I ought to. It wouldn't be fair. I can't help but feel that I would gain so much more than you.'

'How can you say that? What the hell do you even mean by that? This is not a property deal, it's a marriage. Two people who love each other deciding to share their lives together. How we do that and where we do that are decisions we've still to make, but there's no point in discussing them if you aren't sure that you want to try.' He swore viciously under his breath, wondering how the morning could have gone so wrong. 'Is that what you're trying to tell me, that you don't even want to try?'

'No. Yes, of course I want—I have never in my life wanted anything so much as to marry you, but until yesterday the possibility of us having a future together hadn't even occurred to me. I don't even know what my name is. I don't even know if you *can* marry me, if it would be a legal marriage, with my name as Carstairs on the certificate.'

'I'm sure you can't be unique in your situation. It's hardly a reason for calling off the wedding. In fact, we've both got the same problem, for I've no idea if you'd be marrying Dominic Thorburn or Dominic Caldwell.'

'I don't care.'

'No, nor do I.'

She pushed back her chair. 'I'm tired. I'm overwrought. I should probably go.'

He got up, taking her hands, gazing at her searchingly. 'I understand all your doubts, but I don't share any of them. My life will be better for sharing it with you, and that's the beginning and the end of it as far as I am concerned. There is only one way that you could fail me or disappoint me or let me down, and that's if you let yourself believe that you're not good enough for me. I don't want you to change. You don't have to aspire to be my wife, and you certainly would never be a hindrance to me. You simply have to be you, exactly as you are. Think about that, will you? Take all the time you need, Prudence. I'm not going anywhere.'

Prudence walked home deep in thought. Dominic's words had shaken her to the core, for they demonstrated an understanding of her deeper than her own. She had never been able to see in herself what he did, nor did she have his unshakeable belief in her. He thought her extraordinary, but she simply could not bring herself to believe him. He saw her through love-tinted glasses. He didn't see her as almost everyone else did, and it was one of the many reasons she loved him, but she could not convince herself that the opinion of everyone else didn't matter. Marriage to her would damage him. She wasn't good enough for him, even if he thought she was. He deserved better.

Defeated, she crept into the quiet house and hurried up to her bedroom, stripping off her bonnet and veil. Her hair had dried into a wild tangle, and her lips were decidedly smudged. Their lovemaking had been a delight beyond her imagination, the pleasure as much in the joining of their bodies and the communing of their flesh. When they'd made love, it had been as equals. She knew that what she was feeling, he was feeling. But there was more to marriage than love-making.

Prudence stared at her reflection, trying very hard to see the woman Dominic loved. Was she honestly giving up the possibility of a future with Dominic without a fight? Wasn't it possible for her to try to live up to the person he believed her to be? Think about that, he'd said. Take as long as you like. She didn't need to make any rash decisions.

The doorbell clanged and a few minutes later Lizzie tapped on her door. 'A Lady Sarah Fitzherbert-Wright has called, miss,' she said, handing Prudence a calling card. 'I told her you didn't receive callers without an appointment, but she insisted I tell you she was here.'

'It's fine, Lizzie, she's a friend, there's no need to worry. Will you bring a tray of tea to the drawing room, please? I'll be down in a moment.'

'If you're sure, miss.'

Prudence tidied her hair and applied some powder mixed with glycerine to her mouth.

What on earth was Lady Sarah doing here? Curious and relieved to be distracted from her own travails, she made her way downstairs.

'Lady Sarah, this is a surprise.'

'Miss Carstairs. How do you do? I am staying with friends not far from here and I thought I'd pop by. The Rasenbys—do you know them?'

'The Rasenbys! They must live at least fifteen miles away.'

'Really? It didn't seem like any more than five or six. I left my horse with my groom at the village inn. I hope you don't mind my calling unannounced in all my dirt.'

'You don't look as if you've ridden more than fifteen feet, never mind fifteen miles. Please sit down. Are you hungry? I've asked Lizzie to bring tea and cake, but if you'd like something more substantial?'

'You are very thoughtful, but cake will be fine. How are you, Miss Carstairs? Or may I call you Prudence? And you must call me Sarah, for we are friends now, aren't we? You are looking very well, I must say. That dress suits you admirably. How is your brother, is he at home?'

'I have no idea.'

'We had a very pleasant day in London together. I expect he's told you all about it.'

'Actually, no. He said almost exactly what you did, that it was a very pleasant interlude.'

'Well, and so it was. It was something of a surprise since we have almost nothing in common.'

This was patently true, so when the door opened to reveal not Lizzie but Clement bearing the tea tray, Prudence was astounded. 'We have a visitor, Clement.'

'Lady Sarah! What a surprise.' Her brother set the tray down, looking not in the least surprised. If Prudence didn't know better, she might think that this visit was pre-planned, and she was not the intended focus.

'We are flattered you have come so far out of your way, aren't we, Prue?'

'I do have an ulterior motive. Aside from a desire to call on your sister, I wished to look up the parish register here. I have become interested in my mother's family—rather too late, sadly, to discover more from the horse's mouth, so to speak. I have been going through her papers and was astonished to discover that she had an aunt I knew nothing of, a most extraordinary woman, by the sounds of it. I know that she was born near here, but I had no idea tracing her would be so complicated.'

'I could help you with that, actually,' Clement said. 'We historians are used to wading our way through registers and the like. If you give me the details I can see what I can dig up.'

'That would be extremely helpful. Perhaps if you are free tomorrow?'

'I might be at that.'

'I don't know what possessed me,' Clement said to Prudence half an hour later when Lady Sarah had left and they were alone again in the drawing room. 'I can't really spare a whole day. But there was nothing to be done, she all but railroaded me into it.'

'Indeed,' Prudence agreed, biting back a smile.

'It's not that I particularly wish to spend any time in her company, if that's what you're thinking. In fact, I find her rather exhausting. She has a great many opinions, some of them rather radical.'

'Clement, do you think that there is any record of me in the parish here? A baptism certificate, perhaps.'

Her brother ceased his absentminded consumption of the cake crumbs from Lady Sarah's plate. 'What makes you ask?'

'Nothing in particular. I'm curious, that's all.'

'Come on, Prue. You've never expressed any curiosity before. You know that Mercy and I always think of you as our true sister, don't you?'

'I do.' Touched, she got up to give him a quick hug. 'And I feel the same. This is my home. Mama and Papa are my parents. But as far as the law is concerned. If I wished to…to get married, to use an outlandish example.'

Clement raised his eyebrows but said nothing. Prudence began to stack the tea tray. 'Do you think you would be able to do some of your historical digging on my behalf?'

'I can, if you wish, but I don't know what I'll turn up.'

'I'd like to know, whatever it is.'

'I'll do my best, but are you sure you know what you're doing, Prue?'

'It has nothing to do with my feelings for you or Mercy, and Mama and Papa will always be Mama and Papa, but I would like to know, at the very least, what my name is.'

'Then I'll do my best. I don't want to interfere, Prue, you know your own business, but if there's anything I can do to help, even if it's just a brotherly shoulder to lean on, I'm here for you.'

'Thank you. I am perfectly—I will bear that in mind.'

'Good.' Clement kissed her left cheek and patted her on the shoulder. 'Leave it with me.'

Chapter Nineteen

Prudence sat in the turret room at her circular desk, staring out at the walled garden. She had been studying the plans for a housing estate intended for what the charity termed the 'reputable working-class', which Dominic had obtained. There were any number of schemes being considered by various charities, though none had progressed beyond the planning stage. Some were eminently practical, some utterly fanciful, and all, it seemed to Prudence, came with extremely judgemental caveats about their intended occupants. Dominic wanted her to feel useful, and to include her in his own intended project which was becoming more ambitious with every visit he paid to the city, but the more engaged he became, the more she felt her own isolation.

It was a week today since they had made love

that first and only time. He had been at great pains to give her the thinking time she needed. Their conversations had revolved around the business that lay before her and had not touched on their own future, but she knew the subject was looming. They were losing their ease with each other. Their kisses were careful, with Dominic keeping a tight rein on his passion, while she was afraid to lose control of hers, afraid of what she would say. The truth was the only progress she had made was to confirm her initial instincts. Their marriage could not be a happy one, and the fault would be entirely hers.

'Prudence!'

She whirled around, her heart leaping at the sound of his voice. 'Dominic! I didn't expect you back until later today.'

'The city was unbearable in this heat—yes, even I found it hot,' he said, smiling at her. 'I finished my business early with Doncaster this morning and decided to come home.'

'Home?'

'It's where the heart is,' he said, putting his arms around her, 'that's what they say, isn't it? And here you are.'

Alone and waiting, she thought, but did not say, wrapping her arms around his waist and burrowing her face into his chest. His clothes smelt of smoke, of the city, of another world from this one. She tightened her grip. She didn't want to lose him.

'Prudence?'

She looked up. 'I love you so much, Dominic.'

'Oh, Prue, you know I love you too. So very much.'

Their lips met and clung, and his arms tightened around her, and she pressed herself against him. Desire shot through her, and need, and a feeling of rightness. She tilted her head to deepen the kiss, wanting to show him how much she loved him, wanting to prove to herself how strong her love was, and when he lifted his head to gaze deep into her eyes, his breathing already ragged, she pulled him back for more kisses, pushing his coat aside, undoing the buttons of his waistcoat, tugging his shirt free, to smooth her hands over his skin, the taut belly, the hard chest, the peaks of his nipples, the rough hair of his chest.

'Prue,' he said, dragging his mouth away, his eyes already glazed. 'Oh, God, I've missed you so much.'

'I've missed you too. So much.' She ached for him. She could feel him, pressed against her, aching for her. 'I need you, Dominic.'

'Yes. Oh, yes. Why do you wear so many clothes?' he said, tugging at the lacing of her gown, shedding his coat, shuddering as she clutched at his buttocks through his trousers.

She wriggled free of her bodice, and he buried his face in the swell of her breasts, kissing and licking, loosening her corset enough to push it apart, and finding her nipples. Pleasure shot through her. She stroked the length of him through his trousers, and her body began to scream, urgently, to have him inside her. They sank to the floor, Dominic discarding clothes as they kissed, touched, pulling her on top of him, her skirts billowing out over both of them, and then finally, at last, he was inside her and she could feel herself tipping over, just taking him in, holding him inside her, leaning over him to kiss him deeply, a primal instinct taking over, her hips moving, his hands under her skirts, on her bottom, her cries mingling with his as her climax took her, and his quickly followed.

She fell, panting, onto his chest. He wrapped his arms so tightly around her that she could hardly breathe. His chest rose and fell against her. Under her skirts they were still one. This, Prudence thought, was all the proof she needed, surely.

* * *

They sat at the kitchen table, gazing besottedly at each other. It was late afternoon. They had bathed and restored a semblance of decency to their attire. Dominic poured them both a glass of Madeira. Frank was asleep on his favourite chair by the range.

'I went to a bathhouse in Jermyn Street yesterday,' Dominic said. 'It's not been opened long, and I'd heard it had a pool for swimming.'

'And did it?'

'There was a marble pool, though it wasn't big enough to swim in or deep enough—in fact it looked more like an ornamental fishpond. There was a deeper pool with extremely cold water that one was expected to jump into after lying sweltering in the hot room. Very similar to a hammam baths, which is what they have in Turkey and which I presume is what this was supposed to replicate. There were a great many gentlemen lolling about wrapped in towels, smoking pipes. The coffee was excellent though.'

'But you didn't get your swim. Poor Dominic, you will have to build yourself a pool here.'

'That's an idea. The thing is, Prudence, I met someone I know there. My old Colonel, in fact. He seemed pleased to see me.'

'And were you pleased to see him?'

He shrugged, shook his head, then smiled rue-fully. 'It was the oddest thing. I felt—nothing. He made no mention of our last meeting, not at first, tried to talk to me as if nothing had happened. Then—I don't know, perhaps it was because I had nothing to say, he began to bluster and all but apologised and made noises about looking into having my medals and commendations restored.'

'That's wonderful. Isn't it?'

'What would I do with them? I'm not a soldier any more.' Dominic swallowed his wine and got to his feet. 'I'm starving. Would you like some bread and cheese?'

'No, thank you. Do you really—don't you care at all about your medals, Dominic?'

'That part of my life is over. I don't want to be one of those men who is forever harping on about the glorious deeds he performed in his past. The future is much more interesting. I've been thinking, Prue, that you might be right.'

'Again!'

He laughed, sitting back down with a plate of food, which he immediately pushed to one side. 'Seriously. Do you remember what you said to me—it must have been about ten days ago now, when I first showed you those photographs of our project. You asked me what I was going to do about it. You didn't mean the houses I own, you meant what was I going to do to tackle the problem at its roots, didn't you?'

'You're already doing far more than any other landlord, Dominic.'

'Yes, but it's not enough, is it? What about all the other landlords?'

'The members of the club you don't want to join, you mean?'

'You can't change the rules if you don't join the club. I've been thinking about that a lot, Prue, while I've been out and about. Some of the sights I've seen, you wouldn't believe. Did you know, by the way, that the water companies don't even go to the bother of putting a tap on the supply in some of the poorer areas? The water just comes pouring out once or twice a week, however inadequate a time it is that they switch it on for. Aside from the waste, it makes a mud bath. I was thinking...'

The afterglow of their lovemaking burst like a bubble, taking all her certainty with it. Prudence listened as Dominic enthused about his plans, grand and small. She had always known he could be much more than he aspired to, but it was bittersweet to see him literally growing before her eyes, for she could feel herself diminishing with every word. It wasn't that he was leaving her behind. Far from it, he was making a huge effort to include her, but he simply couldn't understand what was very clear to her now. He was taking on a public mantle. One that would require him to attend dinners, formal functions, balls. Events where his wife would be expected to be by his side.

'You're very quiet,' he said, reaching across the table for her hand. 'I know I'm contradicting myself in a way, talking about taking up my seat in Parliament, for goodness' sake. But I've realised what you've been trying to say to me all along, Prue. It doesn't matter whether I call myself Dominic Caldwell or Dominic Thorburn or the Earl of Bannatyne. I'm still me. Tragedy and fate handed me this inheritance. I can rid myself of it as planned and do some good in the process. But if I walk away, I'm leaving behind the opportunity to actually change things. I'm not naïve, I know I won't necessarily succeed. I'm probably setting myself up for a fall, but it's trying that counts. It's taken me a while to understand that, but I do now. You've always known. You are so much wiser than I.'

I wish I wasn't, Prudence thought disconsolately. Tears clogged her throat. She got to her feet. 'I have to go. I have a headache.'

'Why didn't you say, instead of letting me prattle on?' Dominic pulled her into his arms, kissing the top of her head. 'Shall I walk back with you?'

'No!' She freed herself gently. 'No, I'll be fine. It's the weather. I think there will be a thunderstorm later. Stay here, have your bread and cheese, I'll see myself out.'

The rain started as Prudence approached the Manor gates, a sudden torrential downpour as if a tap had been turned on. And left on, by an irresponsible water company. She leant against the gatepost, unable to walk any further, and stood for a long time, her mind frozen, her clothes saturated, but her eyes dry behind her veil. It was over. Everything she had feared was coming to pass. Today had set the pattern for the future if she married Dominic. Her waiting at home, trying to make herself useful. He in London, actually getting things done. He'd praise her efforts. He would do his best to include her in everything, it wouldn't be his fault that her contributions would become less and less. How could she help fashion a world she was not part of?

She pictured herself earlier this afternoon, gazing out of the turret window into space. The way her heart leapt when she saw him, the joy of making love and the closeness she shared with him. That too would change, when it became the only thing they shared. Would she come to see making love as a duty? As her only contribution? She couldn't imagine it now, but in the future—it was possible.

'There is only one way that you could fail me or disappoint me or let me down, and that's if you let yourself believe that you're not good enough for me.'

She wasn't good enough in the eyes of the world, and that was what counted. In the eyes of the world she was a poor maimed creature forced to live her life behind a veil. She didn't want to, but she had no option. Her scars defined her. She couldn't let them define Dominic too.

'You simply have to be you, exactly as you are,' he had said. *'Think about that...'*

She'd thought about it. She had no option but to be her, exactly as she was. Hawthorn Manor had been her sanctuary. If she married Dominic, it would become her prison.

* * *

When she reappeared in the kitchen half an hour later, Dominic's plate of food was untouched, his wine glass full. He jumped up when he saw her and pulled a woollen blanket from the back of one of the chairs, seating her in Frank's chair by the range, as if he had been waiting, expecting her to return.

'When you kissed me today,' he said, after she had stared mutely at him for some moments, 'I thought you had decided I was right. That our marriage was right.'

'I wanted to. I thought that if we made love— I thought I'd prove it to myself.'

'It won't make any difference if I tell you that I won't do any of the things I mentioned earlier, will it? If I tell you that none of them matter to me if I don't have you, Prudence?'

'I won't believe you. You don't really mean it. They do matter.'

'They do. But nothing and no one matters to me as much as you.'

'It's because I feel the same that I can't marry you.'

He flinched but made no move towards her. 'The problem is, you can't see yourself as I see you, and it seems nothing I can do or say is going to change that. Which is ironic, since it's entirely down to you that I now look at the world differently. You've made me comfortable in my own skin in a way I've never been before.'

'You would have got there without me, Dominic.'

'I wish…' He took a breath, clenching his hands. 'What's the point? You are determined to be right, and do you know what, Prudence, I think I finally agree with you. Our marriage would be a mistake because you would not let it succeed.'

'That's not true! I want to marry you more than anything, but I would ruin you.'

'No, you wouldn't. I told you once that your scars don't define you. I was right about that. They don't. Unless you allow them to.'

Chapter Twenty

Prudence morosely shuffled through the pages of her notebook, but the designs she had so carefully drawn of fantastical water features failed to engage her. It had been delivered by hand the day after she and Dominic had parted company for ever. Two weeks ago yesterday. There had been no accompanying note. She had not seen Dominic since. She did not expect to. There was nothing to say and nothing to be done, except get on with the rest of her life.

Setting her notebook aside, she pulled a sheet of paper towards her with the aim of writing to Mercy, but ten minutes later the ink had dried on her pen and she hadn't written a single word.

'Prue! I thought I'd find you moping in here. I have news for you.'

'Clement. Good morning to you too,' she said,

rising from her desk. 'I'm not moping, I was trying to compose a letter to Mercy.'

'Ah! Well, if that's true I'm not surprised you're struggling. What the deuce do you imagine happened to have her return from Baden-Baden after only a week there? All she said to me was that she'd decided she preferred the English countryside. If she meant that, why isn't she here?'

'And, more to the point, where is Harry?' Prudence said. 'He's not with her.'

'Well, that's a blessing, as far as I'm concerned, but it wasn't Mercy I came to talk to you about.'

'How is Lady Sarah?'

'She's in perfect health, so far as I know. Very robust constitution. Did you know she's never even had measles?'

'I didn't,' Prudence said, once again marvelling at the intricacies of her brother's mind. 'May I ask how on earth you know that?'

'It's a natural enough question, isn't it? Childhood ailments, family medical history, that sort of thing.'

'Under what circumstances, would that be…?'

'Talking of childhood ailments,' Clement interrupted. 'I think you'd better sit down.'

'What is it?'

'Do you want a cup of tea?'

'Clement, you're frightening me. Is someone ill? Dead?'

'No, no, nothing like that. Well, they are dead, but— Look, the thing is, Prue, you remember you asked me to look into the parish records for you?'

'Oh.' She sat down suddenly. 'You've found something?'

'A great deal, actually. Are you absolutely sure you want to know what I've dug up?'

For the first time in days—no, in two weeks— her interest was piqued. 'Yes, of course I do. Go on.''

'It was a tricky bit of work. Interesting. I had no memory whatsoever. Mercy didn't either. I wrote and asked her. Mind you, she's two years younger than me, but it's astonishing all the same. The thing is, Prue, what I found was that there *was* a baby, a girl, born within a few days of your birthday, to our parents. Virtue, her name was, can you believe? Virtue Carstairs. Makes me feel marginally better about Clement.'

'What happened to her?'

'She died, poor little mite. Registered, baptised, died, all given the same date. That doesn't mean they all occurred on the same day; it's simply how they were recorded. It explains why Mercy and I don't remember her. We'd have been too young to know that our mother was expecting, and if the babe was ailing from the start, they'd have kept her from us.'

'How tragic.'

'Yes, but the question is, Prue, what does it tell us about you?'

'I don't know that it tells me anything, save that we were almost the same age.'

'It was Sarah who got me thinking. She does charity work at a lying-in hospital. Not do-good stuff, reading tracts and making arrowroot jelly, she gets her hands dirty. A woman who has lost a child—a baby—it can affect her mind. They lock some of the unlucky ones up, according to Sarah. It's a temporary form of insanity, but it can make a woman behave very oddly. Steal someone else's baby, for example. No, don't look so horrified, our mother didn't actually steal you, but she did take you on as a…a replacement for the one she lost. Like a ewe will take an orphaned lamb on, you know—if it's wearing the dead one's coat. Not that you… I don't mean that you…you know how much our mother doted on you.'

'Clement, slow down. Are you telling me that Mama—what? Took me from a workhouse or a wet nurse?'

'Orphanage, though you'd only just arrived. It was in all the newspapers at the time. That's how I found you. I checked the date of your birthday. It was quite a sensation at the time.'

Prudence paid off the hackney and stepped onto the roadside, checking that her veil was in place. Clement had offered to accompany her, but she had insisted on making the journey alone. The row of terraced houses had been built about twenty years ago, when the landlord finally gave in to pressure and knocked what remained of the previous dwellings down. These were brick-built, like thousands of others which were being constructed all over London, with a substantial appearance, as if they had been built to last, when in fact they had been designed and constructed as cheaply and flimsily as possible. The cracks were already apparent above at least two of the window frames, a sure indicator of subsidence. There was one water pump at the end of the street. No sign of privies, which meant at least the current occupants had their own at the rear of the property.

She walked along the street, counting the doors. This was where the house she had been born in had stood. It too had been brick-built. Georgian, with a low roof. Her parents had lived in two rooms on the first floor, above a cobbler's shop. She was their third child. Her sister and brother had died the year before in a cholera outbreak. There had been repeated complaints from her parents and several other tenants of water damage to their home. The roof leaked. The windows leaked. Water oozed up through the floorboards. The walls ran with damp. A group of the tenants had written to *The Times* about the roof. The letter was reprinted a few weeks later, after the accident.

She had been sleeping in a drawer in the front room when the roof fell in, while her parents took their dinner in the back room. They had both died of their injuries. There had been four other deaths, twenty-two others taken to hospital. And one baby who, if she recovered, would be scarred for life. The landlord's agent was lambasted in the press, but the owner had never been named, let alone shamed.

A young woman with a basket in one hand and a toddler clinging to the other came out of the door to the house. 'You all right, love? You look a bit lost. Not from these parts, that's for sure.'

'I'm fine, thank you,' Prudence said. 'I don't suppose you know if there's anyone who lived here before—before this terrace was built, I mean?'

'You mean before the collapse that killed those poor folk? My mum lived here back then, but she's out in the countryside in Hounslow now. Were you looking for someone in particular?'

'No. I was curious, that's all.'

'Terrible time. If you ask me, another five years and these houses will be going the same way. Excuse me, I must be getting on. Good day to you.'

Prudence watched the young woman hurry down the street. Why had she bothered asking about previous residents? She wouldn't have had the courage to speak to them. Though she had spoken easily enough to that young woman. She already knew more than enough about the family she had been born into though. Like Dominic faced with his ancestors, she had felt little attachment to the names in the newspaper reports Clement had found for her. What she had felt, and what she felt more strongly now, was anger. What had been the fate of the other people injured and maimed in the accident? Who had paid for the burials, for the doctors and the medicines? If a quirk of fate had not deprived her Mama of Virtue, where would Prudence be now?

And what of the man who owned the house, where was he? He had prospered enough to rebuild, and he had managed to detach himself sufficiently from any guilt to build them just as shoddily. Her blood boiled thinking of him. The man was nothing short of a murderer. Exactly the kind of man whom Dominic was setting out to battle against. Alone.

It was not far from here to Clerkenwell, where Dominic's houses were. She had come this far, alone and veiled, without suffering anything more than a few rude stares. Prudence decided to risk going a little further. When she got there, she recognised the street from the photographs. She also recognised the man who owned her heart talking to another man in brown overalls. Dominic was wearing neither hat nor gloves. He was wearing a coat she didn't recognise. He had had his hair cut. She shrank into the shadows of an alley, watching him point and gesticulate, watching the man take notes. The pair of them laughed, then Dominic slapped the other man on the back and walked away.

Prudence felt such a devastating sense of loss that she staggered against the wall. She loved that man with all her heart. He had wanted to marry her. He had offered to build his world around her. And she had rejected him.

All the way back on the journey to the village, after walking the streets of London until she found a hackney, she sat in the first-class carriage of the train, her mind in turmoil. She loved Dominic. She wanted to marry him, but she wanted to be his equal in that marriage. Not Poor Prudence who would make him unhappy.

Poor Prudence.

She stopped in her tracks at the gate to the Old Rectory. Was that really how she saw herself? It was how everyone else saw her, thanks to the inheritance a slum landlord had given her. It wasn't how Dominic saw her, he never had. But really, was it how she saw herself? Poor Prudence, condemned to spend her life behind a veil, ashamed of her face. What had happened to her was shameful, yet she was the one who suffered. Was that right? These were her scars. This was her face. She had never found herself repulsive, but she was acting as if she was. And it wasn't her fault!

She missed Dominic. Almost the last time they'd spoken, he was full of enthusiasm for the battles he planned to take on, against men like the one who had ruined her life, and she had walked away. Abdicated. She could have been part of it, but she had declined because she was Poor Prudence.

Poor Prudence, who had travelled up to London by herself today. Poor Prudence, who had survived a horrific accident, had been given a new family and a second chance, who had a brother and sister who loved her, and a man, a wonderful, brave, heart-stopping man who wanted to spend his life with her. Was this a Poor Prudence?

Dominic had come to England intending to rid himself of what he had inherited, to sell up and go back into hiding. Now he was claiming his inheritance for his own and making something in his image from it. If she could follow his example, she would prove herself worthy. Not to him, but to herself. Finally, she understood what he had been trying to say to her, but he'd got it wrong. Her scars did define her. The question was, what story did she want them to tell?

Chapter Twenty-One

The leaves were beginning to turn, though it was only early September, the result of what even Dominic would admit had been a long hot summer. He had been in England almost three months now. He had not managed to save a single lettuce from the marauding snails, but he had had a decent crop of everything else, including his cucumbers. In November, he would take his seat in the House of Lords. Doncaster was urging him to make some sort of announcement in *The Times* about his reclamation of the estate, but he'd fobbed the man off. He had no idea what they made of his continued presence here in the village and couldn't bring himself to care.

It had been nearly three weeks since he had last seen Prudence. He did not for a moment doubt that the decision they had taken had been the right one, but he wished they'd not had to make it.

'Life goes on,' he said to Frank, ruefully aware that he was now reduced to talking to a cat. He'd have six goats to converse with soon. 'Life just gets more and more exciting.'

He dropped onto the bench and studied the garden, trying to distract himself by planning for next season. Work on the estate in London had temporarily come to a halt. Contract disputes, Doncaster muttered every time he asked. There were any number of tasks that he could do in the meantime, but too many of them reminded him too much of Prudence. How many privies? Should there be a bath house? Why couldn't she see…?

'Am I interrupting?'

His eyes flew open and he jumped to his feet. He hadn't even realised he had fallen asleep. 'Prudence.' His heart leapt. He ignored it. 'How are you?'

'I am well.' She smiled at him. 'I'm very well, Dominic. May I talk to you? I have something important to tell you.'

Prudence had managed to deliver her well-rehearsed speech without faltering in the midst of Dominic's exclamations and questions, his astonishment and anger, his sympathy and his admiration.

'I can't believe I didn't see you that day in London,' he said. 'I remember it. If I had known you were standing just a few yards away, that you had come to London on your own—but that was the point, wasn't it, you had to prove you could?'

'I didn't know it at the time but yes, that was partly the point.'

'And what now, Prue?'

Her heart began to pound, and butterflies took flight in her stomach. 'I asked myself, do I want to be Poor Prudence for the rest of my life, or do I want to take a leaf from your book and make my inheritance my own? And I decided that I wanted to follow your example.'

With shaking fingers, she handed him the large brown envelope. 'Open it.'

He took the photograph out, exhaling sharply when he saw what it portrayed. It was a long time before he spoke, studying it intently. She had insisted on the photographer taking several images from different distances and at different angles. The one she had selected was of her head and shoulders, showing her face in profile, the right-hand side exposed to the camera. Her hair was pulled tightly back, and the photographer had powdered her face, to provide a better contrast with the scar. There was no backdrop. She wore a plain-necked blouse with no trimming. There was nothing to distract the viewer from what she wanted to display.

When Dominic set the photograph down carefully, his eyes were bright with tears. 'I have never seen anything so moving and so beautiful and so incredibly brave. Never.'

'I want you to use it, Dominic. I want to be part of the fight against unscrupulous landlords and the need for adequate housing.'

He nodded, lost for words.

'And if you still want to marry me...'

She was in his arms before she could finish her sentence, and no words were necessary. Their kiss said everything that needed to be said.

Epilogue

The shockwaves which had reverberated through polite society when the announcement was made in *The Times* that the Seventh Earl of Bannatyne had established his claim to the estate and the title had barely died down when the announcement of his betrothal was posted.

In the middle of October Prudence prepared to walk down the aisle of the village church on her brother's arm and become the Countess of Bannatyne. Following the fashion set by Her Majesty, she wore a plain white silk dress with a white lace veil. The church pews were full, the village having turned out in force to witness this most astonishing event, the marriage of a man who they had not known existed to a woman who had spent the better part of her life trying to hide her existence. Prudence had invited only one guest. Her sister Mercy sat in the front pew, accompanied not by her husband, who was confined to his bed, and by all accounts unlikely to rise from it again, but by her friend Lady Sarah. They would both be staying at the Old Rectory for an extended visit following the nuptials.

'Ready?'

Clement smiled down at her. Prudence nodded firmly, and her brother gave the signal for the organ to strike up. Dominic was waiting for her at the altar. He had broken with tradition to stand facing her. She walked confidently towards him, her heart swelling with love. Her brother let go her hand and retreated. Dominic smiled at her. And Prudence lifted her veil, smiling back.

'Now everyone can see you as I do,' he whispered.

* * * * *

Historical Note

As usual, a vast amount of reading and research has gone into this book, and you can find out more if you're interested, on my Goodreads page and on my blog.

I am particularly indebted to Liza Picard's *Victorian London*, and Judith Flanders' books *The Victorian House* and *Victorian City*, for all things plumbing and London life. Simon Heffer's *High Minds*, and Cecil Woodham-Smith's *The Reason Why* were just some of the books that gave me background on the Crimean War and Dominic's experiences in the army. Sarah Wise's book *The Blackest Street* gave me a very personalised insight into life in a Victorian slum and was the starting point for Prudence's back story—which is entirely invented but sadly not at all unlikely.

The content of *The Times* which sends Dominic hotfoot back to England is based on an edition of the time, with the exception of the train crash, which is entirely a product of my own imagination.

Prudence's precious shower bath is actually slightly before its time, and of course her water features are very much an anachronism, and more steampunk than Victorian Gothic. And the railway to Bognor Regis wasn't actually completed until 1864, so I've taken a bit of artistic licence there—and a few miles of track.

There was no formal process for adopting children in 1862, so my use of the word is an anachronism. Children could be made wards, or informally absorbed into families, but there was no legal process to grant them inheritance rights.

Until 1837, following the Births and Deaths Registration Act and the creation of the General Register Office in England and Wales, births, deaths and marriages were not centrally recorded. Parish registers were the main source of information, but not all births were entered there. The law viewed children—and wives—as the property of a marriage, however, so Dominic would almost certainly have been recorded as the Earl's son, no matter who his true father might have been, in order to avoid a scandal.

London in the eighteen-sixties was one big building site, with work on the Embankment and the creation of the various pumping stations associated with Joseph Bazalgette's revolutionary sewage works causing uproar. The pumping stations and the sewage works were indeed tourist attractions, and the subject of endless articles in the press of the time—including a 'virtual' tour of the sewers published in Dickens' *All Year Round*, and real tours of the sewers in the early eighteen-sixties—obviously before they opened. Work started on Crossness Pumping Station in 1859 and was finished in 1865, so the construction probably wasn't as far on as I've suggested when Prudence and Dominic visit.

Octavia Hill and the Peabody Trust—both of whom opened working-class estates around 1864—inspired Dominic and Prudence's efforts to provide decent housing for the poor.

And, finally, some of you might have noticed the Armstrong family popping up again. I simply can't leave them alone. Poor Harry, I'm afraid, takes too much after his father to survive much past this book.

There—I hope that has whetted your appetite for the next!

COMING SOON!

We really hope you enjoyed reading this book. If you're looking for more romance, be sure to head to the shops when new books are available on

Thursday 28th October

To see which titles are coming soon, please visit

millsandboon.co.uk/nextmonth

MILLS & BOON

THE HEART OF ROMANCE

A ROMANCE FOR EVERY READER

MODERN
Prepare to be swept off your feet by sophisticated, sexy and seductive heroes, in some of the world's most glamourous and romantic locations, where power and passion collide.

HISTORICAL
Escape with historical heroes from time gone by. Whether your passion is for wicked Regency Rakes, muscled Vikings or rugged Highlanders, awaken the romance of the past.

MEDICAL
Set your pulse racing with dedicated, delectable doctors in the high-pressure world of medicine, where emotions run high and passion, comfort and love are the best medicine.

True Love
Celebrate true love with tender stories of heartfelt romance, from the rush of falling in love to the joy a new baby can bring, and a focus on the emotional heart of a relationship.

Desire
Indulge in secrets and scandal, intense drama and plenty of sizzling hot action with powerful and passionate heroes who have it all: wealth, status, good looks…everything but the right woman.

HEROES
Experience all the excitement of a gripping thriller, with an intense romance at its heart. Resourceful, true-to-life women and strong, fearless men face danger and desire - a killer combination!

To see which titles are coming soon, please visit

millsandboon.co.uk/nextmonth

MILLS & BOON

Coming next month

UNWRAPPED BY HER ITALIAN BOSS
Michelle Smart

'I know how important this maiden voyage is, so I'll give it my best shot.'

What choice did Meredith have? Accept the last-minute secondment or lose her job. Those were the only choices. If she lost her job, what would happen to her? She'd be forced to return to England while she sought another job. Forced to live in the bleak, unhappy home of her childhood. All the joy and light she'd experienced these past three years would be gone and she'd return to grey.

'What role do you play in it all?' she asked into the silence.

He raised a thick black eyebrow.

'Are you part of Cannavaro Travel?' she queried. 'Sorry, my mind went blank when we were introduced.'

The other eyebrow rose.

A tiny dart of amusement at his expression—it was definitely the expression of someone outragedly thinking, *How can you not know who I am?*—cut through Merry's guilt and anguish. The guilt came from having spent two months praying for the forthcoming trip home to be cancelled. The anguish came from her having to be the one to do it, and with just two days' notice. The early Christmas dinner her sister-in-law had spent weeks and weeks planning had all been for nothing.

The only good thing she had to hold on to was that she hadn't clobbered an actual guest with the Christmas tree, although, judging by the cut of his suit, Cheekbones was on a huge salary, so must be high up in Cannavaro Travel, and all the signs were that he had an ego to match that salary.

long while, her gaze studying him. 'The offer is very… generous,' she said at last.

'I don't care if it's generous, Miss Peverett. Is it *tempting*?'

He wanted her to say yes, despite the voice inside whispering a warning, *you are tempting fate.*

She nodded, but her words were wary. 'Yes, it is.' She was still suspicious.

That voice inside was more insistent now. *As well she should be—you are concealing your true purpose from her.*

Ferris refilled their glasses, ignoring her suspicion and his twinge of conscience. 'A toast, then, to a new partnership.' The idea of having her here should not please him as much as it did, nor should the thought of his undisclosed agenda sit so poorly with him. He didn't like the feeling that he was misleading her.

Anne had summed up his offer correctly. He did want to keep an eye on her and she needed the space. There was just more that he'd omitted telling her. Perhaps the omission wouldn't matter in the long run. They both had what they wanted and people would be served by the arrangement. But the 'ends justifying the means' reasoning didn't quite assuage his conscience as well in practice as it had in theory.

'To teamwork.'

Continue reading
LORD TRESHAM'S TEMPTING RIVAL
Bronwyn Scott

Available next month
www.millsandboon.co.uk